Apricots from Chernobyl

Apricots from Chernobyl

narratives by

JOSIP NOVAKOVICH

Josip Novakovich
6/14/95

GRAYWOLF PRESS
Saint Paul

Copyright © 1995 by Josip Novakovich

Publication of this volume is made possible in part by a grant provided by the Minnesota State Arts Board through an appropriation by the Minnesota State Legislature, and by a grant from the National Endowment for the Arts. Significant additional support has been provided by the Andrew W. Mellon Foundation, the Lila Wallace-Reader's Digest Fund, the McKnight Foundation, and other generous contributions from foundations, corporations, and individuals. Graywolf Press is a member agency of United Arts, Saint Paul. To these organizations and individuals who make our work possible, we offer heartfelt thanks.

Published by Graywolf Press
2402 University Avenue, Suite 203
Saint Paul, Minnesota 55114
All rights reserved.

2 3 4 5 6 7 8 9
2 4 6 8 9 7 5 3
First printing, 1995

Library of Congress Cataloging-in-Publication Data

Novakovich, Josip, 1956-
Apricots from Chernobyl / by Josip Novakovich.
p. cm.
ISBN 1-55597-212-8 (pbk.)
I. Title.
PS3564.0914A67 1995
813'.54–dc20 93-35921
CIP

This book is dedicated to my brothers, Ivo and Vlado,
and to my sisters, Nela and Nada.

These pieces have been published in a different form in *The New York Times Magazine, Threepenny Review, Boulevard, Witness, New Letters, Hungry Mind Review, Seattle Review, Massachusetts Review, New England Review, Antaeus, Icarus, The Sun, Chicago Review, Briar Cliff Review, Four Quarters, Western Humanities Review, The Gettysburg Review, Manoa, Pequod, Vassar Quarterly, Gulf Coast,* and *Ploughshares.*

I thank the editors of all these magazines for their support, and I especially thank Scott Walker, Ann Czarniecki, and Gordon Thomas for helping me to write this book, and Fiona McCrae for publishing it. I am also grateful to The National Endowment for the Arts, Ingram Merrill Foundation, Vogelstein Foundation, The Fine Arts Work Center in Provincetown, Villa Montalvo, Centrum, and Yaddo for giving me enough leisure to write the book.

contents

Via Negativa

ঌঌ

I don't remember when I learned the word *God* because the word floated in the dark bedroom – probably as much as *Mama* – and my mind floated in the word. *God* preexisted the formation of my consciousness, and by the time I could begin to wonder what God was, a lot had been spun around the word, so that *In the beginning was the word* worked in my case.

The word came from my father, who would teach me how to walk and not long afterward show me the stars and tell me how God made them and kept them afloat. God was everywhere, keeping things from bursting into the dark nothing.

Pantheistic elements permeated Father's theology. Daily he repeated his favorite verse: *For the invisible things of him from the creation of the world are clearly seen, being understood by the things that are made, even his eternal power and Godhead . . .*

Wearing a fencer's net around his face and a straw hat on his head, Father led me to his beehives in the garden. To him bees were the sixth book of Moses, the fifth Gospel, and each bee was one letter from the book of Psalms, each drone a letter from the Apocrypha. Bees fulfilled the Old Testament laws, by their perfectly regulated lives, and both testaments, by their perfect love for the Queen bee. But, there was a down side to the buzzing letters of Revelation: they stung. Upon stinging, a *B* fell upon the dank soil, coiled into a letter *C,* trembled, and died, while my lips swelled. My father claimed the stings cured his heart.

And his heart needed curing. It was the largest heart in the county according to the doctors, which – though a terrible thing according to them – made me proud of him. On X-rays the heart filled his chest. He had emerged from a horrendous life. He was forced to leave school after the fourth grade, despite the headmaster's pleading with his father, who replied, "If you will stay at our house in my son's place and work twelve hours a day, carving clogs, to feed my family of ten youngsters, he can go on with school."

After serving in the Yugoslav army for two years, when the Second World War broke out, he was forcibly drafted into the Croat Guards. He deserted and joined the Communist partisans, whose atheism he could not tolerate and who could not tolerate his preaching – they repeatedly pushed him into the front lines against the enemies, clearly hoping to get him killed. He deserted the partisans. At the end of the war partisans captured him, tortured him, starved him – his kidneys collapsed – and, though he was ill, forced him to serve two years in the Yugoslav Federal Army.

Father had been religious even before the war. Although a Croat he protested the Croatian government's burning a Serb Orthodox church in Kutina at the beginning of the War. But after the war, as he faced high taxes for his small enterprise – clog making (the official ideology considered all private enterprise the enemy of the people) – and close scrutiny by the police, he became extremely pious.

He became so zealous in prayer that thick crusts of blood covered his knees. When I was about eight years old he began to have visions and speak in tongues. Several people from other parts of Croatia and Bosnia gathered. They laid their hands on whomever was around, and everybody got the gift of tongues, except me. That evidence of my lack of faith alarmed me.

One day, behind closed doors, Father and his younger brother calculated the date of the Second Coming of Christ. It turned out to be only three years away. Although Christ did not arrive, Father died exactly three years after the calculations. As his brother commented, Christ came for him. (My uncle's comment taught me that the coming of Christ might refer not to a physical event affecting the world, but to your own death. That idea guided me to see religion as a beehive of metaphors for the inner reality rather than as cosmic apocalypses.)

Father's death was perfect. Several months before, he had begun to honor Fridays because of Muslims, Saturdays because of Jews and Adventists, Sundays because of most Christians; he wondered whether he should not honor Mondays, too, because of certain branches of Hinduism. He begged many people for forgiveness in the name of Christ for the sins he had wittingly and unwittingly done. He repaid those he thought he had got the better of in business. He still worked four days a week, hard, from sunrise till sunset, and then prayed most of the night. After the nights, he'd be strangely radiant. I am not sure that he slept much (like Kovrin in Chekhov's "Black Monk").

One night he wrote his will in clear handwriting, said to my older brother, "I'm going," screwed up his eyes to the ceiling, and began to die. My brother prayed, but Father said to him, "Don't pray for me, I'm safe. Pray for yourself." My brother woke me up, shrieking, and we both prayed for Father as gurgling sounds and foam came out of him and a trickle of blood from his nostril down his lips, while the wall clock clicked midnight, between the sixth (the number of man) and the seventh (the number of God) day of the month. Mother looked for the doctor on duty, but he had left the hospital and was gambling and drinking in a tavern in the woods to the rhythm of Serb folk songs, so by the time he paid a call, Father was stunningly lifeless. Faith in God perhaps curtailed Father's life but gave him a dignified exit out of it.

Resentful that I had to grow up without Father, I dared to question the sacredness of my father's death. I demythologized it and thought that he had gone mentally ill with paranoia – delusions of persecutions and grandeur. Persecuted he was most of his life, so I could not say that he was deluded on that score. Grandeur. It was a miracle that after facing death many times in the war he came out alive, raised a family of five, and played the best tambourine in town: his being carried away in thanksgiving to God struck me not as a sick taste for the grandiose but as something quite realistic and harmonious.

I thought perhaps he had plunged into religion out of cowardice, but then, he faced death quite intrepidly.

I thought that he had shied away from life, but I remembered how much he had loved honey; how he had introduced me to mutton at a village fair where he had sold two hundred pairs of his wooden clogs – with what gusto he had eaten, humming with pleasure; and I remembered with what thrill he had played the violin. He had rejoiced in life so gumptuously it was all the more remarkable that he died so willingly.

His faith left a deep mark on everyone around him. His oldest son became a lay minister, besides being a doctor. My brother is a mainstay of his church in Daruvar, Croatia. To the question "Why do I believe?" he gives a deflated but admirably honest answer: "Because I have been raised to believe. My grandfather believed, my father believed, and I believe." His theology boils down to respect for the dead.

Father's oldest daughter studied theology. Her faith is a classic case of misapplied theology. In the fall of 1991, when Vinkovci was under siege by Yugoslav Federal Army and Serb irregulars, she believed God would protect her. So while almost everybody else had left the town or hid, she walked in the streets. Shrapnel struck her and penetrated her liver; she was operated on without antibiotics, the hospital was bombed in the meantime – it took her half a year to recover.

I, too, studied theology, at Yale Divinity School, finishing a three-year program with a euphonious title, Master of Divinity. I cannot say for sure that I wanted to attain faith like Father's, but I do marvel at how thin mine appears and how robust his. The more I studied theology, the more skeptical I became. It could work the way Pascal conceived: the heart tends either toward God or away from Him, and for those who would believe, there is enough proof in the Scriptures to confirm this faith, and for those who would disbelieve, there are enough stumbling blocks in the Scriptures to help them turn away from God. I enjoyed weaknesses in theological arguments, and thought that my approach was the *via negativa:* after eliminating all the paths to God, the true one would emerge.

Although I read philosophy – Plato, Spinoza, and Hegel – and works of mysticism – *The Cloud of Unknowing* (there were a lot of small herbal clouds of unknowing all around New Haven in the late seventies) I remained *the fool that I had been before.*

Maybe I self-lacerate analyzing my spiritual path, until I realize that this self-abnegation could be a part of my religious heritage. Can I see my path in a good light? I started studying medicine in Novi Sad, Vojvodina (now Serbia), then psychology, then theology and philosophy, and finally, fiction. From liver shrinking in formaldehyde to imagination: from material science to less and less substantial, more and more ethereal, subjects. I think and I hope that I have mirrored my father's spiritual life, even if indirectly, in a muted way. Perhaps according to his kind, ecumenical theology, I could find something religious in my resorting to writing, which requires faith and forces upon me the rigors of a mendicant life.

When I go to Croatia, I visit my father's grave, where the epitaph *Death, where is thy sting?* reminds me that my beehive is empty. My faith is a starless dawn compared with the depths of the night, Father's faith, in which the Milky Way spiraled out of God's mouth as mist in the frosty cold.

Revising Memory

❧❧

I began to write stories in the States out of nostalgia when I dodged the Yugoslav Federal Army and could not go home. *Nostos-algia*, the Greek components mean *return* + *pain*: the pain that drives you to return. But I could not return, because in addition to politics, time banned me. I missed the times and places and people of my boyhood. I thought I could stay in touch at least with the people and the place, if not the time. I wrote a long letter a day, under the illusion that I was reaching beyond the ocean and plugging my spirit into my native soil, through that bit of a tree, the page, which contained the traces of being rooted in a moist black soil. In return for the long letters, if I was lucky, I'd get a few postcards.

I thought I might just as well give up on the lousy lot of my friends and brothers. But by then I was addicted to remembering through writing, and so I wrote to the wall in front of me. I described the places of my childhood in more than a hundred pages, and my fingers walked and ran, barefoot, as I used to in summer days: through a brown wooden gate on rusty hinges into the narrow passage between our scaffolded home and our neighbor's whitewashed house, both windowless to the passage, past laurel hedges and flower beds on one side, and a heap of sand on the other, past two cherry trees, where the yard opened up next to an apricot tree that my tabby and I climbed onto a balcony. Beneath the balcony, with its nose sunk to the dust, crouched an old Mercedes ambulance, which died when I was eleven. Next to it hid an old well, boarded up since I was nine. Father had managed to convert us from a spindle-well pulling tribe to faucet suckers, a miracle that diminished the yard: the dark, mossy, dank, echoing well, with cold moist air rising, that underworld was shut. Past the balcony around a walnut tree stretched out, supine, belly-up, a large pile of fine sawdust, on the surface dry, soft, good for wrestling and jumping in, but prickly to your eyes with the gusts of the wind.

Over a tilted red-brick wall on the western edge of the yard I often saw an old woman walking clockwise around her spindle well, pushing the rosary beads with her trembling blue thumbs, her swollen lips twitching. As a Baptist I was awed by her superstition, and our neighbors were by ours; our father often lay prostrate on the ground, in prayer, before entering his workshop.

A pale sister and her brother – children of a man who had come out broken after a long penal servitude for having been drafted as a lower officer in the defeated army of Croatian regulars during the Second World War – gazed through the wire fence, their small fingers bloodlessly clutching the wire squares; their eyes, glazed, playless, haunted the yard as my best friend, Danko, son of a Communist, and I shot arrows and wrestled.

Behind tall piles of wood trunks, thick wires laden with oxhide tanning in fallow stretched to the beams of Father's workshop.

After Father died, we quit making clogs. The pile of sawdust grew darker, rotted, and became soft soil, with red roaches crawling in it and red worms creeping out of it.

Next to the swing rotted a pigsty, without pigs because of the town ordinance. When I was six my brother-in-law slew the last big pig with a knife he had made from a broad and thick piece of iron. The knife stuck in the pig's throat, widening its larynx; the screams came out magnified, shrill, gurgling with blood, as the pig dragged sweating Kornel, who held on to the knife, around the yard for a long chilly time until only gusts of wind and blood came out. In the pigsty my middle brother (two years older than I) played doctor, inserting a thermometer into the asses of the neighborhood girls and boys. On the pigsty I fastened a silky American flag that I had torn from the antenna of a black Cadillac parked in front of our pink courthouse.

Farther down at the end of the yard opened up a frog pond, a green eye staring into the clouds. Beyond the pond stretched the soil that my mother turned to make way for tomatoes, potatoes, onions, strawberries. Half a dozen neighborhood boys, my brother, and I built teepees in a fallow corner and shot flaming arrows dipped in gasoline and threw knives at one another's chests, with straps of thick leather beneath for protection. Since in our town no garbage was collected and exported to city dumps, we took care of our own garbage in the fallow corner, burying some, burning the rest, and it never grew unmanageable because hardly any of our food was packaged and almost every box and bottle could be reused.

Between the two southern quarters of the garden, blue grapes covered the path – old vines crookedly growing and shooting their new vines into wires and wooden posts, making a dark, dank alley. The vines curled around pear trees, contributing to my father's theory that the snake in the garden of Eden was in fact a vine that curled around a tree and gave Eve wine that first made her shameless and then shameful. Drunkenness was the original sin.

I could have gone on and on, but I realized that the place was out of my grasp. Even before leaving Croatia, I'd been exiled from the place of my boyhood.

In the late seventies the Yugoslav government confiscated and paved our garden for a parking lot and a handball court. My brother Vlado moved to the ground floor of our home, tore down the wooden gate, erected an iron gate, paved the entrance to the yard, and built a stone wall so that you couldn't see the neighbor's yard – the neighbors had died or moved away anyway. He put rocks and sand into the frog pond; the frogs died. He sold our beehives, and though I couldn't say that bees had brought me much joy with their pricking and my swelling, I missed the buzz of their swarming.

Then I could not have acknowledged that the vanishing of those things comprising the world of my youth had somehow created a void in me, a phantom of alienation, as though my limbs had been severed and my nerves still recreated their aura. In the States, however, I could give physical expression to this alienation. Now there was an ocean and two seas and nine mountain ranges between me and my town. I had become a certified alien, with an alien registration number (green card), and therefore, though still a young man, I could torture people around me with stories of a time and place when I was not an alien. And I strove to return – through my memory – to the home that was not alienated, but redolent with images, gaining in beauty through the haze and mist of uncertainty. Sometimes the images became mere phantoms, metaphorically speaking, but recently, literally speaking.

These days Serb irregulars and Yugoslav federal soldiers are shelling the town; mortar strikes close. A projectile from an air force jet hit the newly built school of concrete on the edge of the old garden, setting its roof ablaze.

On national holidays we used to watch from our windows federal soldiers firing blanks at one another and raising smoke screens to make us feel safe and protected. But it looked as though they would attack us, which in fact they are now doing (November 1991): the Federal Army, which has with our money for decades paraded as our protector, is destroying the towns of Slavonia, with Vukovar already gone.

I expected that my original place would fade in my mind, but I didn't expect it to be destroyed. Before, as the state stole the garden and my brother cemented the yard, my original place seemed to me paralyzed, sick, sorrowful, but now it could be dead, or at least its skin, Yugoslavia, has died and is peeling off.

Now that Yugoslavia has died, and I can't return, my nostalgia has become grief. The first circle of Dante's hell bears the superscript: Desire But No Hope. Grief as longing and despairing, however, does not open the foul vistas of hell but casts you into the pains of purgatory.

To accept grief – give it priority over the practical daily routines – and express it, makes for mourning. All the paths of my imagination end in the place extant now only in my mind – and perhaps in the minds of others – but not out there. My imagination and memory almost solipsistically delve into my mind in an odyssey in which rather than myself I find the bricks from my childhood, the bricks that have cracked, burned, crumbled, collapsed. *Mourning.* Is it accidental that only "u" distinguishes it from *morning?* Perhaps it is, but it's a good coincidence. Mourning is the end of a night, and the beginning of a day. Maybe soon I'll see more clearly?

How could I have such Edenized memories of a place apparently surrounded by terror? My memory must have deceived me, must have made spontaneous revision, but now in the light, in the dark, of what has been going on lately, I must revise the revision.

Perhaps if my recall had been sharper, I would have been glad to be out of that muddy Croatian town for good. But I could not quite remember the features of the beeches I had climbed (the knife cuts in the bark after merciless lovers had carved out their initials and hearts) and I could not recall the sounds of quarrels and insults, and the quiet jealousies and hatreds between Serbs and Croats. Perhaps I remembered my hometown out of resentment just as much as out of love, out of fear as much as pride. Perhaps I wanted to annihilate the town through satire and sarcasm, or to raise it, through humor, for I believed that by playing with my memories I could have fun. The town would become the type of place often made into movies, particularly Czech movies, in which a spirit of drunken benevolence makes everything lighthearted. (Our town is the center of the Czech minority in Croatia.) On page I recreated my hometown, "as I remembered it," or chose to remember it.

And now it's clear just how selective my memory is, now that my childhood friend Danko has joined a band of chetniks to shell our town from the surrounding hills. This is how I recalled him years ago in a story:

> *I invited him to the sawdust, where we played dead, burying each other. In summers we knocked down green-skinned walnuts, and smashed them open with pebbles, as though cracking skulls, and indeed, out came little brain hemispheres. We chanted Dundu-Rundu, Dundu-Rundu, Dundu-Rundu, meaningless syllables with a good intoxicating rhythm, feeling as unfettered as cavemen, and peeled off thin walnut skins from the little brains and chewed the sweet meat.*

I thought I had written something quaint, but now that the friend, as an adult, has probably cracked real skulls, I see in the passage the obvious aggression to which I had failed to pay attention. I remembered the spirit of the childhood experience incompletely, or did not understand what I remembered. It's perhaps the incompleteness of my memory, something unsaid and at the time ineffable, that intrigued me, made me wonder and write.

Here's another example of how an incomplete memory generated my imagination: when my father was dying, my brother Ivo called me. By the time I got to the deathbed, I do not think that Father was conscious anymore. A trickle of bloody foam was sliding from the corner of his mouth onto his chin. Ivo had witnessed most of the stages of Father's death, but it was I who wrote the story of Father's death, seventy pages long.

So I think an experience not quite fathomed gives me the strongest impetus to imagine. The moments just missed are the ones that drive you crazy, crazy to live in an imaginary past, a past of your own, like an idiot.

That dwelling-in-the-past-narrowly-missed is by no means

unique to me: it is common in Croatia and Serbia and the Balkans in general. Homer narrated about past enmities between two continents, and six hundred years after these events embellished from his memory (or hearsay), Greece and Persia were at war; maybe the poetic memories contributed to the war? Similarly, Serbs eulogized the Kosovo battle of 1389, in which they had been defeated by the Turks. Legends arose about the Serbs almost defeating the Turks. And now almost exactly six hundred years later, rather than the beautiful oral epic tradition, we have reports of Serbs slaying and raping Muslims ("Turks"). And Croats, too, out of vague rumors and vaguer memories of kingdoms past, have sought independence at all costs, creating a new country, perhaps. And perhaps the new state might turn out better than Yugoslavia; perhaps the eyes of the secret police will not peek over the fence; perhaps neighbors will learn to respect one another's religions. Memories do lead to creation, but equally, to destruction.

I can't attribute any colossal consequences – constructive or destructive – to my storytelling, but I hope that I will soon be at peace with the town of my youth: so that there will be no need to go back and change, to "revise" the past. But it is clear to me now, that in my writing, my town has been mostly imagined. It is my town, crisscrossed not with streets but with stories.

Static Travel

The most fascinating of all the buildings in Zagreb for me when I was eighteen were not ancient buildings in the old town, or the skyscrapers in the new, but a building that did not distinguish itself in any special architectural way. Although the building was not much to look at, I looked at it keenly, so much so that I concluded I was nearsighted, which later proved to be true. An American ruffled flag hung from the building into the streets. Through the exhibition windows on the ground floor I looked at the pictures of Apollo astronauts landing on the moon. Sunshine reflected from the glass and instead of seeing what was inside, I saw the other side of the street, which was behind me. I wanted to lean my forehead against the windows, so I would make enough of a shield against sunlight, to look into the Moon country. Yet I was too scared to pay such close attention to the U.S. consulate lest the Yugoslavs should term me a pro-American traitor, and the Americans, a spy.

I heard that one could read American books in the library, but I did not dare to climb the steps into the library on the mezzanine floor. In default of reading American books, I resorted to the British consulate. For a long time I stood next to the door with a brass handle, a lion's head, listening to the rustling of newspapers. The door opened, and afraid of being caught standing, as if eavesdropping, I walked in. Behind a heavy counter, a woman with black hair and stark white streaks in it looked at me as if accusing me of something. In English I asked her, "Could you please tell me whether the general public . . . one . . . might use . . . hhh . . . the library . . . " Pronouncing these words, I was sticking my tongue between my teeth, to form the *the* sounds, feeling embarrassed for making the obscenely suggestive gesture with my tongue. My *r's* seemed to me now too rolled, now too slurred. "Da," she replied in Croatian curtly, though it may have been Russian just as well. She sized me up and down as if telling me: "How dare you, puny provincial, use this cosmopolitan, imperial language!"

In the manner of a starved rat caught in the light of day, I scurried next to the wall into a corner behind bookshelves and stared at books as at sliced cheese. The cheese had turned colors into gray, brown, black, though some of it still seemed yellow inside. I smelled the books, and through them printing shops, lead, years of lounging in shades and elegant spaces. Attracted to the idea of leisure bound to the books, I dared touch a book and take it into my hands. It was Aldous Huxley's *Time Must Have a Stop.* I sat at a huge varnished table. I bent over the book, like an embryo, trying to envelop myself into the book covers. Although I could understand the English of the book, my thoughts were not in it. The glossy surface of the table reflected changes in light, passing of shadows of eerie readers. Now and then a board of the floor squeaked so lightly that I was not sure whether it was the wood or the Oxbridge leather that squeaked. It must be the dry leather, I concluded. It squeaked like dry snow in the winter when I trampled through it, pressing hard just to hear it squeak crunchily, because it made me feel decisive and unstoppable. Finally I could not resist looking around, behind the shade of my hand and thumb fitted over my eyebrows – to guard me from the sight of anybody who might wish to keep track of what I was looking at, as if I were cheating on a high school exam. A man on my far left sat straight and read a huge newspaper with very fine paper. Why such large area for a newspaper? – as if it were a world map, and the larger it was, the more precisely one could focus one's scrutiny on small areas, colonies.

A tall man walked in, his head tilted back as if he wished to observe the chandeliers hanging from the ceiling even though there were none. His well-lidded eyes looked around horizontally, nowhere in particular as far as I could tell, like the eyes of someone used to watching distant horizons. I could not tell what color his suit was. Despite the attitude of the head, and the quality of his suit, he stepped into the room not at all stiffly but rather comfortably and with an imperial air said: "Now then . . . " He said something else, but I was already perplexed with the possibility of the present and some other time coexisting. This British metaphysical Weltanschauung of having then and now at the same time showed me clearly the narrow horizons of my provincial mind. Now the woman of severe dignity who had treated me so haughtily turned into a charming girl. She blushed and curtsied. Then some girls walked in, moving with ease as if the library were a skating rink. Although they were Yugoslav girls, they were just as free as any English girls. See, what it is to be a city person! I thought. Gradually, however, I began to dare, more out of spite than courage, to look around and soon I realized that nobody ever looked at me. I was not quite sure whether to be pleased at these findings, and I walked slowly to the bookshelves again.

On another occasion of my visiting Zagreb from my town "hid behind God's back," I walked to the American consulate. I breathed carefully outside of it, walked up and down the street, stood now and then, looked at old ladies in white gloves walking their spongy poodles, as if that was what interested me. I wished to enter the U.S. library and felt the same excitement as when I had considered telling a girl whom I had accompanied home, "I love you." I had walked around her; I looked at her hair, touched it, and wondered aloud whether it had split ends; I talked about all kinds of things, yet the more I did all these things, the more impossible it seemed to tell her. Now, the more I walked around the U.S. consulate, the more it seemed to me that I was loitering, and there was no way a bum could walk through the doorway on the side of which golden plates said: The United States of America.

So I walked away, bought a Coca-Cola, and drank the hissing liquid. The intensity of hissing diminished, and the frequency rose. I walked into a narrow curving street. The buildings had ornate façades and various miniature busts and friezes on them that one noticed only by accident. If you walked for the hundredth time down the street, you might for the first time see some shocking angel stick out at you a split tongue from his mouth. "Wow," you would say, "how is it possible that I never saw him before?" And from that day on, you could not walk through the street again without seeing that split tongue. So many demons and saints lurked from the roofs at me gleefully that it seemed I was in some cathedral of the Devil. In these old buildings spiteful history jeered through blind stone, without irises. In the street there were two consulates (the West German and Austrian) with their libraries, as if the primary mission of consulates were to educate foreign masses. I wished to walk into the German consulate but it seemed safer to walk into the Austrian.

A kind thin old man greeted me. He had gold-rim glasses. A smooth skin covered his bald skull – such as could be found only on bald skulls, finer even than the skin of babies. "Oh, wie nett! Ein junger Herr besucht uns! What would you like? How could we be of service to our young gentleman?" The kind man gave me a tour around the library as if it had been a large one. "Oh, it's so lovely that a young man is interested in German books! Nowadays they all want to speak English! No, I don't blame them, it is the language of the future, yet mein Herr, nothing could be more beautiful than the books of the bygone times. Ach, they do not know what they are missing!" He shook his head, like a tortured Jesus who raises his voice, "Forgive them, for they do not know what they have done!" as if it had been their fault that we now lived in the future. I sat at a table and read Zweig's *Schachnovelle*, rather, pretended that I read. The old man looked at me with so much joy and zest, scrutinizing every trait of my face as if the meaning of the wonderful story would soon show through and beam onto him the distilled drama. He looked like a hungry cook who had just prepared most painstakingly a cleverly spiced trout for his special guest, hoping to taste his own food through the transfixedly teary eyes and burning lips of the eater. Yet the salty tears could tell nothing of the coldly sweet brooks where the trout had leaped, and mine could show no intrigue from the book. Fearing that I should grow fatigued quickly, the old man brought me in his trembling veinous hands, with a gold ring on his annular finger, a glass of water. I drank it and it tasted like the walls through which it passed (at least as I imagined it, though I hadn't tasted the walls).

Then I visited the West German library, which was even stiffer in manners than the English. Equipped with *Das Kapital*, pleased with how heavy it was, and with *Die Phenomenologie des Geistes*, covered both from the material and the spiritual grounds, I walked into the American library. Yet as soon as I walked over the threshold, I lost my self-confidence but not my determination. I walked to the librarian and asked her whether I could read there. "Oh, sure, no problem," she said in English. I sat down and put my unreadable German books in front of me. Unlike the British books, American books were in special plastic jackets, and each one of them bore a large U.S. seal, a whole pale circular relief, seemingly intended for the fingertips rather than the eyes. People around me moved in a spacious way, which put me at ease provided they were not close to me. New people were coming and old ones leaving at a high frequency so that I had doubts as to how much they had read. Nobody asked the librarian for permission to read. So, my having asked her must have disclosed me as a provincial, but that made no difference to the librarian, or to anybody else. I liked how much at ease I could feel there.

I piled many books around me on the table, but, instead of reading, I glanced around the room.

At the library surprising manners prevailed. A young man sat in such torn jeans that his knees showed through the holes, and his left ball hung out. Now that is liberty! I thought. These Americans really know how to be free. He was hairy and almost everything on him was bushy: his chin, eyebrows, tip of his nose, knuckles, ears. The only parts of his body that had no hair were his eyeballs. Although it was summer time, he had a llama sweater. He read some book with a picture of a hairy guru who was in the lotus position with a smug expression on his face, as you would expect from someone with ten million dollars in imperishable assets. The young man sat with his legs thrown over the table. How can capitalism thrive with so little respect for things? I wondered. I for my part had always considered things more worthwhile than myself so that I had to sit at a table without touching it. The only contact with tables I might have was through books, cups, and plates. Leaning elbows against the table to support my head was a degradation of human dignity, which had incited teachers to shout at me: "Is your head filled with lead? Are you in a tavern?"

The comfortable American swagger showed clearly that they were not accustomed to walking through narrow doors, corridors, and alleys, and that they never needed to give way in the streets to anybody, not even to cars. True, there was not much grace in the swagger, but what is grace compared to luxury? A mere surrogate. They stepped on the floor firmly as if certain that they had all the right in the world to tread on the earth. Fear of stepping over broken glass and nails sticking out of wood planks seemed foreign to them. I for my part had to worry at home not to step on the parquet floor lest I should make it dirty. And I was not to sit on the floor, because my trousers might thereby become dirty. These Americans even sat on the floor. This is liberty! America reeks of liberty the way cigar smoke reeks of tobacco, I thought. As I admired these casual manifestations of liberty, a huge young man walked in. His neck looked like a tree trunk rising out of the ground, with roots outlined over the bottom of the trunk. I had never seen a young man like that. True, a butcher in our town did look like that. He had an enormous chest and neck, and his face was as red as the international Communist flag, and the meat that he handled – and ate, as the rumors would have it, raw.

Generally, I was taught to behave as if I did not exist, whereas most Americans I saw, it seemed to me, behaved as if the world did not exist. They walked as if they could push a bull out of their way, and I as if a fly could push me over. Yet in the library as long as I had the heavy German books on my side I was safe.

A girl in a tennis outfit walked into the library as if she could play right then and there. Her outfit was completely white. Even her teeth and her underwear were white. Only the little balls on her short tennis socks were not white, but rosy. Her legs were smooth and hairless, which I admired, not yet having heard that American women shave their legs.

I borrowed several books from the library and was too lazy to read them, let alone return them. I did not bother to return them because I thought America was rich enough to absorb such minor losses. As for the warnings from the library, they could not harm me in my Communist country. In fact, they contributed to my feeling of being a good Communist youth, through my showing contempt for the American materialist culture. I wavered between extreme respect and neglect in relation to the consulate and the States. I yearned to go to the land of opportunities and absurdities. Our newspapers were always filled with anecdotes from America, and the general sense was that such absurdities could happen only in America. I longed so much to visit the States that nothing could stop me. But to go there, I would first have to go to the consulate to see the consul himself.

Crossing the Border

On the train approaching the Swiss border my fellow passengers stare at the Black Forest where patches of deciduous trees are radiant with sunshine. I have a sensation of homecoming because I am about to visit one of my best friends, whom I have not seen as long as I have been away from Yugoslavia, more than five years. Yet, instead of being joyful, I am nervous. I always grow nervous when approaching a border. Sometimes I dream I am being taken off a train to a police station of a border town, to be tortured with burning cigarettes.

I think that many exiles dream similarly. The border crossing arouses a feeling of doing something illicit, of violating the mythic line between one land and another. In many countries the very possibility of such transgression has been turned into fantasy, a surreal possibility (which is to say impossibility): a form of transcendence. The transgression of borders becomes an obsession with many Eastern Europeans, and it is this challenge rather than their dissatisfaction with the lack of potatoes in stores that entices many of them to cross the borders. The border in their minds becomes a frontier between the real and the imagined, between a technological junkyard (East) and a computerized perfection (West), between the drab and the brilliant.

Leaving your motherland for the first time is a rite of passage, a sort of birth: You establish your being-on-your-own. Abroad you find a precise, concrete, artificial, alienated fantasy land in which the trains run punctually and without clanking, in which all the reality as you know it has been scrubbed away, the friction of matter is gone, and gloss shines and glares at you. You drift and slide like a child left in a hockey rink on skates for the first time. Now the reverse challenge occurs: to come back. Now you live the Odyssey, the ode of the essay of return, and to do it you must cross the borders from your surreal deodorized laundered permanent-press existence back into the old country, where you feel you sucked life directly out of the crumbling soil. The borders are again obstacles, more mythic than real. Breaking through them back into Motherland, the sphere of your childhood, is incest. You shudder at the thought of that body that you feel you must not penetrate.

Now the thought of the border arouses my body and mind. Images of exiles who must not cross borders come to my mind: a pale sleepless East German woman in West Berlin walking the streets and telling me how much she yearned to go back to East Germany, but her plea to return had just been rejected by the East German officials, and she was doomed to hang around the wall and to look over Alexander Platz, the ugly Muscovite space with highrises, toward the green brass roof of a church next to her old home.

An Albanian who ran across the border to Yugoslavia in a suit he had made of rubber tires so the barbed wires would not electrocute him. In a storm, when police dogs could not smell him, he stumbled over stones, branches, holes. Now he works in a New York pizza parlor, pretending to be an Italian, because he thinks it's better for his business to be an Italian.

An East German mathematician I met in Budapest, where he

hoped to sneak into a Greek truck and hide among hot green peppers and tires, to pass the Hungarian border into Yugoslavia, which used to be the exit land of Eastern Europe. He didn't have enough courage to follow through with his plan. Two years later by marrying a West German teacher he got his exit visa. I don't know what he does these days. He owes me two hundred dollars, and I guess to him communicating with me isn't worth that much. At any rate, he cannot go back to East Germany.

A Rumanian who swam across the Danube to Yugoslavia, almost freezing to death and drowning, in his spasms of shivering, but he made it, and went to New York. Although he was an architect in Rumania, because he has lacked the proper papers in the States, he is a construction worker. I bet he dreams of borders. He deserves to. He is a real exile, unlike me, who probably could not even attain the status of official exile, exiled from exile.

I could list many cases of people gazing across the Hungarian-Yugoslavian border, into freedom, and I have done the same, except in my case, I was staring, or at least I thought I was, from freedom into the almost certain enforcement into the military service. I am there at the border near the bank of the river Drava, whose waters after many rains are light brown. No border patrol in sight. All I see on the other side is a muddy peasant riding a muddy bicycle unsteadily, and a muddy dog limping after him. I expect the slivovitz drunk, which I surmise him to be, will fall at any moment, but he pedals on. Can you imagine? This is the celebrated Iron Curtain! It looks more like a mud curtain.

But no reason to think of the Iron Curtain now: I am approaching Switzerland, the land of absolute liberty. I reproach myself for the pounding of my heart. I expect dark blue police and laugh at myself. And lo and behold, a policeman comes straight toward me. "Passport please!" I show him my Yugoslav passport, he looks carefully through it, slaps it across his left palm (which I experience as if he were whipping me), and puts it into his pocket. "You get off at the border, Badischer Bahnhof, next stop, please!" I feel robbed without my passport. Something must be wrong with my appearance. Whenever I am tired – and after bumming through Europe for two months I certainly am – I think I look very much a Slav. These "free-world" policemen are like dogs trained to smell us out, which in many cases quite literally should prove possible! I am the only one dragged into the police station, while others admire what a free country Switzerland is, where nobody even bothers so much as to look at your passport.

The police ask me to empty my pockets. I turn them inside out and lay my miserabilia on the table. Two policemen quite unashamedly feel my thighs and ass, which tickles me. With clinical concentration they examine the stuff on the table. It is an obscene invasion of my privacy, more so than if they had turned my asshole inside out and inspected it under a microscope – any microbiologist could tell you that there we are remarkably similar. In pockets turned inside out you can see how we differ. They take my old student ID from which a sticker has fallen off, leaving an incriminating word: Void. My picture plus my name equals void.

My ID dreams flash through my mind. Asked to show my identification papers, I hand over an empty white card. Not that, a real ID please! I give them another one, with my picture but no name. The officer is angry. I search my pockets and with a sense of salvation feel the plastic of a card. The officer examines it through a magnifying glass, and shows it to me in a rage: my name and above it a Chinese face. I snatch the ID and find another one. My face and Li Hao Chu below. Then my name and a picture of a cat. And so on until I wake up.

Recalling the melange of my ID dreams, I chuckle. The policeman looks at me as if it were illegal to chuckle. "Why would you like to visit Switzerland?" "To visit an old friend." "His name? Address?" I give the information. "His occupation?" "An exile." "There is no such occupation," the cop hisses. "Yes, there is; it's a full-time occupation, day and night," I say. The cop goes to the computer, looks for my name, does not find it, and enters it; his two index fingers hit the keys like the beaks of two slow woodpeckers; his eyes stare at the keys with the same type of green light as the computer screen. Now I am in their records. "What do you have in your bag?" I offer my bag for rape like Lot his daughters to the mob of Sodom. There is plenty of linen there. I hope that pieces of my shit stick to the cotton and that the cop's fingers sink into them. But my linen looks spitefully clean; I had been scrupulous about my linen and washed it just before the trip through Germany.

They look at the contents of the bag with squeamish disgust thinning their lips; they look through the French and German bank notes of low value in the heap, at the addresses on torn pieces of paper, mostly people I've met on the trains, in the streets, pubs, at the Siberian conference in Paris, etc. – all the addresses that I would regret throwing away but do not have enough enthusiasm to enter into my address book. I would still like to write to these people one day; their traces accumulate in my pockets, warm them up, make me feel like I need not be alone, call me to write. All that is childishly innocuous, but now exposed on the table it looks immoral to me. It seems wrong, and if it is not wrong in my eyes, it seems to me it must be wrong in their eyes; everything about me one way or another must be wrong and illegal. I've had it. I'm angry.

"Your occupation?" the green-eyed policeman asks me. Though I sometimes become witty when angry (perhaps the only time I do), his question leaves me with a speech impediment. I mumble and stumble over words. Ordinarily I would meet the question with cheerful insolence: "I am a bum," the effect of which would be that I would not be believed. Now I feel guilty because I have no ostensible occupation. I feel as the unemployed must have felt under the pharaohs of Egypt, who, according to the liar Herodotus, asked that once a year each citizen of Egypt demonstrate to have made a living in an honest way during the year; whoever could not do so was to be executed. Although I'm on a writing fellowship from Vassar, I cannot say I am a writer since I haven't been published. I cannot say I am a minister, since despite taking a degree in divinity, I haven't been ordained. My life is being assessed, and reckoned worthless. My German fails me, English and Croatian spring up in my mind, and I break into eloquence in English explaining that I have just finished my religious studies in the States and am touring in Europe for personal edification. It sounds so simple and acceptable that I immediately translate myself into an easygoing and thoroughly incorrect German, and the cops laugh and beg me to spare them.

They tell me I may go, and they show in a bearded relic from the sixties and order him to empty his pockets. They don't even look at me to see whether I am leaving, and though I could not say that I miss their attention, I feel curiously abandoned.

I am in the streets of Basel, free to go wherever I want in Switzerland, and I enjoy the privilege of treading the cobbles and of climbing into the tram, which takes me past gilded buildings on to a sooty stone bridge over the poisoned river Rhine. The dark old architecture surrounds me like historical ghosts.

The border crossing has shaken me up somehow. Without it the city would appear free and beautiful. But rather than to take the border harassment merely as a necessary evil that misportrays the free country, I suspect it to belie a police state.

That crossing into Switzerland took place in 1984. I've had many border crossings before and since, each one distinct in its own way. Crossing the German borders from Holland I was thoroughly searched for drugs; a bony cop squeezed one-third of my toothpaste before he began to believe it did not contain cocaine. Crossing from West Berlin to East Berlin, I was interrogated for a couple of hours. I was sent back from Dover to France because I did not have enough money to be allowed into England; thrown off a train in Denmark because I did not have a Swedish visa. In my entry into Hungary a customs officer looked through my papers, mostly diaries and stories, sat down and read them for a quarter of an hour, making cynical comments and laughing whenever the narrative struck him as stupid. My luggage was searched through in my crossing to Yugoslavia for smuggled coffee. A Soviet border policeman ate all my bananas.

Almost whichever border I cross, the police take out their books and search for my name among the names of terrorists, murderers, rapists; and not finding it, they look at me as if meaning, "All right, not yet, but we'll catch you some day!"

In the summer of 1988, it annoyed me that I needed a French visa on my U.S. passport, but a Frenchman said to me: "When a Frenchman wants to go to the States, he has to undergo the insulting process of a obtaining a visa, so why shouldn't it work the other way round?"

It strikes me now that I've taken my border crossings too seriously; after all, since I am past the drafting age and have a U.S. passport, I can go back to Yugoslavia. For many people border crossings have been more trouble than for me. For example, after World War II it was nearly impossible to leave Yugoslavia. A man from my town cut the ceiling of a train and hid in the narrow "attic" between the roof and the ceiling. In the darkness he couldn't read his watch. To make sure that he would get off the train abroad, he waited as long as he could and when he got off he was right back where he had started from: in Zagreb. The coach had been to Vienna and back. He was caught and sentenced to several years of enforced labor; the fiasco killed his spirit. He was raving mad once he left the labor camp.

Before World War I my grandfather attempted to emigrate from Austria (the part that is now Croatia) to the United States. He could not obtain a passport. He thought it was so absurd that his cow had a passport (for sale abroad) that he took a preposterous chance. On the passport of his cow he traveled to the United States and was admitted into the country! I wonder what the U.S. immigration officials thought when they saw "450 kg" for my grandfather's weight.

Nowadays the U.S. consulates do their best to frustrate potential visitors: in India thousands of people wait for days in front of the U.S. consulates to petition for visas; if you are lucky you get an interview with a petty official, which turns out to be an interrogation. Many people enter illegally, through fraud – buying passports, green cards, copying visas, or plainly crossing the borders where they are least attended, risking a not-so-gentle treatment by the U.S. border patrol. People are driven by poverty, or by a desire for wealth, or by hardship of one sort or another, greed of one sort or another, to move to another country and seek a new life. Even where life is not hard materially, it may be hard spiritually. You can run into many Dutch, Swedish, German, Japanese, and other immigrants in the States and other countries. It's not that materially they didn't have good chances at home, but they just needed a throwing away of their strict upbringing in a country where different customs rule – a breakthrough into a new life, through borders not as obstacles but as thresholds to imagined freedom.

Unterwegs

❧❧

Wiggling my shoulders out of the backpack straps, I stand at a tram stop in Basel. Not far from me stands a gentleman whose moustache doesn't hide a slight smile. I imagine he's complacent at being Swiss. A tranquil young woman in a jockey outfit of leathery tones basks her cheeks in the setting sun; she seems to be a cognac ad from the Sunday *New York Times*, torn out and made three-dimensional. I wish to ask her for directions, but, cowed to be as decent as possible – among the Swiss, you can't be like a Roman – I ask the complacent Swiss gentleman. He replies he's a stranger too, just come out of Germany. I am about to ask the ad, but an elderly woman with a large shopping bag, having overheard me, tells me to take the number two. I thank her while the ad looks at me, her hazel eyes translucent in the sunshine and streaks of blond hair slanted like Sahara sand in the wind. Behind the curve, a green tram, number two, rings.

Gilded rims of buildings glow. It must be terribly expensive to rent here, I think, yet you can stroll by the medieval splendor and stare at it for nothing. I remember I haven't paid the fare.

Images of my previous visits to Jonah, in Zagreb, nearly ten years before, hurl into my mind like stones thrown from the sling of David; they hit me and only because I am not Goliath, they don't harm me. I speak of what to me is as old as the Stone Age, of my fire-red bearded friend slicing cheese and onion in a stale basement of a stone building in Zagreb. When Jonah spoke, whatever he'd experienced, read, heard, became an anecdote. A musician constantly interrupted him there to hum his tunes that he was certain would make him an instant hit. He'd seize Jonah by his jacket – he had actually so little confidence in the catchiness of his melody – and hum into Jonah's ear. We all fought for his attention; the basement was bursting with talent though nobody among us wrote or drew a line of anything. He was the champion arm wrestler in Zagreb although gesticulating while talking was the only exercise he got – a considerable amount, actually. Of course, I idealized him now, after many conversations where nothing made the difference, why not make a difference now? This is the man who, without seeing me for years, invited me to live in his apartment as long as I wished.

After passing through the layers of new sensations – golden, gray, green, blue, brown – that visiting an old city for the first time usually gives, each one in a different way, I am at his doorstep, pressing a little bell-button, a red nipple on a small white breast. We shout greetings and nonsense when he opens the door, like two American girls who have won a pizza in a lottery, except in deeper voices. We sit down and finish all his alcoholic reserves, three bottles of wine and half a case of beer, in no time. He tells me France is only one hundred yards away from his apartment, and Germany two hundred. He would take less than twenty minutes to go shopping for wine and cheese in France and for bratwurst and bread in Germany – if the Swiss police finally gave him a temporary pass. As an exile, he's in limbo, waiting for permits. He tells me that only a little more than ten years ago one of the Swiss cantons gave women voting rights, such is the Swiss democracy. He talks about the roots of Croatian words in Persian; Croatian sailors in Teheran can converse with the Iranian sailors, using no foreign languages. Curious information keeps coming out of him.

We are not alone. Five or six strangers stay with him: three Spanish street musicians, one English guitarist, one Croatian exile. He bought six used mattresses to accommodate the homeless.

The musicians fall asleep late in the evening. In the morning, they rub their eyes, finding Jonah and me talking with the same zeal as the night before. The second evening, they are about to fall asleep, yet they stare at us talking as before. In the morning, catching us in the same elation, they seem to be waking into a surreal world. Propped on their elbows, in the third evening, they watch us like a TV set – a live broadcast of a contest for the longest continuous conversation, for the *Guinness Book of World Records.* Close to dawn, we awake them, bursting out into laughter. They stare at us with bloodshot eyes, as sleepless flesh at apparitions.

Jonah lowers his voice, giving it full volume; his face outlines puzzles, increasing its creases; and solutions, dispelling the creases. He feigns being insulted, his hand akimbo; he feigns anger, stretching out his hands to your throat as though to strangle you. He has a tremendous voice. Voice is one of the critics' favorite tools, a platitude really, but the written word cannot have it; written word can't make it, can't raise a voice out of a cavelike, barreled chest.

After three nights and two days of sleepless conversation, I surrender to the spirits of sleep. Jonah sleeps for only an hour and goes to work with Ivan, the Croatian exile. They call themselves Freemasons because they work part-time as construction workers. The part-time gives them the sense of freedom.

The sunlight in the room tells me I am a lazy bum. I crawl from the mattress and sit up. In an armchair in front of me, Leo from Manchester, with a cigarette hanging from his lower lip, is changing a string on his guitar. He rolls the knob and the plucked string whines higher and higher. He greets me cheerfully, the way only the awake can those still half-asleep, shouting that the breakfast's on the table – he's made an extra omelette for me. And he walks out into the street to play, as he had been doing for twenty years.

Leo plays in a narrow street in the center. The higher the street curves, the narrower it grows and the more southwest German in style: the house skeletons, beams, form squares and triangles right on the surface – resembling a starved man whose ribs and jaws are no longer concealed by flesh. The people, too, express an openness; although they do not seek your gaze, once they meet it, they don't shun it – they look lucidly as if they had nothing to hide and you had nothing to hide, and all that passes without a tinge of anxiety. Asking for directions to come to Leo's street, I chat with several people. Just as easily as the conversations start, they end – there's no progress and no regress. I lose all the desire to talk because in the easygoing openness, the people are cut off from me profoundly as if their beams, high cheekbones and white teeth, were there only to support the shining skin, while their essence stayed safely away in their bank safes. Outside of the interior Swissness, among comfortable eyes of the people, I relax as though in a sanatorium, where rich catatonic schizophrenics OD on Thorazine. Envious of their wealth and spiteful toward their high civilization, I am of course bound to twist the basically pleasing impressions.

Before I could make out any other voices, I hear Leo's gruff voice, "How many roads must a man take to be a man?" He smiles; I never knew you could sing and smile at the same time, even with a wide-open mouth. His eyes shift from face to face, his head sways in the rhythm. He opens his eyes, showing his large eyeballs, as if suggesting something crafty and funny. I am thrilled and proud; thrilled by his voice, and proud, because I know him. His eyes touch my face too; I smile. His eyes go on, abandoning me; his eyes establish a brief intimacy before they move on to another face in the rhythm of his string-pluck. Little children, old ladies, youngsters move with his rhythm. Several girls astride their bikes gaze at him, their lips and eyelids loose and moist.

I walk on. At a corner before an ancient apothecary, a child in a silk shirt and pearls in her ears plays the violin awkwardly. People drop coins in her small violin case. It strikes me unfair that this child, apparently from a well-off family, pockets the money that could go to homeless musicians. Perhaps the child's parents insist that she earn money for her lessons, teaching her some kind of entrepreneurship – to be able to grow richer in adulthood.

I walk over a stone bridge over the Rhein and sit on the riverbank steps among many young people, who read, chat, knit, laugh, smoke pot, gaze at the passage of water under the mild sun. Bare feet, loose hair, loose skirts, loose shirts; the whole scene is loose, a relaxed Swiss interpretation of postmodern punk hippiedom. They affect the love of nature as only cement-bound city kids can, using the only nature they know, their bodies, half-naked and babyishly sloppy. Some eat nuts and roll their own cigarettes. Red paint on girls' finger- and toenails give me an impression, my Rorschach, that the nails have been torn out of their flesh – in a medieval torture chamber during the Counter Reformation? No Nuke badges show the youngsters stand for good in some way. Old people passing on the promenade above pause, lean over the fence, and inspect. Some Turkish guest workers, timidly grouped together, drink red wine from bottles and lustfully and incomprehensibly stare, painfully left out, uninvited.

Leo shows up, and a brunette with blue eyes and flushed cheeks in a purple skirt coils over her feet at his feet, her hips curving into a likeness of a mermaid, come straight out of the Rhein. Leo leaves, and I talk to her; she's enthusiastic. The three Turks now sit next to me and they butt in on our conversation, and gradually, I am pushed out. The woman listens to them enthusiastically. A Swiss young man in a white suit behind me laughs as he chews his lunch; he comments about the pollution of the Rhein and invites me for beer. Kurt works as a masseur, but would prefer to be a concert pianist.

Later, at home, Leo reads a little, listens to some music, transcribes songs, drinks orange juice, and says he can't sing for several days because his throat is sore. He'll rest his vocal cords. He invites me for a beer to a pub with a peasant-worker atmosphere, and talks there:

"I like Basel. People are generous, the police don't bother you, except that there are too many rules here. We are not allowed to play between noon and four in the afternoon, and we can't go on after nine-thirty. Silly. I don't mind. I can't play all the time."

"You are lucky you can make a living, working so little."

"There's more work involved than what meets the ear. Yes, of course, I am fortunate. But it's not everywhere you can make money. In France, seven or eight years ago, people would drop you one-franc coins into your hat. They still do, but the one franc is now worth three times less than before. If they made a new currency, with one unit worth three times more, they'd drop those. There's just something in the number one, some kind of completeness. Here, too, I get mostly one francs, but those are Swiss francs."

As he talks, he spreads a pile of nicked coins and stacks them; they resemble refinery tanks seen from afar. When he's done, a waitress gives him blue bills in exchange. He has made ninety francs (sixty dollars) in two hours.

The transubstantiation of the coins into respectable bills fascinates me because I have no way of making money while bumming through Europe.

"It's summertime," he goes on. "The living is easy. People are carefree, they open up like tulips, they give. But wait for the autumn! I have to save up. But I can't."

He laughs and orders a beefsteak and a couple of large beers, one for me. He rolls a cigarette and wraps himself in light blue smoke. His straight black hair shines dark blue; cut straight above his eyes in the middle of his forehead, it looks like a wig. His face is burnt with sunshine, smooth, except for two deep creases aside his lips, which form a lower part of a capital *A* with his nose forming the upper part. Below his bright blue eyes spreads a marshland of broken capillaries, which makes me suspect that his kidneys are bad. One of my roommates in the medical school in Yugoslavia told me that darkness below the eyes almost inevitably signifies poor liquid drainage, that is, poor kidneys.

"You must have played with many people," I say.

"Sure. What gets me is that Patti Smith used to pass the hat for me. I thought she was too lousy to sing with me steadily. We slept together on the same narrow bed and I got no hard-ons. And now she's a sex symbol! A superstar. I don't know which is more incredible. I guess, her being a superstar."

"Wouldn't you like to have become famous?" I ask him, pushing him into the past tense of unfulfillment.

The meal has been lowered and is steaming in front of him as he digs his knife and fork in. "I stay in the streets. Several times I was invited to do studio recordings, but things always fell through. I don't know why. I played in a band once, but I couldn't take orders; I like to be my own boss. I am happy to play in the streets, make contact with passers-by, there's nothing more beautiful. I get tired of the streets, but there is nowhere else. You go away from one street, you find you are going through another."

Recalling my neglected ambition to write stories – and thinking that I experience nothing and some people very much – I wish to hear whether he knows a good story.

"Well, a crippled painter spent his afternoons in a café, near where I played my music, having his drinks, his laughs, and making sketches. One day he was taken to the hospital. There, he walked on his arms to the window, climbed it, and by the rain drains went down, six stories. He slipped off around the fourth, and was smashed to pieces on the pavement below . . . Better red than . . . white."

Leo blows his nose on the side of the table into gravel. "I liked him. I realized how much I missed him at that café table, sketching over his bifocals. Can you imagine? During his life he was always poor, a beggar practically, and after his death, he became well known."

At home, Leo and I cook a meal, very little to my taste, macaroni with bacon, for four of us; Jonah, Leo, Ivan, and me. The grease makes me sick after the first bite. Leo enjoys it and asks me to clean up the kitchen, which I flatly refuse. I go out and buy two bagsful of groceries from my supply of money, for common use. Still, my refusal to put in "actual labor" pisses him off.

Before Ivan and Jonah got their free masonic work, Leo had treated them to quite a few meals at the neighborhood pub. He continues to treat them, repaying them for their kindness.

We go out for a meal another evening, and he treats Jonah and Ivan, but not me. He says: "These Spaniards! They play out there at least seven hours a day. They must make five hundred francs a day. Still they've bummed Jonah and Ivan for cigarettes – their last ones! If Ivan and Jonah have only macaroni to eat, do you think the Spaniards care to notice and share their roast beef?"

None of the Spanish speakers are Spanish. The violinist is Moroccan, the guitarist Argentine, the young woman who accompanies them (not in music, in person) Basque.

The Moroccan says nothing at all, looks at nobody, and sits in the armchair with a sad expression on his face evening after evening. In the streets his violin moans out gentle pathos. The noble pain in his face seems at odds with the cigarette-bumming story. I try Spanish on him, but my Spanish-Quechua mélange, picked up in a two-month hike in the Andes, is defunct. I try my poor French. He livens up and gesticulates, most appreciative. Afterwards, he treats me with respect, which is mutual. The lanky Argentine and the Basque bask on the mattress, inseparable. I never see them touch each other, let alone embrace, nor do I hear any erotic panting coming from them at night, nor do Leo, Jonah and Ivan, who comment on it as some kind of terrible aberration, while I remember that Leo slept like that with Patti Smith. Perhaps the couple are so cultured that they avoid making a female pant with sexual desire in front of five young men, that is, beasts.

The couple prop themselves on their elbows, whisper to each other, and deposit their lanky bodies back onto the mattress. The Argentine's skull shines; his brown beard cushions his lengthy face of the sad countenance. The Basque mirrors his face, in the same elongated manner, except that her eyes are larger, calmer, delicately framed with long eyelashes.

The Spanish speakers speak no English. Leo, who speaks no Spanish, keeps addressing them in English. After several days of that abuse, the Spanish speakers show up with a miniature dictionary, one by one and a half inch, Spanish-English.

One evening the Spanish speakers offer us glasses of wine – it's the Basque's birthday – and Leo thinks the wine is too cheap, and suspects that when we are gone, they'll drink champagne.

Next morning, while Jonah and Ivan work, Leo speaks to them; the shocked Moroccan, who, it turns out, does understand English, translates. "In a month you have contributed nothing – rent, food, cleanliness – everything is expensive. You should pack and leave."

Flushed with anger or shame, they do.

When Jonah comes home and finds out what has happened, he is furious, he wants to run out into the streets to invite them right back.

My picture of seven people living in harmony despite poverty was torn apart and thrown into Swiss garbage. Leo and Ivan tell me that if some other people were there, unimpeachable harmony would fill the little apartment. Jonah nods.

Later, Leo comes home all excited. A rich middle-aged woman has given Leo a fifty-franc note and invited him to play at her gallery opening for another one hundred and fifty francs. Leo accepted and asked whether he could bring along a painter, Jonah. She replied, "Of course, I'd love it if you did."

Leo comments on how rich people always say, "I'd love to," "I love it," "How lovely!" They love everything, and liking is just too weak for them. "But then again, maybe this one does love." Leo folds the bill to clean his nails with.

Jonah, Leo and I walk a long way, sweating, to reach the gallery. The sculptures exhibited are cute representations of idealized Swiss peasant life. Little axes stick out of felled miniature trees, real pygmy fir trees; piles of wood, no thicker than matches, neatly frame the scenes.

Wine, cheese, crackers, orange juice, I notice them before I notice the people. The sculptor is grinning in the limelight. The gallery woman tells Leo to wait a little before he starts playing. Leo and I walk out for a breather. Three braless girls in torn T-shirts, standing through a Volkswagen sunroof, shriek at Leo; the car beeps, they stop and chat with him. The gallery woman comes out, her golden necklaces and bracelets rattling, and tells them not to make so much noise in front of her gallery, to leave at once. Is she jealous? The bug is gone, and the gallery woman loudly laughs, and while talking, she breaks into dance as if she simply couldn't control her vitality. All her movements, far from spontaneous, strike me as measured, and she is pathetic in trying to present an image of enjoyment, freedom, and youth. Her inviting Leo may be one of her little whims.

Unpacking his guitar, Leo shouts, "I'd like to play a couple of songs!" His voice is oddly gruff in the fine space. Nobody pays any attention. He clears his throat and repeats, "Hey, folks, I'd like to play a couple of songs!" Now only a couple of people acknowledge him; they stare neither welcoming, nor disapproving, but with a slight air of surprise, as if to say, This thing doesn't belong here, does it?

Leo, sensitive to failing to gain attention, realizes he should try something more formal. "I find it a great pleasure to have the honor of being among you, Ladies and Gentlemen, to present . . . "

Several people take out their handkerchiefs and wipe their foreheads. It is hot even in the gallery – in a cool country like Switzerland, air-conditioning isn't a must. They walk around, and lean forward to examine the works, their arms locked in the back for balance.

"You know, I am usually out there in the streets, an outsider to the beautiful settings like this, so it really is a great pleasure to . . . " Leo stumbles into unfamiliar ground and stammers;

Jonah, Ivan, and I worry for him. Of course, he doesn't belong, but he's been invited; he deserves none of the insulting treatment, mostly in the form of the lack of any. "Although I am an outsider here, I hope I will manage to give you pleasure with my songs." And, in a Joe Cocker voice, he begins: "How many roads must a man take to become a man!" He sings extra loudly as if to regain the lost territory, but there's no territory to regain. Several people turn toward him, their glasses of green wine calmly nestled in their pale fists, and measure him, wondering perhaps how it comes about that on a quiet Saturday afternoon, on a hot day, somebody grows so eager to shout so loudly. But most resume walking and bending toward the sculptures. I eat a lot of cheese. The song over, Leo asks, "If you have any requests, I'd be happy to play them for you."

One elderly gentleman with white-blue hair makes a request, and Leo sings and encourages the man to sing along. Leo wants a happening. The man does sing along, and Leo encourages him to take over completely, at which the poor man doesn't know what to do. His weak voice fails. His embarrassment grows; it looks as though Leo is making fun of him in revenge for having been tacitly made fun of himself. They are sorry they have gotten themselves into the mess. Even before the song is over, the gallery woman seizes Leo by his arm, and says, "Leo, I think it would be better if you played outside, so we can hear you as a *gemutlich* background."

She walks with him arm in arm as if on a promenade, and pushes him out. A man in a black suit, with the air of a mortician, brings out a chair for Leo to sit on in front of the gallery.

Leo shrugs his shoulders, breathes deep, tilts the chair back as he sits down, and grabs his guitar as a drunk grabs a fence post. He plucks the strings contemplatively, playing for himself, plucking out a problem. He hums along his étude and makes eye contact with us and the passers-by, and a small circle forms.

When Leo is done, and the gallery woman has thanked him

financially, he asks, "Could you now take a look at my friend's drawings and paintings?"

"I am too busy. He could leave them here and come to pick them up tomorrow at nine in the morning. I'll tell him what to do with them."

Throughout the exhibition, Jonah was out of his element, partly amazed at what he was seeing, partly disgusted, and he didn't like standing on the sidelines like a mute beggar.

Next morning he and I walk to the gallery. We are there at nine o'clock, sharp. The gallery is locked with a Sunday hangover depression about it. Fifteen minutes later, a tall man, a senior executive type of appearance with hangover hostility, comes to the gallery entrance and unlocks first the grates and then the door.

"We've come to get the paintings we left here last night with Mrs. . . . "

Without looking at us, he walks inside. We wonder whether he has seen us at all. Several minutes later, his hand, his white shirt cuffed, peeps out of the door, holding the bundle of paintings. The fingers are loose and the bundle is about to slide on the cobbles, but Jonah grasps it in his hands. There's no statement of opinion, written or unwritten, from Mrs. . . . , unless this extreme rudeness is one.

There's no time for us to say anything. The door is closed. Jonah holds the bundle of his works like a rabbi his Torah. We walk to the nearest pub. He looks relieved, although he's harbored hopes that he could make a living selling paintings. Yet from the start, as he saw the gallery woman, he was suffused with exasperation that he should depend on a creature so plastic, so intent on disguising her wrinkles, which probably wouldn't have been ugly if they hadn't been acquired in petty pretension.

Of course, it is doubtful that vanity produces one kind of wrinkles and genuine suffering another, for even vanity boils down to suffering. Self-pity, the bottom of vanity, brings about perhaps the same physiological reaction as does compassion: the same acidic effect, corroding the face. Yet when a person tries to hide the creases through surgery, makeup, and loud jewelry, the person expresses poverty of spirit. Why use the artifacts? If the eyes are alive, they overpower the wrinkles, illuminate their history, the trial, the drama, the character. The light of the eyes shows the evidence of heavy loss in the empty trenches, that is, in the creases, and bestows an aura of wisdom, that is, resignation, after defeat as well as after victory. The open eyes state, No more powder, gun or cosmetic, should be dragged back into the trenches.

Mrs. Gallery must understand the power of radiance – she has attempted to produce a glow, a light around her. She must have had an inner light – it came out a little when she was generous to Leo, and was eclipsed when she was in her setting among her class, eclipsed by gold. Attempting to produce radiance, the effect rather than the cause, she has smothered herself.

Still, no matter how you acquire your creases, if right now you look straight in the eye of another human creature, trying neither to hide nor to show anything, you will be absolved of all your vanity by a sort of grace – the grace many Christians believe in; no matter when you join the faith, you are on equal terms with those who'd been there for decades. A fake man in a moment of true frankness is as graceful, even radiant perhaps, as Moses. So, although the woman looked ignoble, empty, decadent, if she were in a moment to lose herself, her plasticity would melt away. But many people, perhaps especially those who hang around galleries, around the art of seeing, avoid insight. That's how I think, and my thoughts mix well with the foam of beer, especially as I remember that I contradict myself, that the open eye of many Swiss struck me not with grace but emptiness.

What an insult for my generous friend this rejection has been! He hoped to share his work in the mood of intrepid piety. When your work gets into the talons of a red-nailed vulture that looks more like carrion than vulture, you shudder, jolted into a state of becoming a miserable moralist, as I am now. The woman has enough paint on her to cover a whole tribe with war colors, and whether she knows it or not, she has declared war. The trumpet of loud colors has awakened my friend and me; we can look now into the society of trade and into ourselves, to see whether all in us is a commodity too, whether we can be bribed. If she turned around and offered my friend a lot of money for his paintings and me for my stories – wouldn't we sell? We would, and we wouldn't have to worry about insights, but, rather, about Swiss bank accounts. Isn't our philosophical mood merely a cover for defeat?

Yes, it is.

So, Jonah and I drink our bitter cups of poverty, beer. Hardly any beer is bitter enough. Sometimes beer is only cold when it should be bitter. We let the bitterness grip our taste buds. It sinks into your blood through your tongue, away from the surface, and tightens your muscles.

I look at my barrel-chested friend – his ignited eye, his fiery red beard. True, that's something surface, but I believe there is a hierophany, a revelation of the spirit, from a good soul within. Jonah has always been soulful and passionate. For passion he forfeited formal education – he had preferred to shriek out poetry in bars to going to school to recite it by rote. Nothing could corrupt him, I am certain as I look at him.

Next morning, Jonah wakes up, eager to work as a construction worker, not a Freemason. Soon, his salary comes, he pays his rent, feasts, and invites a new crew of street musicians to stay with him.

The morning after the feast I take a walk along the bank of the Rhein and run into Kurt the masseur. There's something bitter about him today.

"Remember those Turks who talked to the girl when I met you? Well, they raped her. Can you believe that?"

"How do you know?" I ask.

"I saw her a day later. She wept and told me."

"They gang raped her?"

"No, the husky guy with a mustache took her for a ride and raped her in the woods. The police wouldn't write her report because she had no witness. I am going to kill him! Here!" He opens his coat and shows me a gun below his armpit. "I bought it just for him."

We drink in the same pub as before. He uses, whenever he remembers, High German, but always relapses into Swiss German. He repeats himself so much that I manage to piece his story together:

"I used to be married. I had a wife and daughter I loved. One day, I cooked a meal while they went shopping. I set the table with flowers and candles, and I sat and waited. The bell rang. They shouldn't ring the bell, they had a key. I was puzzled; we never had visitors. I opened the door. The police came in. 'Sir, we are sorry to have to tell you this, but we have to. Your wife and your daughter have been killed in the street fifteen minutes ago. A cab knocked them down on a pedestrian crossing.'

"Every evening I cooked the same meal and set the table, with flowers and candles, and I sat and waited. I believed that they would still come, that they were not buried and dead. But the bell never rang. I began to avoid the apartment, and whenever I can, I am out in the streets. I hate the indoors."

Kurt and I shake hands; I feel his wedding ring. Serious, he looks me straight in the eye, with tears in his. Can you believe it, I think to myself, he is Swiss, yet passionate. He's destroyed my prejudice and my desire to have any prejudice.

Why am I writing all this? I was at a loss what to write, so I took a bath and read "Luzerne," a story by Tolstoy about an Italian street musician. As the paperbacked story disintegrated under my fingers, I decided to write "Basel," a story about an English street musician. But instead, I wrote about the Swiss border police; then, my friend Jonah occupied my attention – and would deserve more – so that Leo remained on the sidelines, in a way appropriately – being an outsider was his central theme. He slipped out into the streets, forsaken, eliciting a flicker of friendship in passers-by, before they'd drop him; and before they could drop him, he'd drop them, to make sure he had a say and wasn't merely a passive dropout.

This is a story, a history, I don't care what it should be called, let it be outside categories to fit the spirit of outsidedness.

Anyway, almost everybody is an outsider and exile. Why pretend? Everything is in a flux, so that even if you stay in the same place, you are adrift. You can hit the road, catalyze the change, crassly throwing yourself out of your deceptive home – the structure that gives you an illusory sense of permanence. Drifting with the flux, or a little ahead of it, you may find more constancy – albeit in change – than at home. Luther said that you should consider yourself a guest wherever you are, nothing belongs to you, you are *unterwegs,* on the road, and you must always be ready to pick up your stick and go on. You should consider your stick as something rented, and likewise even your body and your soul.

You needn't feel utterly helpless. You can make this your motto (Joshua 1:9):

Be strong and of good courage; be not afraid, neither be thou dismayed: for the Lord thy God is with thee whither so ever thou goest.

I've tried to make it my motto, but I always forget it. From multitudes of impressions, my senses blur, my thoughts drown. Out of the sensations, I have to pick up my stick and go! For now, I don't want to leave Basel.

Jonah and Ivan tell me the Biblical picture is incomplete unless I look into astrology. I say the only thing that could induce me to take a look at it, aside from vanity, is that Taurus is supposed to be the most skeptical sign, and since clearly I am skeptical, paradoxically, there could be something to it. My doubt makes it believable. To follow their discussions, I decide to learn the basics, and while I am drawing charts and counting the degrees between Mars, Jupiter, and Venus, several Croatian exiles show up and argue. I detest politicos, so I don't want to listen to them, but I overhear.

A man has brought photocopies from the Basel library, about a Croatian thirteenth-century priest, who was, on the account of refusing to renounce his unorthodox beliefs, tortured and executed. The Catholic authorities tore up his body on a stretching machine and threw his bones into the Rhein. The event took place before Jan Hus, the Bohemian precursor of the Reformation.

"The Czechs have made so much out of Jan Hus, and you Croatians always keep silent," says a voice. "Jan Hus is a hero; Andrija Jamometich is buried in obscurity, to be dug out by German scholars."

When the man who speaks hears that I am a "minister-in-abstinence," he brings the papers to me and beseeches me to do something about publicizing them. The case intrigues me at once, but I refuse to admit it, thinking how tedious scholarly work would be. Moreover, I shun anything nationalistic. The man feels that and asks me whether I am a Croatian.

I deny it.

"Well, what are you then?"

"A mixture of Slovenian, Croatian, Hungarian, and Czech ancestry."

"A mixture," they all scoff at me now. "Do you think the world goes by such definitions?"

"I don't need definitions."

"Don't be silly," they say. "You can't think without definitions. All right, where were you born?"

"Slavonia."

"That's Croatia. Where were you raised, what language did you speak, whose air did you breathe most of your life?" Without waiting for my answer, they say, "Croatia, Croatian, Croatian. So why don't you call yourself a Croatian, why does everybody shun the word? This little nation has been oppressed for a millennium in various empires, and her own people renounce her!

"Do you want to hear what Engels writes in *Neue Rheinische Zeitung,* with the blessings of Marx? – He says that Croatians are a little Slavic nation, by nature reactionary, a bunch of vagabonds and adventurers who roam the earth and spit on everything and foremost on themselves and their own soil."

"Marvelous!" I say.

"That fits you, doesn't it?" they say.

"Perfectly," I say.

"Engels wrote that after Jellachich and his Croatian regiment had put down the Hungarian Revolution of 1848. He failed to see that the Croatians had been oppressed by the Hungarians – that a Croatian National Revolution had taken place. Marx and Engels despised small Slavic nations and loved the big Germanic nations. Seeing that you have been brainwashed by Marx's disciples to hate Croats, Slovenes, Slovaks, you still refuse to call yourself a Croatian?"

"I do."

"Typical Croatian mentality. You want to claim you are an internationalist?"

"No. International contains the odious word *national.*"

"And you think you are pleasing anybody by refusing to identify yourself? Do you think people will respect you if they see you can't be faithful to your own people?"

"Every nation is filled with assholes. I wouldn't like to affiliate myself with any. A human being is a human being. If someone proves to be a human being, I don't care what nationality he or she belongs to."

"Do you think it is any different for us? But you must identify yourself, and from there respect others in their own right. You have to have a nation, even simply just to know what it is to have a nation you love, because most people do."

"I don't understand what a nation is."

"Remember what Engels says about you?"

"National problems should be transcended, they should be made an anachronism."

"You've been brainwashed, my boy."

"You've been brainwashed."

"Where do you live? Don't you see what is happening in

Ireland, Iran, Iraq, Israel, India – just to mention the countries that start with *I,* let alone Albania, Armenia, Angola, Afghanistan . . . The whole world is in turmoil because of unsettled national identities. The sooner you get your identity straight, the better."

We all shout.

"You are blind," Jonah says. "You think I emigrated for fun, like you – and I don't believe you did it for fun, you can't be an exile for fun! I wanted to found a Croatian Evangelical Church, and after I publicized it, the police – most of them Serbs – interrogated me, twisted my arms, spat at me, searched my apartment, threw everything around, threatened to kill me if I went on with my plans. I got a notice to show up in court. It was a matter of jail for using the word *Croatian* or *exile.*"

"Why did you insist on using the word *Croatian?*" I ask.

"Why not? Everybody has a right to call himself something."

"But the Croatian Nazis killed thousands of Serbs."

"Yes, a small minority of Croatians did – conquered by Hitler. Do you think they all had a say? Some among them were quislings – they saw a chance to gain power. Others would have allied with the devil himself to get rid of the Serbian dominance, which had oppressed them since the First World War. Just like the Ukrainians against the Russians, or Slovaks against the Czechs. But most were dust in the wind. And anyway, Serb fascists killed a lot of Croats."

"Serbs have all the reason in the world to mistrust Croatian nationalism. You don't need to insist on national terms. Why not simply be a Yugoslav?"

"*Yugoslav* is a neologism; Yugoslavia was created on a drafting board in Versailles – Woodrow Wilson needed the neutral zone because the First World War had begun in the Balkans."

Ivan tells me that he was harassed by Serbian police in Croatia for trying to introduce a real Croatian dance in a folk ensemble. "It's harder to be a Croat than a German, Italian, Russian, English.

Nobody questions the right of a big nation to exist – no matter how many atrocities it has done – a small one everybody spits on."

"I didn't know you all were that political."

"Of course we are. We have no choice. Our apartment, even here, is under surveillance by the Yugoslav secret police," Jonah says. "The agents are everywhere. For all I know, Ivan could be an agent in disguise."

"Maybe you are," Ivan says to me. "Maybe Jonah is. We are all in a cloud of suspicion. You've got to get used to it before you can stop being afraid – and do something for your people."

Jonah gives me a typewritten list of the Croats killed abroad by *UDBA,* the Yugoslav secret police – nearly a hundred people on the list, more than twenty in Germany. He shows me another list – Albanians killed by the Yugoslav, that is Serbian, secret police. They tease me that I, too, am now listed for having visited and stayed for so long with the anti-Yugoslav elements.

I sulk. Either they are paranoid, buying émigré lies, or they are right. The generous musical apartment has even further lost its harmony. I listen to Luther's call, to pick up my stick and go, *unterwegs* – on the road, or, literally, under the roads.

A View from the Slope

Spring 1983 at the Károlyi Foundation

"May I remind you that it's my turn?" I spoke in as gentle a voice as I could muster lest I offend my opponent by pointing out evidence of her senility – she had made two moves in a row, without waiting for my move.

"Yes, that's what I am reminding you of. If you don't want to move, I will." She smiled slyly, boomeranging the suspicion of senility, her pale eyes covered with a milky haze.

It was true. I had taken too long, staring more at her than at my board, thinking about how I was playing history. My opponent was the ninety-one-year-old first Hungarian first lady, Countess Katharine Károlyi. Her husband, Michael Károlyi, had formed the first Hungarian government after World War I, distributing his lands to peasants as an example for other landowners to follow, and in turn was ousted as a selfish exploiter by Bela Kun in the Soviet-engineered Socialist revolution. In exile in France Count Károlyi bought a Medici villa on the edge of Vence and formed a colony for young artists.

For days all of us fellows at the colony had waited to see the countess – she would be the first noblewoman I ever saw. And one morning as the mists and clouds drifting in the valley beneath us made it look as though we were in heaven, the countess walked down the stone steps in Adidas sneakers.

I pretended to be a writer although I hadn't published anything, which, to my mind then, should have counted in my favor. The secretary of the foundation told me that only because the countess wished to have somebody Eastern European – and nobody from real Eastern Europe had applied (Yugoslavia did not count) – was I admitted.

Now, I threatened to fork Madam Károlyi's queen and rook by preparing to jump my knight onto her f-7 pawn, but she made a maneuver, first checking my king with her queen's bishop and then withdrawing her bishop on the h file to protect her threatened f-7 pawn. She smiled again, leaning over the board and peering at me. Her gray-blue hair with her pale blue eyes, the creases engraved and stretched between high zygomatic bones, her thin nose and raspy breathing gave me the feeling that a ghost was experimenting with oxygen, getting high on it, while she could very well do without it.

"Hungary has many good chess players. Portisch and Adorian," I said.

"Yes, Adorian has a charming beer paunch," she said.

While we played, her maid – not a servant in the old sense, but an employee of the Hungarian government, whose task it was to take care of the countess's well-being – brought us tea at four o'clock. The maid kept swearing in Russian under her breath, perhaps for my benefit.

The countess took a book off her bookshelf, her autobiography, and opened a page, her long fingers trembling. Their dry skin wrinkled in waves like an oversized glove that had once fit a sensually plump person seventy years before; a picture in the book displayed a beauty with hazy turns of cheeks and a monalisaic smile.

She urged me to read the opening of the book. Her parents, who lived in a castle atop a hill, yearned for a son, an heir, but all they had were three daughters. So, when the mother gave birth to the fourth child, a messenger ran down the hill into the village, shouting, It's a boy! A feast started. The second messenger came down the hill, slowly, and announced it was in fact a girl. The feast stopped. No sons were born to the nobles, and Katharine lived under the impression of having betrayed her family for not being a man. "Yes, men have it much better, don't you think?" she asked me when I turned the page. "You can go into politics, you can do anything. Of course, as a woman, you can too, but it took me too long to understand that because everybody kept telling me the opposite."

We finished our tea and returned to the board, but made no more moves. "I love Yugoslavia," she said. "Why do you live in the States? In exile my husband and I first went to Dubrovnik – the happiest time of our life. It shouldn't have been, but it was . . . the marketplace with fish, young men singing at every corner . . . After World War II my husband arranged with the Swiss government to have a large shipment of medicine sent to Yugoslavia. But Tito sent it back, saying, 'We have everything; we need nothing.' He was so proud. Such wonderful pride!"

"I don't think so. If he had needed the medicine himself, he would have taken it."

"I know." She sighed. "We people around the Danube have so much in common; I wish there were some kind of Danubian confederacy – Austria, Hungary, Slovakia, Croatia, Rumania, Moldavia . . . "

"It sounds too much like Austria-Hungary."

"I mean confederacy, not empire."

"Europeans have no talent for confederacy. Somebody would dominate."

We stepped out on the balcony. The maid came running up the road, wailing and exclaiming, *Bozhe moy!* My God! She pointed at a black cloud and ran into the basement as though the devil were going to pounce on her from the sky.

"You don't often find such wonderful superstition anymore. Marvelous!" Madame Károlyi said.

The countess and I talked two times a week at teatime. However, my privilege soon faded because a friend of mine, Boris, whom she immediately preferred, visited me from Croatia for a week – actually, he would stay five months, while I stayed only three – with his blue guitar.

Boris did not intend to outstay me, but, getting ready to study English literature in England, he needed a good place to prepare. The old handyman had just had a falling-out with the colony administration. He had gulped from the barrel of oceanic dark wine he couldn't quit (nor could I one evening when I visited him) and had gotten into a fight. In the morning he showed up with a black eye, trying in vain to fix a pipe. Later in the evening, drunk again, he banged on the doors of the female residents in pitch darkness, and when that did not work, he tried to enter the scattered bungalows through the windows. So in the morning he was fired. Whenever something went wrong, people came to my bungalow, asking for Boris. Since Boris readily helped – hauling gas tanks, lighting up stoves, changing fuses – the countess offered him the job of part-time handyman: free residence (sharing my cottage) and five hundred francs a week.

Although Boris did not have a driver's license, he drove through the narrow Provençal streets a Russian Volga the Hungarian government had given the countess. The government had long given up hope of communism's working, and the resentment against the old aristocracy turned into unabashed admiration. Boris chopped wood for the countess, blew into the fireplace until he turned red and until flames caught, while the rapturous countess clasped her hands in gratitude. She played chess with him and showed him her old manuscripts and letters. I felt a little jealous, as though he had stolen my girlfriend, a woman of ninety-one! Later, when she died, it turned out she must have been ninety-eight at that time – when she died three years later, she was one hundred and one, according to Boris. Perhaps she did not want to ruin her amorous prospects by revealing her age.

The colony perched on a steep rocky slope with cypresses and cedars. The bumpy trees grew in waves like huge candle flames; when the sun assailed the trees, the emerald curves wavered in the heat, their green quenching and cooling the intense blue light. The Provençal landscape explained to me the realism of French impressionism. The rich, oily, aromatic oxygen, the foothills of the Alps on the north, the azure sea on the south, the red wine – what a setting! Art, the mythical bird, should perch on a cliff and fly into the waters like an osprey, climb above the ice . . . but my art faltered, which I blamed on my German electric typewriter, an Olympia. You were supposed to believe at least in German perfectionism. Every time the repairman in Nice fixed it, it worked beautifully in his shop, but in Vence the old problem recurred at once. The spacebar did not work – all my letters stuck together. As I was no experimentalist – especially not under forced circumstances – and did not wish to write a novel as one word that would stretch for four hundred pages, I tried again to repair the typewriter, but there was something deeply wrong with it. Or with me. This was the first time that I was absolutely free to write – I expected the leisure would lure out my demons to "create" – and yet for hours I sat and stared over the typewriter at lizards meandering among the stones and sparrows panicking at the new twists in their imaginations while nothing twisted in mine. I tried to write a story about a man who loses his soul while trying to save it. He feeds the poor but one poor drooling man disgusts him so much that, instead of giving him another morsel, the benefactor stabs him to death with the kitchen knife. At that moment, the benefactor's soul leaves him and wanders into the universal void, and he soon becomes the U.S. secretary of state. Every ten lines I quoted from the Greek New Testament, without translating, and I imagined that this would do for sophistication – certainly better than quoting French. Soon I lost the threads of the story.

So I spent the days hiking above the town, past horses I fed with fallen apples, past ruined churches, across a creek, past a bunker. You could hike in any direction, over the mountain onto another, and you would not run into Private Property and Keep Out signs, as you would in the States. I understood why exiles loved France.

In the morning I shopped at the farmer's market in narrow cobbled streets within the walls of the old town, buying onions, fish, fruits, cheeses. I shopped at a supermarket – a long haul past a town waterfountain, up a steep alley, past loud dogs – and borrowed books at the British library run by two old English ladies. And I had an American dentist, who was scared that my check would bounce, rebuild my tooth. Biting into a crusty pizza in Nice, the tooth cracked, and when I chewed my own tooth, I complained to the waiter that the meat was not deboned; the waiter laughed and told me to look at my angry mouth in the mirror. In the evenings Boris and I often drank red wine. I had not drunk much wine before, and now the tart tightening of my gums would, I hoped, teach me some French secrets. I was not alone in that hope. An Australian painter, an American Chicana writer (Sandra Cisneros), a Canadian sculptor who rented a duplex in town (a red-faced white-bearded bon vivant), Renee Butler, a Jewish sculptor who made various tents out of transparent silklike cloth (she claimed it was her ancestral nomadic nature that drew her to tents) – in fact, there were dozens of people in nearby villages and in Vence who came from the States, Germany, Sweden, in pursuit of art: a whole subculture of either artists or winos. In some the two combined productively, in others destructively.

One man outleisured us all. John, an Englishman, lived above us, high on the mountain, with a goat and a rooster. His hen died. One day he wrote me a note, begging for a forty-franc fellowship to buy a potentially egg-laying chicken that would make him and his rooster exceedingly happy. I denied him the application. It came at a bad time, several days after he and I went to a museum in the Magdh Foundation. I had to pay his entry fee, twenty francs. Afterwards, I made dinner for him. The following evening the same. While his cheeks bulged with my cheese, he told me that I was too materialistic, that there was a better way, less matter-bound, wiser, less harmful to the world, and that this way was his. He peeved me, but later I regretted that I hadn't given him the mini-fellowship. A hen would have given him an egg a day to supplement the goat milk; he had a sack of flour for pancakes. He ate wild onions, roots and, later on in the season, wild berries. He drank from a spindle-wheel well. In the evening, he went to sleep with the setting sun, and now and then burned oil in a two-millennia-old oil lamp he had found in the ruins of Carthage. Every night he woke up at three to study the constellations of the stars. He kept a stargazing and bird-watching diary. He looked as though he were in his late twenties – a young Don Quixote – and in fact was in his mid-forties. For twelve years he had traveled through Asia, Africa, Europe, visiting temples and monasteries. I spent many hours talking to the meditative man, who outbohemianed us, though he had tough competition.

Sandra Cisneros, on an NEA grant, wrote poems in the morning, and at noon laughed reading letters from her friends, and in the afternoon sat at the cafe blowing the coffee steam away from her cup. "It's important to spend an hour a day looking like a writer," she said. "That's the most enjoyable part." Interrupting her sips of espresso, she startled young men by complimenting them on their eyelashes, lips, and nostrils. It entertained her to see them blush. "You have to take liberation seriously," she said. "Women should be able to say whatever they like. And it's good for the fragile boys." But she was not quite ready when a fragile German – three hundred pounds, six-and-a-half feet – whom she had met in Florence with four other Germans – arrived. Sandra had given the Germans her Vence address to be penpals, and when Ludwig showed up, exhausted after a five-day hitchhike from the east of West Germany, in love with her, he frightened her. She asked me whether he could stay with me. I said fine – I wanted to improve my German anyhow. So this scorned pining giant now had to listen to Croat German. So he wouldn't die of depression, I took him out to climb the mountains with me – he ran out of breath and nearly died from the effort. In the evenings, he drank beer, bouncing it in his bulging cheeks, and slurping more. He stayed for ten days – until I freaked out at him because the German typewriter did not work, as though that were his fault. Although he invited me to stay at his home for a month, I told him to go home, to Saxony: *Sachsen wo die schoene Maedchen wachsen.*

Many people stopped by and a dozen stayed. A tall Pole and a chubby Pole emerged from a lemon Mercedes one dusk. The chubby man – his neck covered with cotton and bloodstains, his fly open – said he was a fashion designer. Under heavy eyebrows the tall man's eyes scanned the slopes, bushes, bungalows. "Women? Any action here?" In his paintings thousands of female buttocks rose from sandy earth, beyond clouds, like the tower of Babel – and above it floated the painter's tormented self-portrait. "The way to heaven, man!"

In February an official representative of the Hungarian government arrived. Sara Karig, a distinguished translator from Russian and Bulgarian, would help take care of the old countess. She had spent nearly ten years in a Siberian camp, where she perfected her Russian and learned Bulgarian, and she never quite recovered from the freezings.

In the dark villa, she complained that the stone floor was too cold. Siberia was in her bones. When she heard I was a beginning writer, she told me she was an editor – however, that I should not be afraid but show her what I had written at the colony. I did. She liked one story and said that she would publish it in a leading Hungarian magazine. I was happy about that: what absurdity, to be a native speaker of Croatian writing in English and publishing in Hungarian! Madame Karig asked me one morning, "Do you keep a journal and take notes? Do it. Whatever strikes you as trivial and silly now may one day delight you. If in a novel you write a scene at a train station, rework what you scribbled down while waiting for a delayed train – and so strengthen your credibility. And you may need a countess one day. Take my advice."

When it rained, Madame Károlyi lay in bed with bottles of oxygen flanking her as though she were scubadiving in a pernicious ocean. One afternoon she, Madame Karig, Boris, and I sat and planned to form a colony on a Croatian island, where taxes would be lower, the climate sunnier and warmer, neighbors friendlier. From the sale of real estate in France a much better colony could be established on an island. She had already talked about it with some Japanese sponsors. She had a dreamy look, rasping, barely opening her mouth, visionary, as though she were outlining a revision of paradise lost. In a blue dusk the rain ceased, the clouds bled pink reveries, and I left the room of the noble dreamers.

The following dusk it stormed, and the electricity went out in my cabin. On my way to see Boris, who now stayed in a low stone cottage next to the villa (where the exiled president had first slept in France) I saw Madame Károlyi on the terrace. "Do you have electricity?" I asked.

"Oh yes," she smiled broadly. "Electricity I have! . . . but I've lost everything else."

Boris lay on a cot in the cottage and read Herodotus. It was good that he had moved so I could finally work. He complained, "Every five minutes, she shouts 'Boris, Boris!' It's as though she were a five-year-old and I her parent." And sure enough: feeble, imploring cries, "Boris, Boris!" whiffed through the curtain. "After hours, I am not answering!" He laughed in a low voice, the way I and almost everybody else from our hometown, Daruvar, laughed.

A year later Boris told me that after he'd left she had named her German shepherd Boris. "She was so used to shouting my name!"

My story, as far as I know, never got published in Hungarian. I visited Madame Karig in her apartment below the Fish Castle in Buda. She told me that the story would be published if I cut it by 30 percent to make space for the illustrations a cartoonist had already drawn for the story. She was curious to see what my concept of revision was. I did not try to tighten sentences, because I would lose the leisurely rhythm, but I eliminated the beginning, the end, and one long digression. She said, "That's exactly how I like to edit." But later nothing came in my mail in the States, and when I visited Hungary with my wife in 1990, Madame Karig's name was not in the phone book. Jeanette and I walked to her apartment on the steep street in Buda. I had imagined she would invite us upstairs and serve us blue grapes swimming and bobbing in cold water in a crimson pot, as she had before, and that she would show me her fortieth novel translation from the Bulgarian. But her name was not on the address plate where it should have been, where it used to be, nor was it on any other plate in similar-looking buildings in the street. So I feared that she had died.

Now in 1991, eight years since my stay in Vence, the countess and probably Madame Karig are dead. Books and articles about the countess, by people who had stayed at the colony, appear. Sandra Cisneros is a well-known writer. I am still waiting for my first novel, *Salvation and Other Disasters,* to come out, after two years of delays (Salvation and Other Delays?). From London John the hermit called Renee the sculptor (who had gotten divorced in the meantime), asking her to buy him a one-way ticket to the States so he could tend goats in Montana. Boris kept in touch with the Polish painter (who had remained in France), got his Ph.D. in English at an American university, and became a professor. He's just called me up, tired of the computer-modem news from our Croatian town – hospitals and schools bombarded, old men mutilated; abandoned and lonely cows and pigs wander through mine fields, blowing up and bursting red into the rainy sky. Boris left for Croatia to ask for a machine gun so he could defend his country.

Just eight years, and things are so much worse, almost for everybody!

Writing in Tongues

"Relax that tongue. Let it move. Praise the Lord! I hear the sound! Let your ego go, don't think about it! I hear the word! Hallelujah!"

Under my father's and my brother-in-law's palms, my skin began to feel hot, and crackles of static convulsed my scalp with cool shivers.

"God is working! I hear the word!"

I suspended the tongue between my jaws, offering it to the electricity, but when nothing seemed to take place, now and then I rolled an *r,* plopped my tongue against my incisors into some kind of *t* . . .

"Get your ego out of the way, let the Lord do it!"

I relaxed the tongue again, a new wave of static shivered down my forehead into my eyes, where blue light appeared on the hitherto dull dark-brown screen of my eyelids and the light grew almost white.

"The Lord is releasing a waterfall of his grace over you!" The men prayed frenziedly, as though God's offer depended on the strength of their plea. Air whistled through their teeth as they tremblingly breathed – and evoked for me a steam-engine train in the snow, whistling out the smell of oily coal. I tried to get the train off the screen of my eyelids, because God no doubt wanted me to be receptively blank. The whistling in the men's teeth lowered in frequency, my eyelids became brown again, the train vanished, my scalp grew cool, and the men, dangling their hands along their pockets, said, "The Lord was very close to giving you the gift of speaking in tongues, but there's something in the way: your pride."

I stood up from the artificial rug, my knee popped. Just before I touched the door handle a spark pricked my fingertips.

Then it was my brother's turn to undergo the laying-on-of-hands. Soon he broke into a song, in a strange tongue, with varied vowel and consonant combinations. Ivo walked out, luminous – in addition to salvation, a vague and unprovable theological concept, he had acquired a concrete skill, a new tongue. All I got from the tongues was envy – not a gift but an anti-gift. I envied the way Cain envied Abel, though I was the younger brother, who did not plan to kill the elder.

But a year later, the Lord had not arrived yet, my father died, our Baptist church suffered a schism into the charismatic and the non-charismatic branch, and rather than salvific powers, speaking in tongues seemed to exert divisive if not destructive ones. Still, the aura of something divine in speaking in another language stayed with me. In the attic I found an old Political Rand McNally Map with America in the middle and Asia split in half. I smoked cigarettes and gazed at pink China, green America, yellow Soviet Union. Most countries were pale, all without mountains, most with black rivers.

To political geographers, rivers seemed more important than mountains, or they were simply easier to do, which itself must have been some kind of statement about American leisure. The map came from my grandmother, who had moved back to Cleveland, Ohio, after divorcing my grandfather in a village near Kutina in Croatia. She had visited a couple of times and given me crisp dollar bills. Yugoslav money, mostly red and blue, could boast no crispness; it creased, creases became cottony, oily and dark, and slowly disintegrated at the sparse seams. We taped the vulnerable creases since shopkeepers would not accept a bill missing a corner and banks would compensate you only a percentage of the shriveled money. On our bills bosomy women harvesters bent and factory workers bared their chests, clenched their fists, out of control and emotional, but on the American bill a tranquil gentleman, resembling my grandmother, his neck wrapped up in cloth, had no need of baring anything. The trans-Atlantic money seemed as clean as a starched bed-sheet, self-confident and erect. I read the bill, *One Dollar, In God We Trust, The Great Seal, Federal Reserve Note.* I knew *In, We,* and *One.* All the kids on our block knew how to count in English, German, and Hungarian, at least up to five, and how to swear in these languages, plus in French and minus in English. From the world map I learned some English names of countries. Germany, which used to be *Njemacka,* literally meaning the land of the mute ones in Slavic languages, from now on would be Germany for me – easy to remember because *germa* meant *yeast* in Croatian.

English was everywhere: on the radio (Tom Jones and the Beatles), in undubbed movies in the cinema (*Goldfinger* and *Spartacus*), in sports (soccer, basketball, tennis), in fashion and cars. But still, it seemed to me an impossible language to learn, with shifty vowels, tongue-in-tooth consonants, slippery and flowing like an eel, albeit, an electric eel, but for that all the harder to catch.

So, when I had to sign up for English or Russian, two hours a week at school, I thought that I could learn only Russian as a Slavic language, but to take it I would have to transfer to the morning classes and I preferred to stay in bed till late, neither awake nor asleep, lethargic, guilty, until I smelled fig tea and eggs with onions – my mother brought my favorite breakfast to bed, to stir me out of my sloth (that I read novels late into the night counted only as more sloth) – and so, probably not out of great love for the West nor hatred for the East I began to study English, in the afternoon classes, though study is a strong way of putting it, since I studied nothing during those years of pubescent yearnings. Some basics – like *My name is Mary, and what is yours? Mine is John.* – I did learn although the classes were conducted in Croatian and I doodled birds and skipped school – and English – as much as I could get away with.

When I was sixteen, I badly sprained my left ankle, and stayed in bed for several days. My brother Ivo, aspiring to learn English in order to become a rock-star, had bought a dozen Langenscheidt's books in simplified English, with the vocabulary of 450, 750, and 1200. I grabbed the one with 450, *Greek Myths.* As a kid I used to read fairy tales, and now I would not have admitted that I wanted to read them – and to my mind myths were nothing but tales. Under the guise of learning English I read the book in a couple of days, amazed that the meanings of the words came across, through a shroud of letters, from a long distance of memory and guessing – the chaotic letters ordering themselves through my leaps of faith spoke of men and women changing into animals, gods into lusty men, and after that, that I should understand a language seemed modest and natural, no hubris. Then I read *Dr. Jekyll and Mr. Hyde.* Jovially I wondered whether the new language would change me into a half-man half-goat or a donkey or, equally astounding, a foreigner? When I returned to school a week later and the teacher asked me to translate a text the class had studied in my absence, I did it unfalteringly. My grade jumped from D to A. Where Christianity had failed to give me a quick command of a language Greek pantheism succeeded.

At night I listened to Voice of America, BBC, and Christian broadcasts on the short wave. In the dark I loved ominously sonorous Texan voices announcing "The Hour of Decision." I'd wake up early in the morning when the stations went off the air, to a buzz sliding up and down the frequencies, like waves crashing against my walls and my ears. One morning I wrote the radio station because the announcer had promised a free New Testament. (That was the second letter I had ever written in English. The first I had written with a dip-in steel pen, in calligraphy, to Roger

Moore, who sent me his autograph, which I kept with autographs of my dead father.) Along with the New Testament came the station's monthly magazine with my letter printed and highlighted – evidence that broadcasting the Good News into the Communist bloc worked. Seeing that my words, not Croatian but English, were printed in Canada, gave me indeed a great confirmation in the faith – not in Christ, but in the word: the English word had become flesh or at least lead on cellulose. Hitherto, English had been a myth – sounds travelling ethereally, sailing over tempestuous oceans, partly as particles, partly as waves, to torment me at night, metamorphosing me into a prisoner, locked in language, or lack of language. I could not speak back but now, look at it, my name, in black on orange paper, in the secular and sacred language had spoken, written, back!

Though I detested going back to church, I still went because now and then English speaking missionaries visited. One Sunday afternoon the president of Liberia gave a speech, and I got to shake hands with him, the first president, and actually, the last so far that I have shaken hands with.

The library in our town, Daruvar, got a present of one hundred books in English from the U.S. Consulate in Zagreb. I read *The Old Man and the Sea* without a dictionary. Then I read the dictionary, marked the words I lusted after, wrote them down on lists, and walked in the park, memorizing fifty a day. During history lectures, I took notes in English. I gave all my friends English nicknames, and some stuck. A Boris became Bobby and many people still call him that; Zeljko, a name derived from *zelja* or *wish,* became Willy, since Desire did not seem to be a man's name. I remember where I learned some words: *obtuse, obtrude,* and *obese* I learned with my feet dangling in the town swimming pool, in water green from algae and brown from the spring rains. *Mob* I learned at the cool water fountain in the park, Juliesbruenn – a German name from Austria-Hungarian days – as I let the water pour over my forearms to cool my blood. *Bog* I learned while bathing in a large oval marble Turkish bathtub in our hot springs – the letter sequence meant *God* in Croatian.

In 1973, when I was seventeen, my brother, a friend of his, and I decided to travel in Europe on InterRail passes, inexpensive even for us because the Yugoslav economy was at its peak. Wherever we went, it was I who had to ask for directions, so I lost all shame in English. In my new tongue, I could say things I could not say in Croatian – words did not have emotional histories, they were feats of memory rather than disasters of the cardiovascular system; I could easily talk about emotions, while in Croatian, the equivalent vocabulary scared me.

When we got back, my mother commented that we were not normal anymore – henceforth she would trace my prodigal ways to that fateful trip. One of the bizarre steps I took was to quit my medical studies, which I had begun in Serbia (odd for someone from Croatia to study there), in order to transfer to an American college. But to me it was not a bizarre move: I had applied a year earlier to U.S. colleges, but the slow process – in the fast-track society, things worked even more slowly than in ours, where you'd apply to study two to three months in advance – took a year, and my going to the States now merely fulfilled my yearning to study in English.

I had applied first to the cheapest Protestant schools, addressing them with "My dear brethren," although I no longer went to church. But, admissions officers informed me that there was no financial aid for foreigners. Next, I tried the cheapest state universities. Same reply. Out of desperation, I wrote to the most expensive schools, Ivy League and similar, and got enthusiastic responses to apply. Vassar and Brown did not charge any application fee. Vassar's cablegram reached me at the dorm, printed on a pale ribbon, with the words full scholarship. My sister, a nurse in Germany, bought me a one-way fare to New York. The evening before my departure, I found my childhood friends sitting on a terrace in the park. I said, "Tomorrow I am going to the United

States." They made no reply, but continued to slurp coffee and blow out cigarette smoke; some raised their eyebrows slightly and went on with their conversation about soccer. Offended and supercilious I walked away: they did not believe me; I had spoken of going to the States a year before.

I thought I would become a psychiatrist after the interlude of linguistic pleasure. However, at Vassar my plans to become a shrink quickly shrank. After reading "The Death of Ivan Ilyich," I wrote a death story in Croatian. I mailed it off to a Serb friend of mine, the editor of a literary journal in Zagreb. His reply astonished me. "What language are you writing in? Croatian? This is not Croatian: too many Serb words, too much strange syntax – and not consistent enough to be mistaken for experimentation. First learn the language, then write in it."

True, Croatian had been Serbianized for decades to fit the Yugoslav model, ever since the thirties and the dictatorship of King Alexander Karadjordjevic. I could understand why one would wish to distance oneself from Serb imperialism in language – after Tito's death nowhere else was it possible. But whatever vocabulary I had grown up on was a living language, so why not use it and savor its nuances, all the more multiple because of the mix of cultures? The project of having to ethnically cleanse my native language – and of acquiring the slang evolving out of my earshot since I now lived in the States – depressed me deeply, all the more since I did not want to deal with any kind of nationalism. But, had I forgotten my love for English? I read in English, studied in English, wrote papers in English, spoke for many hours in English in dining halls, as was usual with students, who in that respect lived in an old-world rhythm. I lived in English. "Language is the house of being"; couldn't English become my home?

I translated my story into English, brimming with conceit once again. Then my new American friends began to point out my awkward syntax – too many winding sentences and misplaced adverbs and wrong prepositions – and lapses in diction: too much mixture of the high and the low styles and too many British words. This sounded familiar. After all, in the eighteenth century Britain used to be to America what Serbia was to Croatia for a half of the twentieth: a colonizer. In American culture there still lingered a strong drive to purify the language by eliminating excessive Anglicanisms. I fell from the frying pan into the melting pot, in which not many ingredients were allowed to melt. In college, while invited to admire Joyce's word permutations, I was discouraged from experimenting, from deviating in any way from an imaginary standard English. I was invited to admire Faulkner's lengthy acrobatics but held fast to the rules of basic word order and exhorted to copy Hemingway's short sentences – which was all fine, but from my theomythological background in English, the accountability to write in the least common denominator of the language seemed to me deconstructive, inhibitory, humiliating. But soon I realized that the advice to simplify was salubrious; in Croatia, under Austria-Hungarian and German influence people strained the language, writing monstrously convoluted sentences. Under bureaucratic Communism, where obfuscating was desirable, newspapers became unreadable. I had not deviated from the Croatian style: the longer and more confusing my sentences were, the more proud I was.

My teachers now taught me to make "precise" and "vivid" descriptions, to select the "mot juste" – and I still often try to follow that basic assignment. After spending dozens of minutes on making several word choices, I am mightily disconcerted when friendly writers tell me: "You know what? Your being a foreigner is an advantage. You accidentally pair up words in a strikingly fresh way. You probably don't even notice it. We native speakers have to work at it."

And when you don't get a shade of a word because you haven't grown up listening to American lullabies, your friends smile patronizingly; when you don't get accents because you haven't grown up with them while your ear was flexible, your friends treat you as a comic alien, an aquamarine creature – you grope with your fins in the sand (and the sand seems to be English, while the water would be your native tongue). Tell me about the advantage then! My writer friends put me in my place, show me how superficial my project of writing in English must be. Where in me are those soulful contacts with words that can be made only with mother's nipple between your naked gums? Sometimes, for example in the movie *Crossing Delancey,* you find the stereotype of a foreigner who writes in English, and who for that reason is superficial.

Well, thousands of immigrants write in English as a second language, but I can't think of any expatriated Americans adopting a foreign language and writing in it (though there must be exceptions to this). Why? Isn't adventure the spirit of America? Or does "adventure" only come to America, rather than leaving from America? When Americans travel abroad, they notoriously need their Hiltons, cheeseburgers, and even those who seem not to need a layer of air-conditioning wear a thick fur of English language. Sure, many Americans born in America do learn foreign languages, but how often do they go all the way?

I seem to be preaching linguistic expatriation and prodigality, but don't misunderstand me: I merely marvel at the American linguistic unexileability. And perhaps I defend myself against an imaginary charge of superficiality. (I must be imagining things, because who gives a shit about any kind of writing, let alone writing by legal aliens? And I may just as well be superficial, so what? Who cares? But let me go on – it is not clear that nobody cares.) How would the patriotic proponents of only-mother-tongue-is-deep theory know about the superficiality of writing in ESL without ever having dived into a foreign sea to sink breathless and come up with starfish in fists and urchin needles in soles? Those who have not genuinely made a new house of being in another language should not tell us naturalized Americans that we do not know what domestic bliss is, that we are merely bums begging for a quarter to get another suck out of a bottle of Jack Daniels, simply because we have no real home. Just the other night I ordered a beer at a bar, Ralph's Corner in Moorhead, Minnesota, and a man said to me, "You are some kind of foreigner, aren't you?" "No, I am an American," I said. He laughed and then said, "Is your family still over there?" "What do you mean 'still?' Not everybody plans to come to America." In the meanwhile, a big guy shouted at a table next to mine, "One American life is worth more than ten thousand Bosnian lives!" Geez, I am beginning to ramble. But this is my point now: I could go home, to Croatia, and write in Croatian, sucking out the milky depths of my memory in it. I choose not to.

Although I have been tempted to quit the business of words altogether, I persevered, partly because I could not concentrate on anything else with sufficient enthusiasm, and partly because if I needed enthusiasm, I could not only wistfully recall but safely revert to one experience: grasping for understanding through foreign words. I tried to learn other languages to recreate the revelatory sensation I once had with English while reading Greek myths, but after many bouts with German – and some with Greek, Hebrew, Russian, French – exhausted, forgetful, I'd come back to English, like a shaggy dog in heat returning home and collapsing in his shanty, on the old rug comfortingly smelling of familiar urine.

I think I have been accommodated in the beautifully distant new house; the house has become my home, my English, with many loose bricks, shallow foundations, perhaps on sand, but with a large ocean and a big sky airing it. But rhetoric aside (though this phrase itself must be rhetorical), what can one choose? I believe I have chosen English, and each time I write in it, I have the residual awareness of freedom smelling of pine and oceanic salt, and that awareness – despite occasional whiffs of urine – clears my nostrils and invigorates me.

Rock: Twenty Years After

More than twenty years ago, when some of the dead were alive, we were all to become musicians, according to our father, and if we failed at that, physicians, and if we failed at becoming either, the ministers of the Gospel. My older sister entered a theological seminary – and gave birth to so many children that her career was motherhood. My oldest brother, although he had large ears, had no ear for music; he became a doctor and lay minister. My other sister, who sang in the church choir, became a nurse and had no time for song. By the time she had begun to betray my father's hopes, the cobwebbed organ he had bought for Bachanizing his progeny was cleaned. Our mother swept the dead flies and wasp nests stuck in the cracks – made by the extremes of the mini-climate of the attic – in the varnished wood with a broom.

I used to pedal up a storm in the organ; half the keys produced only puffs and winds, noisy jets of air that didn't meet their flutes. Our bristly father, his clean-eared assistant clog maker, my savage older brother, and dirty-eared I carried the organ through the door we had taken off its hinges. We puffed around the box, turning it lengthwise, this and that way, but it wouldn't go through. Ivo and I begged our father: "Please, don't let it go, we will play the organ." "I want to become a pianist." "I want to become an organist."

"Shut up, lazy bones," said our father to us. "If you had wanted it . . . lift it that way!" He had forgotten that he had never offered us a lesson, disappointed by the futile lessons of his older kids. Anyway, he needed to sell the organ to pay the taxes. He took out a block of roof tiles. The organ was roped like a wild bull and lowered through the roof past the swallow nests down the side of the stuccoed wall into a truck. Its flutes moaned, but nothing could save it from the kidnapping. At that moment a vengeful decision to become a musician gripped my throat.

During a Gospel Revival in our Baptist church, our father, who had founded several orchestras in the region, held music classes composed of all the churchgoers who did not suffer from arthritis, although by the way the orchestra sounded, it seemed some people had not yet been diagnosed. Ivo and I got our tambourines and fretted our evenings away with our fingertips and plastic picks. Before each practice we read Psalm #150:

> *. . . Praise him with the sound of the trumpet: praise him with the psaltery and the harp.*
>
> *Praise him with the timbrel and dance: praise him with stringed instruments and organs.*
>
> *Praise him upon the loud cymbals: praise him upon the high sounding cymbals.*
>
> *Let every thing that hath breath praise the Lord.*

The orchestra attracted an unconverted soul, a student of welding, Skala, an emaciated, large-eared, stuttering youth. I was too impulsive to wait through the long pauses, but with a metronome and the stamping of feet, I began to restrain myself. I quickly learned how to read the scores, but I couldn't spontaneously tune into the music, which disillusioned my father because if I were a real talent I would play by ear. Skala did. His ears were so good that he never learned how to read music.

The rock era began for me with the Stones's "Paint It Black," which I got from the son of a Hungarian bartender, Damir, for a collection of stamps from Madagascar. So, it really started with the collection of stamps from Madagascar my brother Vlado gave me to console me for extracting my tonsils in his enthusiasm for medical studies, through my first genuine loss of consciousness, drug-induced, with an acrid bite in my nostrils; something behind my eyes had concentrated on a vanishing red dot, as I swooned toward the exotic spaces of tonsilless existence. The exotic was the key. For Damir it was the magic compressed in the masks of Madagascar on toothed squares of paper; for me it was the sound of a foreign tongue, suspended in the mouth to leave space for voweling and howling. My brother and I borrowed a gray mono record player from Boris, an Adventist recluse. As the world around me was not made of English Rock, I joined two empty cupboards, and there Damir and I sat trading my stamps for his records, deafened by the mono sound augmented by a large wok, in which the record player sat and rolled.

From the roof of our home – a large house made of stone and brick, nearly a fortress, which our father had built as his lifetime achievement – Ivo and I stared through a telescope as thin as a billy club. Besides a crew of storks on the cloister chimney a mile away, the most striking thing was our cousin's walk on the opposite side of the street. His pale blue jeans with a bit of a reddish hue – from being rubbed by bricks – split into bell-bottoms. In the gap in the bells was an orange fabric with red and blue flowers. "He's wearing a combination of pants and pyjamas!" I exclaimed. "That's the new fashion," Ivo commented. "He plays the lead in the rock band; he'll play in the Czech house tonight." With the fear of the Lord in my bones, I didn't dare go to the concert. Our cousin Mrvica – in translation, "Crumb" (because he was short) – had ceased to go to the church, and I considered him tabooed. My brother's cosmology was a bit less permeated with theology than mine: he went to the concert and came back madly enthusiastic about the piercing power of the electric guitar.

Our father died a couple of years before Jimi Hendrix did. With him the church orchestra vanished. I took up my father's violin. A dark snake's head stuck its split tongue out of the crooked neck with asymmetric locations of tones. The strings, high above the neck, cut into my flesh. I could soon play parts of *Die Kreutzer Sonate* and *Bolero* – but my eyes had to focus on the sheets. My brother Vlado's family, who had moved into our large house, asked me repeatedly not to play late at night, and for that matter, not during the day either.

Ivo gave classical guitar recitals in the regional churches. I was nervous for him, wondering whether his sweaty fingers would slip. Three boys from the music school in our town played the same sad Fernando Sor, sorrowful Villa-Lobos, and death-contemplating, transcribed Bach. Ivo began to tutor the reclusive Adventist boy to play the same melodies. The music itself was not as sad as the fact that so many people played it over and over again.

Damir plucked his guitar strings in front of a large audience for the Day of the Republic. He had composed his own song but announced that it was written by an anonymous composer in the late seventeenth century. He read the notes and made some pretty spectacular sounds, but people booed him all the same.

Ivo, Damir, and I banded up into a trio Damir named Fresh Factual Emancipation. We had our instruments custom-made from the best guitar-maker in Zagreb; and they turned out to be superb. We paid for them by my brother's and my work on wooden shoes and by Damir's stealing from his father's bar – he had snatched a certain sum of money every day so that his father would not notice any irregularity. We jammed a lot of sounds. Having no drummer, we were supposed to be particularly rhythmic, but none of us had any interest in that inferior function. I strained to exchange as many tones and as quickly as possible on a theme within a key, but after a while I'd lose the key and the theme. Damir did likewise, and Ivo, who tried to patch everything up, stormed.

Each band needs to have a cellar or a garage to move ahead. Since the death of my gray father and his thirsty car – a corroded Mercedes ambulance that had constantly overheated, that had sat gray beneath the terrace in our yard, that could move half a yard now and then on the power of its battery, and that was taken away by an uncle of mine, who cut it in half with an iron-melting torch – the garage had been empty until several months before the formation of our band. A Yugoslav *Gastarbeiter* from West Germany had brought in a huge washer smelling of acetone, saying that he would open a laundry and that the whole town would be rushing to him to have their clothes washed pristinely. He had overestimated our town's love of cleanliness. For two years we heard nothing from the Germanizer. We failed to throw the grandiose Washing Machine out of doors. It cut the garage in half, wall-to-wall, cramping up the greasy space; broken glass from our soccer playing and archery, spider nets, flat and molding inner tubes, dank air coming out of the doorless cellar from below, all flattened our will to soundproof the space. The cellar was often flooded, potatoes and onions sprouted, and our cat leaped after the high frequencies of an inexhaustible tribe of mice, her whiskers trembling.

We played in the thin-roofed attic among bales of oxhide. Our loud sounds caused the first political awakening in our neighborhood since the Communist Revolution. Democratically, the three blocks of the neighborhood voted to disband us and brought us written notices notarized by the police.

Naturally, the Beatles could be no role model for us, nor the Stones. In an attempt to do away with simple harmonies and keys, we turned to jazz. I had gotten some records of Soviet jazz from a county office clerk, for Austrian stamps from the World War I. But even the jazz stuck to the unfortunate elements of rhythm and harmony, so, under Ivo's guidance, after he had brazenly consulted with a couple of the most prominent composers in the country, we turned to ultraprogressive music, electronic music of the Polish composer Penderecki. To work my way to Penderecki, I was supposed to listen first to Stravinsky and then to Schoenberg, according to my brother. We spent winter nights next to our little iron furnace with wood, and while the furnace almost melted glowing orange and red – the only light in the room as it snowed blue outside – the sharp, brave, cutting sounds of violin, riding on the powerful bass rhythm and panic-stricken winds, absorbed us with their cruelty, exceeding even that of the hardest rock. First we may not have liked it, but our own music got us ready for the modern sounds. It was around 1970; we didn't know drugs, so we used the music and the glowing furnace as drugs. We were full of frequencies emanating out of our strings in all directions, clashing against one another and, now that we knew that we didn't need to play in a key, all we needed was a good place to practice, but the garage was still occupied by a large washer and drier. Two years later, as the band was dissolving, the Germanizer appeared, paid in a noncompatriotic fashion, exactly as much as the weekly rents had amounted to – a handsome sum of money – and he disappeared again, no laundry shop opened, and our people walked in dirty shirts as hitherto.

We celebrated the recuperation of the garage that New Year's Eve. But as it was too cold in the garage, we drank rum and listened to the Band of Gypsies in the living room. I tried to dance but my brother scoffed at me. I fumed and told him that he was as repressive as the church, that even Jim Morrison danced. And, what about *Praise him with the timbrel and dance: praise him with stringed instruments and organs?*

Ivo's friend showed up just at that Psalmodic moment, and when he laughed at the music, I broke his nose, and he left. With the heater and all the instruments on as we tried to counterplay Hendrix, we blew a fuse; we hooked up to an outlet in another room. Damir burped with enthusiasm at "The Machine Gun," and one of his burps was a little unrestrained. He vomited. In search of the bathroom, he vomited in all the rooms in the house, never finding his destination. I changed the fuses, burning them all out so that when my mother came back from the church, where hot herb tea was drunk and loving music played, she was met by quite a sight and stench. She threw Damir out, declaring him a pig. Our band had fallen apart just as we celebrated the ideal conditions for its ascent.

Ivo passed the lead audition for a well-known Yugoslav band, but just as he had packed up to move to Zagreb, he chickened out with stage fright and ulcers, shocked he could become a star. Because of music, he had dropped out of high school and the Baptist church, and now he wanted to finish up. Eighteen years later, he's still a student – of theology in Zürich, having studied physics and philosophy; and, whenever somebody visits him, he plays the same old sad "Asturias" and transcribed, death-contemplating Bachus.

We were not the only musicians in the town. In fact, everybody who had any right intuition about life – and some who didn't – began to play music. One lad, Pop, a couple of years older than I, was kicked out of the school for loud guitar playing and for refusing to cut his long hair. He wanted to play fast like Jimmy Page. Most of our friends criticized him on his preferring technique and speed to the soul of music, but I thought the critique was an expression of envy. He and I were about to form a band with me on the electric violin, but a huge obstacle arose to our friendship. In the match of Spasky-Fischer, he rooted for Spasky. He became a professional guitar player in bar bands, and when that was over, a self-obsessed and witty clinical psychologist. His unwitty explanation for not making it was that he lacked self-confidence, which he'd now regained, albeit too late for music.

Then, Bozho, who later became a writer and politician – leading one of the major liberal parties in Croatia – played the bass with a curly lad, a hater of Israel. During the Six-Day War I had rooted for Israel, and that had done it for my communication with Curly. He ended up in a military academy.

Boris the Adventist went to Germany to study the guitar and live with his divorced parents, who had left him in Yugoslavia to grow up by himself in a house outside the town atop a hill with a crucified Jesus and the two thieves in stone. He passed the guitar entrance exams at the University of Stuttgart but failed the voice exams because, as a recluse who hardly ever had a chance to talk to anybody, he hadn't sufficiently developed his vocal control. He went to Reading University in England, studied Medieval English and is now a professor somewhere in the American space. Whenever I visit him, he plays out "Asturias" and the other same old songs, which grieves me.

Skala the welder gave up industry in all the senses of the word. He quit going to his factory and, owing to his hypersensitivity, he didn't study music. It came to him naturally, and indeed, he'd hear a complex melody once and play it out on the guitar, halting to retune the microscopically unwinding strings because nothing bothered him more than the wrong pitch. He played in city bar bands, but whenever Jesus visited him in a dream, he'd pack up and come back to the church to kneel and to preach against the bass as the instrument of the devil. There was a direct correlation between the excitement of the bass and lewdness. He couldn't even dare to estimate how many illegitimate children his artful fingers had cofathered. The new church band, formed by a minister from Ljubljana, however, soon exasperated him by its lack of pitch. So, he'd go back to a bar band until the further revelations of Jesus. He had succumbed only once to the temptations of bar ladies and showed himself such a great lover that he concluded he must have some Black blood in him. Otherwise, how to explain his enormous musical talent and prowess? And though it was one out of the two times Skala had made love in his life, he was the sexual educator of the town: all the twelve-year-olds knew his knightly performance with the lady, stroke by stroke, as the paradigm of lovemaking. He went back and forth between the bar and the Baptist church so many times that neither would accept him. But that was God's way of telling him to move ahead. He had only to show up in the States and Blood, Sweat & Tears would bleed on their knees, begging him to join and reform them, yet he'd snub them and play in a Billy Graham band. Several times he hitchhiked toward England but got stuck in Germany at some evangelical convention that meekened him, knocking the American dreams out of his head. For years he walked the town, preaching his great American future with Eric Clapton, and he still does it while his townspeople jeer at him, showing the works of inferior Socialist dentistry. Having confessed each thought he had and didn't have to everybody who didn't spit at him and to some who did, he has joined the Catholic church, reconfessing the faith of his forefathers. He is expecting the heavenly orchestra to arrive on earth, to tune up all the untuned instruments and raise hell of a music.

The best one of us would-be musicians was a slant-eyed boy with a curving back, a member of a gang that specialized in stealing motorbikes. I had wanted to beat him blue as a kid, but I was afraid because he led an older gang of institutionalized delinquents – one gang member had axed his own drunken, wife-beating father to death. Instead, when I saw him walk into the park, I showed him *The Brothers Karamazov.* I gave him a speech about what freedom lay in the twistedly passionate and thoughtful people of the book.

"But Dostoyevski is on the reading list for our school, he can't be any good!" he protested.

"Forget our school," I said. "This is where it's at. And that they put it on the list is an accident: they don't know what is wrong, just as they don't know what isn't."

He laughed but was impressed by my cylinder hat and the Mercedes wheel Skala had welded onto my bike.

One day he and his gang broke into the bank and, disappointed at finding no money there, they grabbed several boxes of documents and tossed them from the bank roof into the wind like leaflets. His father – an old mathematician, whose father was killed in the war in front of his eyes by Croatian Nazis – beat him with a dog chain, smashing his muscles. Slavko lay in bed for a month, read *The Brothers,* and played the piano. Catholic nuns had tutored him. From then on he played day in and day out with his windows corked because in his enfeebled state he was feverish and vulnerable to drafts. Once when I visited him, I couldn't breathe. He got dressed, we climbed the roof of his house, and he showed me the rings of Saturn through a telescope.

This summer, 1990, nearly twenty years later, when I visited Slavko, he switched on the light in the corridor by a karate kick. He had earned a black belt. During my brief stay, he gave two concerts – one jazz, anther classical – and both were televised. Healthy, concentrated, strong, he was the music pro, the only one of us dozens who'd stuck with it and made it.

I attended the fifteenth anniversary of my Gymnasium, college-prep, class at a park restaurant. Most men wore business suits; women, makeup and long dresses, commercial scents emanating out of them. A band loudly played electric polka. We drank white wine, Daruvarski Riesling, specialty of our region, mixed with mineral water at the bar, a little removed from the offensive podium. Jun, a Czech engineer, recalled how I had given him a double LP of Donovan. He had listened to the records thousands of times – poor soul – learnt all the songs by heart and sang them to his guitar at all parties. In fact, even at the reunion, after the band quit playing – my wife and I went home then, 2 a.m. – Jun sang and strung out Donovan and Dylan till seven in the morning. Another friend talked about how, with my hair kinky like Jimi Hendrix's, I wore a jeans jacket with rainbows in pastel and how we used to discuss our prospects for preventing baldness in our twenties. For a rock lover there would be no greater tragedy than to grow bald. Growing deaf was no problem. He had gotten some special oil to massage into his scalp twice a day. I remembered that I had helped him with some quadratic equations. He didn't worry to mention his hair – it hadn't left him – nor quadratic equations, but he did (c)rave about Ten Years After.

Damir, the member of the defunct Fresh Factual Emancipation, was now in a lunatic asylum. I saw him on his days off – he got a couple of weekends a month free. He was in the loony bin because he'd gotten in a fight with two Serbs in a bar; he insulted the Serbian national pride. Although Serbs constituted only 12 percent of the Croatian population, they controlled 60 percent of the police force and most of the government posts in Croatia; and Slavonia, our region, was no exception. The two Serbs managed to get Damir imprisoned as a Croatian nationalist despite his being Hungarian. When Damir protested, they stuck him in the asylum. He couldn't deny that he was a drunkard – two years before, sick with his life, which contained no rock anymore, he had demolished his own bar with an ax and passed out, crashing his head against the steps that lead out. He had been detoxicated several times, and now, defenseless, he was being detoxicated with all kinds of toxic drugs. Even after the new Croatian government claimed that all the political prisoners in Croatia were given amnesty, Damir remained in the lunatic asylum in the Soviet style of psychiatry-for-politics, according to him. I couldn't assess whether what he said was true, although by his tone of sincerity, I could tell that he believed it absolutely was. He didn't look insane a bit . . . as long as we didn't talk about rock. But we spent the whole evening talking about Jimi Hendrix and watching Jimi on tape. He lamented that we didn't even have a recording of Fresh Factual Emancipation to prove that we were a band once upon a time.

"The worst culprit was not the Washing Machine," Damir said, "but you. You bought *Melody Makers,* the English rock papers, and instead of practicing music, sat on the floor with a dictionary."

"I had to decipher the lyrics. It didn't make sense to listen otherwise."

"Who asked you to listen? You should have played."

And watching Jimi biting his strings, Damir repeatedly exclaimed: "What spontaneity, what ease, what genius!" After three hours of Hendrix, he and his wife and I and my wife had marital quarrels – marriages on the rocks – and we called it a night.

A Vanishing Country

ꕥꕥ

It is early morning, with black clouds. Crossing from East Berlin to West Berlin at the Friedrichstrasse checkpoint, I slide my passport under a glass divider to a border guard. His booth resembles a soccer stadium box office. I hand it over as if giving my ticket to an airline clerk, who will routinely and politely give me a boarding pass and direct me to my gate. Instead, the gray-haired official scrutinizes me, alternately drawing his eyelids over his gray eyes, as if to sharpen his focus, and drawing them back, as if to show me that I should open my own eyes wide. He compares every feature of my face with that of my passport photo. He studies my visas. I am wiping sweat off my forehead; I had run to catch the city bus. Glancing up, he registers that gesture and flips further through my passport.

"Where have you been?" he demands.

"Magdeburg and Berlin."

"How long?"

"Two weeks in Magdeburg, one day in Berlin."

"Where is your registration?"

"What registration?"

"You should have registered your stay at the police station in Magdeburg as soon as you arrived."

"I thought I'd registered enough. I obtained an East German visa in Zagreb, Yugoslavia – it took me three trips to the consulate. In order to get it I presented an invitation that had been registered with the police in Magdeburg. The border police at Eisenach registered my entry, and now you are registering my exit."

"But they did not register your arrival in Magdeburg."

"I didn't know that I had to register again."

"You didn't know? And what is this?" He shows me several visa stamps, geometric pale blue pictures of hammer and wheat with florid signatures, from Berlin two years before, in 1986. "You registered properly then!"

"Then I visited on a tourist visa, and to activate an official invitation I had to change my visa status, so I visited the police station. I was not aware until now that an extra registration was involved."

"Weren't aware? So how did you manage it?"

"I just told you."

He looks at me grimly as if I have so egregiously violated the law that something equally terrible must now be done to amend my infraction. Even then something will remain permanently wrong because I haven't registered properly. He hisses through his silver teeth, "Step out of the line!"

I can't escape the impression that for some reason this man hates me. There is something in his pursed lips and his glare that the bureaucratic routine alone cannot account for.

I sit at a stone table for half an hour, watching the official scrutinize other travelers. He doesn't seem to enjoy being up so early. Maybe he suffers from arthritis and the sudden shift in atmospheric pressure – it's cloudy outside – has brought on sharp pains in his joints, the personal borders between body and upper arms, upper arms and forearms, forearms and hands, hands and fingers, fingers and fingertips, fingertips and the passport he now examines. There is nothing personal in what he does except personal suspicion. All else is perfunctory, computerized. He orders another man out of line, a Gypsy with a Yugoslav passport, and then a Pole who has a Yugoslav passport as well. The official doesn't seem to like Yugoslav passports. The Pole cracks his knuckles, the Gypsy chews bubble gum. I am anxious that I will miss my train, but even more that I will be interrogated.

An hour later, my empty stomach is growling when a younger but equally stern version of the gray official appears, my passport in hand. He stands two yards from me and alternately glances at me and my picture for a few moments. He pronounces my name distinctly, with a Russian accent, and orders me to follow him. We leave behind the Gypsy and the Pole and walk through several corridors into a small room, a cell. He asks me to sit on a bench beside a metal table. He sits down opposite me; we face each other like chess players. He addresses me in German, and I am disconcerted enough to respond in German rather than in English, where I rather than he would have the linguistic advantage. He grills me: Where have I been? What have I done? Why? With whom? Whom do I know? – banal questions typically associated with New York cocktail parties, but there is provocation in his voice.

I try to make my answers spare and noncommittal.

"Since you didn't register your whereabouts, how can we be sure where you've been? You could have been other places, you could have done something?" He insinuates that they know where I have been; all they want to find out is whether, in addition to having been in these *verboten* places, I will now lie about it.

"Even if I had registered, I could have gone many places and done many things. I don't see what difference one stamp would make."

"A great difference," he says. "And how did you meet your connections in Berlin?"

"They are not connections, they are acquaintances."

"How do you know them?"

"I don't feel like answering that question." I speak the truth, but not very tactfully. Several years earlier I had met a dozen East Germans in an annex of a demolished synagogue in Budapest, where I had stayed for two months. Sylvia, a fluid dynamics teacher, wept about polluted rivers in East Germany and wanted to emigrate but didn't dare to because her parents would lose their jobs. She had hoped to study sculpture, but couldn't, she claimed, because she was not a Communist. Uwe, a mechanical engineer, had hiked two thousand miles through the tundras and taigas of Siberia. Klaus, an electrician, liked his work and planned to stay where he was although he was outspoken in his opposition to the government. "I'm only an electrician, a worker, my opinion doesn't matter." I had slept at Klaus's last night.

"Oh, do you think that we might hold it against your connections? Why should you think that?" the official asks.

"I am not required to discuss my private affairs with you."

"*Private* affairs," he echoes ironically.

"Could you speed up the routine? I have to catch a train in ten minutes. If I miss my train, I will miss the connection to Yugoslavia, and my ticket expires today."

"The routine?" He raises his voice.

I don't answer.

"Don't worry about your ticket."

"Are you going to reimburse me?"

"There are trains from West Berlin to Stuttgart at least once every hour." His voice carries the suggestion that once you are in the West everything is possible and you can't possibly be late. I am not sure that his voice is ironic. "So, where did you meet your friends?"

"What difference should that make to you?"

"A great difference. You could have met at Humboldt University, for example."

I don't answer. I had made an acquaintance, Krause, in a supermarket. He had invited me for coffee and told me he was a professor of history. He asked me about my views on Communism and was upset that I thought Communism could not work.

The more Irish coffees he drank – later, he drank only brandy – the more upset he became, and in the end he shouted that I should not put on airs because I was from Yugoslavia. To be from Southern Europe and from Yugoslavia was despicable in West Germany – *Ich weiss!* – because everybody knows that southern peoples, and especially the Slavs, are inefficient workers. The transformation of this man from a supporter of Communism to a xenophobe amazed me.

"You must tell us where you've been since you didn't register."

"As I told you, I didn't know it was necessary." I could tell him about Krause. So what if the police give him a hard time? He'd deserve it, the bastard, but the way he met me – he may have been a spy, he may have followed me, and he was probably the one who identified me for interrogation!

The official, who pauses just enough between statements for me to drift into a state of anxiety, interrupts my thoughts again. "You haven't convinced me."

"I told you what happened," I say.

"You have a stamp from two years ago."

"I was getting another visa. I wasn't aware of the additional registration."

"He wasn't aware." Eyeing me, he stands up. "Maybe your luggage will talk," he says.

He orders me to remove the contents of my suitcase, item by item. He inspects each one, asking me what it is, even when it is obvious. When I withdraw a pen, he asks, "What is it?" I feel like a student in a remedial language class. Each time I name an object he repeats the word with improved pronunciation.

He tosses and catches the eggcups Sylvia fired for me out of clay. "Your hostess gave you these? She is an Anglophile. Does she speak English?"

"Not very well."

"But she does speak it," he snaps at me triumphantly as though he had unveiled a conspiracy.

"Doesn't everybody?" I say.

"She admires England and she is learning English." Two plus two. "And what did you give her?"

"Schubert records." I lie. I gave her Frank Zappa records. He raises his eyebrows and gives me a sharp glance as though warning me not to lie again.

He flips through each of my books, then holds them upside down so that all my classified documents, or at least some LSD-soaked papers, will slide out onto the floor. He carefully examines the books by Goethe and Kafka, as if the two were illegal reading. He considers *The Return of the Native* by Thomas Hardy with the disapproval of an English literature professor who has revised the canon.

He next seizes my address book. He turns the pages and looks first at the addresses and then into my eyes, straight through the pupils like an ophthalmologist who sees hemorrhaging on the retina. Satisfied, he turns and walks out, my book in his fingers, to check the names against computerized lists. There is one name there I am sure is in the police files. Tim, a diplomat's son, married an East German woman, and funded the emigration of others. His correspondence with some friends still in East Germany landed them in a psychiatric hospital. Once I didn't believe him, but now I do.

It occurs to me that I am not registered anywhere outside of East Germany, except in the East German consulate in Zagreb, as being in East Germany. They could keep me here forever. Who would know that I am here and that I haven't got out of the cell? They will now keep the addresses of my friends on file alongside my name. Will that count against my friends in job searches?

The fluorescent light bulbs cast a shadowless light over the aluminum table and bare walls. Time seems to be a bureaucratic tool. I have been here for two hours.

An hour later the officer is back. He lays my address book on the table precisely in the middle, equidistant from each corner. He stands admiring the symmetry.

"What do you think of Yugoslavia, the GDR, the United States?" he asks in a monotone. He examines the seal that states that my passport was issued in New York, but he doesn't comment on that; he awaits my answer.

"I like the USA, the GDR, and Yugoslavia equally."

"Equally," he echoes, scrutinizing my face for signs of insincerity. Either he doesn't believe that I like East Germany, or if I do, he is trying to make sure that my attitude will change.

"Would you like to visit the GDR again?"

"Yes, I would like to visit again." In fact, I have lost all desire to return, but this seems to be the right thing to say.

"Ach, you would like to visit again!" While bitterly repeating my words he weighs them against my expression, seeking to discern the true meaning – something subversive.

"So, you are an instructor at an American university?" he asks.

"Yes, why not." I fear he will ask me how I was permitted to stay in the United States, for there is no U.S. immigration visa in my passport. I worry that he will discover that I possess an American passport that I've left behind in Yugoslavia (as an émigré, I am a firm believer in passports – I'd like to have three or four; after gaining U.S. citizenship, I didn't give up Yugoslavian) and will suspect me of spying for the U.S. or . . .

"Yes, why not. If it is possible, why not." He pauses. "It must be nice to experience different societies like that, isn't it?" His voice now carries a natural color. The question seems to be off the record.

"Yes, it is," I say. I have the impression he'd like me to go into details, to tell him about American wine, women, and song. I do not proffer any information.

He keeps silent for several minutes as he daydreams. Then, regaining his official poise, he again questions me about why I visited my connections. He warns me I can't leave East Germany unless I tell him. "Who do you think you are protecting by your delay in answering? I thought you were in a rush. So, at whose home did you stay last night?" The more secretive I am, the more he can blame my host, Sylvia, for inviting me and providing me with the papers for my visa. Likewise, to give him Klaus's name and address could harm Klaus. He, I, and a group of engineers drank a lot of Bulgarian wine last night. Klaus has grown fat in the last two years; he used to like his job, now he hates it. He used to be gentlemanly to his girlfriend, now he abused her in front of me – ordering her to cook for us, to clean his shoes, and, noting my surprise, he quoted Nietzsche to me: "Are you visiting a woman? Don't forget your whip." The engineers admired how I clipped my nails casually with a nail clipper; they had never seen one. I gave it to Klaus.

I lie. "I slept in the park."

"Which park?"

"I don't know its name."

"How can you visit a park and not know its name?"

"Why not? Must one read the signs?"

"Where's the park located?"

"Near Smetanastrasse."

"Near Smetanastrasse. You have a friend there, she's a medical student, right?" He recalls the address from my address book, although I had as many as thirty East German addresses there. My address book didn't indicate my friends' occupations, however. He grins at me smugly. "Why didn't you stay with your friend?"

"She wasn't at home."

"But it was freezing last night."

"I was freezing."

"You were freezing," he says, as though since I now lived in the West I was too spoiled ever to be exposed to cold weather.

I don't comment.

He asks me to describe the exact spot in the park.

I describe a slope with benches, near rentable rowboats. "I slept on a bench."

"What color was the bench?"

"There was not enough light to distinguish colors."

He stands up and tells me to wait. "We have decided to punish you," he announces, returning an hour later.

"Who is we?" I say. "Why should you punish me? It was a simple omission."

"You have to be penalized." He is enjoying himself.

"What is the penalty?"

"Depends. Five hundred deutsche marks."

"I don't have that much on me."

He looks through some sort of handbook, seeking how to penalize this additional outrage. "You could serve time," he suggests, as though offering me a bargain. Then he disappears for half an hour.

Upon his return, he says, "We are only going to issue you a warning. It is your duty to know travel regulations before you travel. Is that understood?"

"Yes." I wait. I wonder what else is coming.

"You are free to go."

There is a faint smile on his lips as he walks me to the exit and past two guards into the streetcar station. His smile broadens, and it appears that he is about to laugh at his silly job, which requires him to play the comedy of interrogation stern-faced. He looks cheerful now and he seems tempted to tap me on the shoulder like a sporty cousin seeing me off: "Keep your chin up, old boy!" Instead, he turns abruptly on his heel and walks away.

The orange streetcar – an old type from the time of Hitler; it was preserved underground during the bombings – stops. I enter and sit down. We are above ground, looping on the western side of the gray wall. I am surprised at how thin and new the wall looks from above, with bullet-riddled buildings in the background.

The houses on the western side look sharp, the windows winterized; bright ads bare white teeth and bosoms on their rooftops. The train picks up speed, the tracks are smoother, the jolts vanish, and the train slides underground again.

A pockmarked red-faced man – homeless, most likely – takes a swig of vodka and plays on his harmonica, spreading his thin purplish lips over it. The harmonies are muddy. He tips his bottle and pours a drop into each little square on the harmonica. "Here, darling, this'll perk you up."

A Country Doctor's Rounds

Knee-deep snow on the side of the road translated into a finger-deep slush on the road, enough to make my brother Vlado drive slowly. He stopped the car and turned off the engine. About one hundred people, mostly in black, quietly walked in a funeral procession. A hand-pushed cart with bicycle wheels, rather than a horse-drawn carriage, carried the varnished coffin. Nobody looked particularly sorrowful. There was an unaffected, neither exaggerated nor subdued, solemnity among these people, who had probably witnessed many burials – some had been through two or more wars. At the head of the procession walked a pale, white-bearded Eastern Orthodox priest and two boys. From a backyard, a horse watched the procession, cowed, his breath vaporous, perhaps glad that he didn't have to pull, perhaps sad that people no longer needed him.

"The cemetery is three miles away," Vlado said, turning the engine back on. "They'll spend the whole afternoon in the burial."

The procession passed us from the opposite direction.

We visited two women in a small house that smelled of onion soup. Steam precipitated on the windows, flowing down in jerky drops. The women did not turn on the light – a plain hooded bulb – although the room was dark. A cat slept below the iron wood-burning stove; there was no TV, no radio. The older woman exclaimed, "Curer of bodies, how good that you are here! I have terrible pains in my knees."

"We'll take care of that."

"And who's the young man with you? A young doctor?" she asked.

"No, not a doctor," Vlado laughed. He had wanted me to become a doctor. He'd influenced his daughter and a nephew to become doctors. When I was seventeen he had invited me to picnics several times, convincing me that no profession, neither detective work nor art, offered as much mystery as medicine – how to attack an agent wreaking damage in a human body? You have to trap the agent, assassinate it or bribe it, threaten it, cajole it.

The old woman lifted her skirt above her knee and Vlado found a place, feeling with his fingertips below the kneecap, and injected into it some medicine.

"The Chinese cure people with needles. And a needle stuck in the right place with some medicine in it – not a bad thing altogether."

The old woman didn't blink, didn't cringe, in fact she smiled because she had felt no pain.

"Please, have a seat," the younger woman said to me.

"No, thanks. We have been sitting in the car too much."

In her late forties, a bit round, with fresh shining cheeks, she radiantly exuded sexuality, and as my eyes rested on her, she was pleased as though her philosophy was, akin to my brother's, a young man's eye probing the right place, with a little bit of lust – not a bad thing altogether.

Vlado collected a token fee.

We drove uphill. Children sledded, sliding off the road into thick snow – little rolling bears. We reached a long mudhouse, half of it a stall for livestock, the other half a habitation for people. In the backyard there was a barn with gray haystacks.

"I hope they are in,"Vlado said. "The last time, I honked but nobody opened. They don't trust people."

A woman in widow's black opened the door. It was dark indoors; it was against their grain to turn on the light during the day, while God-given light was on. The cupboard of raw unvarnished wood, resembling a bookshelf, supported a loaf of bread, kitchen knives, and a Bible. Firewood was neatly stacked next to a black iron stove. The two women in the room were strikingly similar – lean; veins; high tendons, bones, and even arteries showing on their arms; their tall flat foreheads were deeply creased, cheeks hollow, lips sunk, noses thin, long, and pointed. One of them was sharp in her eyes. The other wasn't – film covered her vague eyes – and Vlado flashed into her eyes with his ophthalmological flashlight. He gave the woman an injection and prescribed her pills against rheumatism to protect her heart.

The younger woman, ninety-one, said, "Only God understands how much work I have to do for you, what a woe to my life you are."

"Yes, only God knows that," said the older sister, humbly, vaguely, as though trying to comprehend the mystery.

"And you don't know it."

"And I don't know it." The elder sister echoed, penitence in her voice.

"You can't even begin to comprehend how much of it you don't know. Your memory is failing you, you aren't conscious enough to know – only God does."

"Only God does."

"And, Saint Job! Why does it hit me? No wonder that you suffer, after your godless life, but why should I?" She turned to Vlado. "Doctor, you heard that the baker's wife died, and the baker moved away."

"I did."

"Now we have to eat bread made by a sinner, a young drunk. The bread is no longer sweet to me, I ought to bake my own. But I don't have the time." Here, her sharp eye attacked her sister, who sat in the corner, staring blankly, her blue hands trying to warm each other.

Outside, Vlado commented, "The younger sister knows all the Psalms by heart. Today she was out of sorts, but usually she rattles at you long jeremiads with long quotations from the Prophets. She remembers everything, she is the village annals. If you look for stories, you should talk to her." I said that I would like to, but I never did.

"Now, you'll see this poor man. He used to be a giant, and now, he's all bent, thin, a sparrow rather than a man, because of a degenerative disease – a truly rare bird, I'd say."

The man did look like a sparrow. The lights in the house weren't on. The man sat on the bed in his pajamas, and Vlado listened to his heart. He pointed out the man's spine, like a proud architect who has designed a beautiful arch, and he explained the highlights of the exotic disease. The man was so bent that his forehead nearly touched his knees, his hair stuck up, gray, sharp, like porcupine needles. His arms were strangely long next to his short body. On his bed was a cloth-bound novel.

"Any pains?" Vlado asked.

"Doctor, I can't follow the novel. I don't know what's going on." That was his only complaint.

Vlado glanced at the novel, a literary kind, and said, "No need to worry. The author probably doesn't either." Vlado prescribed medicine for the man, and also for a woman who stood by, for her heart. He knew their insurance seven-digit numbers by heart, and the poor folk were flattered by that. "I don't always know the names," Vlado said, "but, as soon as I see a patient, if I'd seen him twice, his numbers pop up in my mind."

Vlado took an old banknote for his service.

"Will you cover the gas cost for the rounds?"

"I don't think so."

My brother made the rounds like a peasant who visits his stables to take care of horses, with the same type of care, in which you can't think of profit. And he looked like a father making rounds to make sure that his children were all right. That he was younger than his patients did not change anything. With his humor, he brought a lot of light into the dark mudhouses.

While I was away from Yugoslavia, I had longed to see the real Slavonian peasants, people of the earth, probably more than I longed to see my friends and relatives, as though the peasants were my relatives in the truest sense, my Adams from *adama* ("earth" in Hebrew). While taking a ride with Vlado, I hadn't planned to see him, to learn from him, but I couldn't fail to be struck by his "medicine man" aura, a doctor and priest in one.

As he drove, he'd say, "In this house I delivered twins, over there, I sewed up a finger a pig had bitten off a man's hand – he still has the finger. In that house I operated on a cataract, using a Gillette blade – the blade is as sharp as any medical tool. I did it by the light of the window – far better for the eye than to shock it with powerful beams of artificial light." He drove, proud of his handiwork. In each house he had fought one demon or another, and he remembered the struggles. When people saw him, they waved, their faces lit up.

"Boy, the people love you, don't they?"

"Sure. Nobody visits them. Young doctors come here for a year or two till they can move to a city. You can't get them to drive out here in the mud. They don't want to dirty their hands, they are scared of having to be the whole hospital. But, look at it! Such beautiful country, people, kind people. I was happy when I lived here." And he looked sad, reminiscing.

Nobody before Vlado in our family had gotten a college education. Our father had made Vlado work full time as an assistant clog maker when Vlado was just a boy. On the way to school, walking, Vlado held his notebook in front of him and wrote his math homework. On the way back from school, he read his assignments. If he slacked off at work, Father beat him with his ox-hide belt. Vlado got so tired of beatings that when he was twelve – together with a cop's son, another hostage to strict upbringing – he ran away from home. The boys wanted to go to

Albania, so that their fathers would never find them. They hopped cargo trains, slept in haystacks in villages, stole eggs, drank them raw. The two fathers posted their sons' pictures in all the major Yugoslav newspapers, with a plea to return the dear sons for a reward. And when the two boys were taken for dead, they showed up, thin, starved, the soles of their shoes gone. Instead of reaching Albania, they had arrived at the Austrian border, where the police turned them back.

My father was careful not to flog Vlado on the first day of his return, but did on the second.

Vlado graduated from the Zagreb medical school with honors, although he had gotten married in the meantime – a match of which neither our father nor the bride's father approved – and had worked in all kinds of odd jobs nearly full time. He became an eye surgeon, and because of his obsession with precision and because he didn't drink or smoke, he turned out to be the best sharpshooter in his army division, ahead of boastful majors.

We visited a retired butcher. Between two long mudhouses the man stood, leaning over the wooden parapet next to a hunting rifle, smoking his cigarette, without shaking off the ashes. Half the cigarette was ash, and it fell into snow when he drew another suck. Around him circled a small orange dog with long ears that made trails in the snow. The man was sturdy, white hair and green hunting cap on his head. His mustache was more white than gray, but beneath his nostrils it was yellow, and his right-hand fingers were stained yellow.

"Good thing you are here, doctor. My back aches."

"What do you expect, for a man of eighty-four, you are doing fine."

"Seventy-seven."

"Seventy-seven? You must be in love to lie about your age."

"Eh, doctor, it's not easy. I hate being alone; it's a sad life."

"Why didn't you remarry after your wife died?"

"I don't want to rush things. They bring me here women that

are too old, too fat, their asses sag, their tits hang, oh, how sad it all is, everything sags as though we were willow trees. And this pain, what can I do about it?"

"What do you do about it?"

"I take my ax and whack over the shoulder where it hurts. I hit pretty hard but the spine tickles, like crawling ants, so I take off my shirt and rub my back against the oak bark yonder. It helps a little. Sad is this life where weakness beats me and chews me."

"Weakness?" Vlado laughed. "If I whacked my back with an ax, my spine would crack."

"Have you heard, Doc, the baker's wife died! What a fine woman she was! He was no baker at all. He moved back to Zagorye – I guess, as a Croat, he couldn't stand our Serbian village. People are at it again, they hate each other, what a life!"

"They'll get over it," Vlado said, as though commenting about a flu epidemic. He had always been scrupulously apolitical.

On our way back we ran across a small graveyard wedged between the railway tracks and the road, no more than twenty tombs, our grandfather's among them. Vlado stopped the car and we looked at the tomb. "What a small cemetery," I commented.

"Yes, Baptist and Calvinist. But our grandfather Pope was a Greek-Catholic. In the war, Pope had joined no armies. Whatever army passed through, he preached against it. After the war, when the partisans executed many Croatian people as well as Serbian royalists without a trial, he went to Belgrade straight to Tito to protest. He had the so-called civic courage. He was jailed, and we weren't sure whether he'd be released or shot. But the Communists released him, with an explanation, 'It's not really his fault. He's lived in America.' If you came back from America – nothing wrong with going there – you were regarded as certifiably insane. And even if you had your wits together, you'd be supposedly so warped by the American loose perspective on life that you couldn't fit in here anymore."

"There's probably truth in that," I commented.

"And, since our grandmother was a Communist partisan, I think she left her anti-Communist husband. Poor Pope, he stayed in love with Grandmother all his life."

Pope remarried, and he continued loving his American wife, who moved back to the States. That story, of his second wife suffering his sufferings, always intrigued me. It was she who raised a big tombstone to him, the biggest in the cemetery. A Midsummer Night's theme, extended for forty years, is no comedy, but tragedy.

We were on the road, and a train ramp was lowered in front of us. I said, "Too bad we stayed at the cemetery so long. Now . . . "

"How can you say that?" Vlado respected ancestry – his religion was not Christianity, but Ancestor Worship.

We drove over twin creeks. "A peculiar thing," he said. "Around this creek I've recorded eleven cases of cancer, and around the other one, none. Yet there's nothing to pollute either creek."

We drove past the woodhouse where Grandfather used to live. Vlado remembered, "At the outset of the war, hundreds of German tanks rolled by our house. Soldiers drew water from our spindle well. I took a log with big nails sticking out and put it on the road to see whether a tank could drive over it or whether it would get stuck. The soldiers shouted at me. Grandfather slapped me over the head – the only time he had ever done that – and said, 'They might shoot at us for that!' He always liked to remember that, and said, 'I knew right then that he'd become a scientist.' "

"Anyway, would you like to come along to my clinic in Pakrac?"

"What for? It's Sunday."

"Sure, but I need to check on a couple of patients." On the approach to Pakrac, soldiers flagged us down. Ahead of us stood a dozen tanks, blocking the road, chewing the asphalt. I was nervous. There had been ethnic tensions between the Serbs and the Croats – it was the winter of 1990 – but I didn't expect to see the army. For a second I had an uncanny illusion that my brother's talking vividly about his childhood in the war magically transformed his memories into new tanks. A soldier with a machine gun told us we couldn't drive through, but when Vlado told him that he was a doctor on the way to the hospital, the soldiers waved us through while dozens of cars stalled. Vlado's medicine-man calm calmed me. We drove slowly over the turned asphalt past the tanks, among young restless soldiers with red noses and red ears in the wind.

Apricots from Chernobyl

Loud clashes of iron dominoed the coaches as our train pulled wheel by wheel onto the broad Soviet tracks from the narrow Hungarian rails. If you stood without support, each clash would knock you off your feet. After about forty such shocks, we were in the famous country.

Several people in our coach sang Serbian folk songs so loudly that a policeman came by to tell them that they had to be quiet in night coaches, but when he learned that everybody in the coach was from Yugoslavia – a tour group – he said: "You can go on. If I was a Yugoslav, I'd be singing too." (This was in the summer of 1990. Now, a year later, the Ukrainian cop may be singing, unlike us, the ex-Yugoslavs.)

It was steamingly hot in the coach. I complained to the chubby steward. He extorted two German marks from me, promising the air-conditioning would work all night. It started up, but several minutes later it stopped. Someone else from our tour group gave him a mark. The air-conditioning ran for a moment but stopped again. Someone gave him ten marks, but twenty minutes later we were all swearing again.

In the morning the red-faced steward knocked on all the

doors, offering free vodka – a mixture of pure pharmacy alcohol and water – as a prelude to buying cigarettes and whiskey from us. When the train reached the hero city of Lvov, we could not get off because the steward, who had the keys, had vomited and dozed off in the bathroom. Our group leader wanted to smash his nose, but that was not necessary; he had already smashed it himself.

Two days later I took a cab ride in Leningrad. As the driver waited for the light to turn green, an old man with a bundle of medals on his chest crossed the street. I said, "A war hero."

"I *tozhe* a war hero." The cabbie knocked on his wooden leg. "Afghanistan. But, who gives a shit."

Thirty banana stickers were glued on the dashboard. "You must admire bananas," I said.

"No. One night some drunk *durak* told me to drive in circles and for two hours I drove and he ate bananas. As soon as he'd peeled a banana, he'd stick the sticker. *Durak!*"

"So why don't you take the stickers off?"

"I don't give a shit."

I got out on Nevsky Prospekt, supposedly the most elegant boulevard in the Soviet Union; Gogol wrote a great story about it. At one end, near the Square of Alexandr Nevsky, Dostoyevski's skeleton reposes in the Tikhvin cemetery; at the other end the latest issue of *Mademoiselle* was peddled, with a picture of models strolling down Nevsky Prospekt over the caption: *The place to be seen.* I could not walk straight through because of a wall of humanity (if the characteristic New York summer smell is urine, Leningrad's must be sweat). Lines of exasperated people spread over the sidewalks; peddlers sat behind fake acid- and worm-eaten ikons, sold cigarettes piecemeal, and offered smudgy photocopies of the American twenty-dollar bill for a kopek each.

I walked into a large shopping mall, a pink crumbling palace, Gostiny Dvor. I hoped to buy a watch. The best watch I had ever had was Russian – not much to look at, but it had a phrase on the back: *protivudarnye,* "blow-proof." Challenging people to throw the watch against the walls and break it, I won bets. Although all scratched up, it kept time perfectly. Ever since losing it, I had wanted to get another watch like that. Now overweight, perspiring women and ill-looking men besieged a counter among empty shelves. I decided I would staunchly bear everything to get a watch, if for no other reason than to convince myself that I had as much endurance as a Soviet. After being knocked around for an hour, seasick, I reached the counter and asked for a watch. "*Vizitka?*" asked the saleswoman. I showed my passport. "No way," she said. "This is only for the inhabitants of Leningrad." "These Poles, they want to buy everything until there's nothing left," a voice commented about my behavior.

In a side street, toward Lygovski Prospekt, at the entrance to a cellar coffee shop it had taken me hours to find, a dog let his tongue hang to the cement, oozing thick saliva through rotten brown teeth. "Our water is so unhealthy that even our dogs are ill," a drunk passer-by explained to me. He joined me at my table and nibbled on a loaf of bread. I asked him about the 872-day siege of Leningrad in which one million people had starved and frozen to death.

He pulled out his muddy *vizitka* and cleaned the letters with his handkerchief: "Survivor of the Siege of Leningrad." He radiated his heroism, but I thought, If you are stuck under a siege, you will try to survive, and if you do, maybe it will be because of cowardice and selfishness, not courage. I had read that the pensions to all the Second World War veterans, including the survivors of Leningrad, immensely burdened the Soviet economy. So, since he got a lavish pension – I was convinced he did – why should he sit here drunk and unable to buy a cup of coffee? But, after all the horrors, perhaps consciousness hurt him and alcohol was a fine way to escape. If not the man, I admired the history in the man.

On the way back, I could not wave down any cabs, but an ambulance screeched to a stop in front of me. The doctor told me to limp into the back of the ambulance and lie down – so the cops would not see me. The trip to the hotel through back streets took half an hour and cost ten rubles. Bottles of plasma dangled above my stretcher. My roommate, a Serb gambler from the Lika region of Croatia, told me he had seen a car knock down a woman on Nevsky Prospekt. She lay dying on the cobbles, but nobody came to help her. The car had backtracked a little, made a detour around the body, and squealed away. I hoped that my "cab" had not been on the way to save her!

On our night train from Leningrad to Moscow, I got coffee for the whole coach – not a great feat of generosity – for an American dollar. Dushan, a big Bosnian Serb, sang raspily at an unbelievable volume. Then Vyera, a Russian woman from Zagreb, Croatia – because she used a Soviet passport, she was the only member of our group needing a visa; a visa to return to her home country! – sang Russian ballads in such a fragile and withdrawn voice that we had to cluster our ears around her mouth, knocking our heads together. The songs floated from her mouth on a chocolaty, warm cloud of Irish coffee. Dushan said, "Motherfuckers! There is such a thing as the Russian soul!"

Suddenly a young blond woman ran into our compartment and began to shout, "*Bozhe moy!*" (my God). Clasping her hands and staring into the ceiling, she presented the innocence of an ikon. "They want to rape me!"

"Who's they?"

"They sold me the ticket at the train station so I wouldn't have to wait in line. I didn't know I would have to be in the same compartment with them. With knives they threatened me."

"Who did?" The big singer jumped up and headed to her compartment.

"She's all fishy," Vyera said. "Throw her out."

But Dushan came back and said: "There's blood on her pillows – fuck it, she's not lying."

From opposite ends of the corridor suddenly two crews showed up, Russians and Georgians. A Georgian grasped the blond woman's arm and whispered into her ear, and when she hesitated in speaking to us, he boxed her in the kidneys so that she gasped and her tears flowed more thickly than before. There was blood on her shoulder. I pointed at the blood, asking where it came from.

I could not understand the Georgian's excited blabber. The Russians came closer, saying that she had made everything up – her nose bled from the weak blood. They wondered whether we wanted to change any German marks.

We told her persecutors to go away and banged the door shut. The young woman looked around. "It's so beautiful here, you have it so good, and where I am, it's terrible. How lucky you are!" And she stared at our luggage.

Vyera warned us the whole thing was a setup so they could get into our compartment to steal our stuff. We got tired of the blond woman's whining and threw her out. Then the four Georgians shouted and one stuck his head into the compartment, looking at our luggage. I told him they should all go back to their coach. He stared me in the eye. It irritated me that he was not backing off. Then he pulled a knife – I was not enjoying the situation – but a man from his pack pulled him back, and they left.

I wondered what kind of police state it was that could not provide security on a night train.

In an ambulance at the Moscow train station, blood dripped from a body in a white sheet. Next to the body lay a wrapped round thing with dark hair, the body's head. People passed calmly by the open ambulance. "Did he come out of our coach?" I asked.

"No, from the train across the platform," Dushan said.

In Moscow, we were in the bus on the way to our hotel from Slavyanskyi Bazaar, a restaurant where we had undergone an eating and drinking epic. The tour guide thought that there was nothing for us to do in Russia but eat, drink, and be merry, so every night we did that, with a lot of Serbian singing, which continued on the bus. I saw two smashed cabs on their sides, so crushed that there had to be corpses in the rubble, but the traffic, including our bus, went smoothly down the avenue.

I was not surprised that the cabs had collided. That day a cabbie had driven – with me in the front seat without a seat belt – sixty miles an hour through dense traffic. He brushed against a car from the opposite direction. His mirror was knocked back, but he stayed cool. Perhaps the cabbie had been psyching the other driver to get out of the way, but the driver was as tough as he. It all struck me, and everybody in my group, as a lack of respect for life or a lack of sensitivity to death. My impression was commonplace; after all, one of the main attractions in the city is the frozen and powdered corpse of Lenin in a glass cage – that monstrosity of dialectical materialism, who, although denying the possibility of eternal life, himself remained on display as though forever.

We lined up outside the Kremlin, next to the eternal fire to the unknown soldier. In about twenty minutes we were inside. We walked down two short flights of stairs and passed in a semicircle around the corpse, the same type of semicircle that the car driver did in Leningrad around the corpse of his victim – except that, in this case, the victims walked around the corpse of the dubious victor. Through cold, air-conditioned air, we walked along his right side, up the stairs, past his feet, down his left side. He was not as large as his monuments; his right fist was clenched over his chest, his left palm was open on his side. Even in death he looked like a fighter. From the satined and Satanic dark, we emerged into the light of Krasnaya Ploshad, Red Square – but in Old Russian, the Beautiful Square. There were enough red buildings around to keep the wrong translation going. Between the Mausoleum and the Kremlin wall, we strolled past the busts of Chernenko, Andropov, Brezhnev, and Stalin; each bust was heavily riding over its corresponding corpse. Khrushchev's was missing.

We walked toward the Basilica of St. Basil, the overly famous church with ten variegated domes that resemble balloons filled with helium, soon to ascend into the heavens. Inside, thick red brick walls arched above the ground, looking like cellar corridors. Elongated, fishy eyes in gilt frames gazed at me from amongst a multitude of red, yellow, and blue flowers drawn on the walls in an excessive way that, anywhere else in the world, would be called tacky or kitsch. But the Russians somehow got away with it, and it still struck us as wonderful art.

Outside and behind the church – or, rather, the museum-a swarm of small boys – barefoot, dirty, some in long underpants, their faces smeared with dust and tears – ran at us, shouting, "Give me a ruble!" I gave a boy twenty kopeks, but that only got him going. He jumped at my legs, grabbed me around my knee, and leaned his cheek against my thigh. "*Davay* ruble!" he cried, tears flowing down his cheeks. He lifted his blue eyes and crumpled his forehead and face around them in an expression of pain far more impressive than the expressions of beatitude in the Basilica of St. Basil. I could not shake him off, and in the heat of the day, the heat of his body was unpleasant. Finally I gave him a ruble. He let me go, ran to a young woman in a green skirt, and handed her the ruble; she slapped his face to keep his tears going and sent him on toward somebody else's leg to squeeze out another ruble. A dozen other children, some Gypsies, some blond Russians, clung to us as we climbed the stairs of our air-conditioned *Sputnik* bus. They cried and wailed as though they were children in Bethlehem during the times of Herod. We could not beat them off, so this was a rape – the weaker over the stronger.

Disappointed by the churches-turned-museums, several of us went into an active, whitewashed church – with blue edges and seven or eight golden pear-shaped domes and bumpy crosses, thickened at the joints like boney arms and legs.

Entering, we heard the monotone of a prayer in church Slavonic. The priest faced the altar, his back turned to the congregation, in the posture of a leader and not an opponent. People stood in the atrium. Bunches of thin yellow candles flickered in front of each of the many gilded ikons, filling the dark church with golden color. It flickered from the frames of saints, from the robes of the Virgin and the serious baby. The candles crackled like static, the light that whispers. A chant resounded from behind a partition; the voices seemed to drift down from above. Some people were sitting – there were only a few seats along the walls – but most continued to stand. A long-hair tabby tomcat lay in the middle of the church and pricked his ears at the higher sounds. He languidly walked toward the partition, seemed to decide there were no mice there, and languidly walked back to where he had lain before. A woman in blue, busy removing the candles that had burned nearly to the end, leaned over to give him a slap, but a pain in her back prevented her. So she nudged him with a gentle kick, for the show. The enemy of the Gospel shrank back a little. I patted him and thought of Gogol's "Overcoat" – the collar was made of cat's fur.

The cat walked over to a corner, sniffing at an azure coffin containing a gray corpse – an old woman with her mouth slightly parted showing her teeth or dentures. One corner of her mouth was glued as though her saliva had frozen in death. Her sunken eyes were not completely closed. A gray cloth protruded over her head with a fancy, jagged paper rim, from which serial Jesuses hailed with their thin fingers, as though voting. The odor made me dizzy; clearly this was not the first day after her death. She looked so sunken and crumpled, as though she had been dead for more than sixty years, like her *tovarish* at the Beautiful Square.

Hardly anybody noticed this woman. The service was not in her honor. She was there because her relatives or her congregation considered it the best place for her to hover before being buried. A dozen people walked by, and their faces registered no change of mood. An old woman crossed herself *en passant* to one of the bearded saints where she lit three candles with hands surprisingly calm for someone that old, in the presence of a corpse.

The cat seemed tempted to jump into the coffin, but, perhaps assessing the corpse as inedible, went to the front of the church instead and sprayed the ancient door, thus reserving his exclusive rights to the next corpse.

The harmonies went on, ordering and reconciling the weak and the strong, the living and the dead. Many people bought candles and lit them. Two women tossed burned-out candle stumps into a bucket. Printed prayers and aluminum ikons stood at an angle, for sale. Kopeks clanged, passing hands. The church was a busy place: some people were singing, others praying; some were whispering to the ikons, others being tourists; some were busy being dead, others lighting the candles; some were throwing the candles into the garbage, others being catty; some . . . and despite it all, there was a dignity, and an understanding that death did not matter.

If I died right there, in Russia, in the church or in a taxicab, it would be the quietest place to go; my death would mean nothing, in a tranquil way. A banal equation popped in my mind, "They value their lives little, therefore they value death little."

Can you respect your life if you drink water from the same glass as thousands of other people? Outside I thirsted, but declined to drink from a slot-machine glass. People came by, sank their coins, drank from the glass, then gave it to the next guy – who sank his coins and pressed the glass down against a broad rubber button, activating a small fountain. There was no way of washing the glass, so the people effectively drank one another's saliva. Like kissing half of Moscow.

The legendary patience was something to envy. Kasparov once commented that, although Ljubojevich – the best Yugoslav chess player – was as talented as anyone in the world, he would never become the world champion because of his Mediterranean rashness. As much as the lines indicated a failing economy, they expressed a patient culture. So when my Yugoslav compatriots spoke with scorn and pity about Russians-and nearly all of them did – I wondered what made us feel superior? Little did we know then that our country (countries) would soon flare up with hatreds – disrespect for life far greater than that in Russia – decapitations, smashed skulls, mutilations, and drunken slayings.

The gambler contemptuously gave waiters ten-ruble notes (the equivalent of somebody giving you twenty dollars) for "coffee." The same man was ten thousand dollars in debt and had to sell his forest for it. He had gambled away the house he had inherited from his father and now lived in a pigsty at the edge of his woods. During the day he worked as a laborer at a state bakery, loading trucks with loafs and taking down sacks of flour. "Everybody in my village gambles. As soon as you start to walk, you throw dice, or stones at trees, for money. Nobody there has gotten anywhere in life. We have gambled our village away in towns. I lost the ten grand to a kid I'd taught how to play poker!" Now a man of forty, single, he hardly spoke to anybody; more precisely, hardly anybody spoke to him.

But still, he stood at the window on the train from Moscow to Kiev, staring at the willowy plains, and exclaimed, "Fuck the poor Russia!"

"The is the Ukraine," a literature student from Zagreb corrected him.

"Makes no difference. It's all Russia to me."

"Just as all Yugoslavia is Serbia to you," muttered the student under her breath so that he could not hear her.

The gambler said, "Only if I could right now dig my way back into my woods, drink mountain water from my brook, eat mushrooms after a cold storm – my dick would stand up like a tree. That's life. Fuck this!"

The train stewardess wanted to marry him so she could move to Yugoslavia. "That'll cost," he said to me as though he were a frugal man. "I'll have to put her up in a hotel. She couldn't stay with me in my pigsty." And while talking like that, he would notice an old woman geese-herding near a swollen, blue-washed mudhouse, and he would say, "Fuck the Sun! How can these people live like that, like pigs?"

After several shifty-eyed Ukrainians and Russians passed by trying to buy cigarettes and exchange money and get a sip of vodka, the Croatian literature student said, "I dreamed of tall blond men with intense gazes, Dostoyevski-types, Baryshnikov look-alikes. Are they all this small?"

"What are you complaining of?" I said. "What impression of Yugoslavia would you have from hotels and night trains? In the States I met a woman who, when I told her I was from Yugoslavia, shrank back and laughed. She had once passed through Yugoslavia on a train. At first she was alone in her compartment, and a bunch of Yugoslav soldiers came by and molested her. The train conductor threw them out and locked her in by herself. But at the next station, the soldiers climbed into her compartment through the window and molested her again. Finally the conductor reappeared, threw them out, and locked even the window so that she nearly suffocated without air. That was her only experience of Yugoslavia, and she drew some conclusions. Do you think that represents Yugoslavia, you, me?"

"Maybe it does." She went into her compartment and locked the door.

I stared through the window at long trains carrying green armored vehicles eastward. I had heard it would take five years of constant train transport to demobilize the Soviet war machines from the disbanded Warsaw Pact.

A steel-toothed woman with silver glaucoma rings in her eyes wanted to sell me aluminum ikons. I bought a Russian New Testament without bargaining and read the Beatitudes. *Blessed are the meek for they shall inherit the earth.*

A peasant got on the train near Chernobyl and offered us stunted orange apricots from a woven willow basket. The gambler handed him a hundred-ruble note: "Here, buy yourself some coffee and cigarettes, Devil take you!"

A Bachelor Party

At Les Amis, as I was about to complain to a waitress that my fresh cup of coffee was not hot, it occurred to me that I belonged to a circle of petulant bachelors. The realization struck me as a revelation, and I was surprised that I hadn't noticed it before. In my mind I ran through a list of the married people I knew and the bachelors I knew. Most active men were married, and most inactive, self-doubting ones were bachelors. I could not tell whether bachelorhood was the symptom or the cause of instability – what came first, the rooster or the egg, the rain or the sea? But am I really a bachelor? Before thirty, I thought the question could not possibly apply to me. Aristotle said that before thirty one should spend time in education, and marry at thirty. I was now thirty-one.

Five years before, my brother-in-law had told me that if I did not get married by twenty-eight, I never would. That soothsaying soothed me then because I had thought that I would, as most philosophers – Wittgenstein, Kierkegaard, Nietzsche, Kant, Hume, Descartes, Plato (whoever I could think of, except Marx, the anti-philosopher) – remain a bachelor. But, I was not a good philosopher; I was too prone to generalize without induction and to specify without deduction. As a bad philosopher, maybe I did not have the mental stamina to take the solitude of bachelorhood?

Although it's preposterous to compare humans to animals, it is equally preposterous not to compare them to animals. It's rare for roosters to tolerate one another, and rarer for active tomcats to hang around in cliques. A tomcat in his prime beats down the others who are satisfied to sit on the woodpile next to the furnace and blink all day long.

So, I wondered, looking around at my haggard circle of bachelors near an artificial fireplace – why do we male animals congregate? Where are the women? Are we the beaten tomcats?

What is a bachelor? An indecisive retreating creature who has not made up his mind to marry. Because of the bachelor's habitual indecisiveness, the bachelor experiments a lot – too much – and his enterprises fail. There are exceptions, and I hoped I would be one, but I could see the bachelor complex and complexity begin to trap my mind into various broodings. What is going on? Does it only get worse?

I looked for the answer, staring at the toms, and despite my brooding, found them a fascinating gallery of characters.

Fernando, thirty-three, awaited the oral defense of his Ph.D. dissertation, or, as he preferred to put it, his "anals." He was the child of a New York Russian-Jewish psychiatrist and a Colombian plantation-owner, who, in a psychiatric session reached a very high degree of transference, out of which, and out of wedlock, Fernando was born – in a Bogotá taxicab that prefigured his mobile and expensive life-style. He was expelled from a Catholic school after he sneaked into the confessional when the priest was sick. Fernando refused to grant forgiveness to the boys who said that they did not masturbate, and those who said they did he sent away with the highest blessings. When I met him, he proposed that we organize an orgy, speaking so loudly that a woman, a good acquaintance of ours, who overheard us stopped talking to us. Fernando's cheeks were always pink and rosy as if he had just walked out of a snowstorm and now faced a fireplace;

or as if he were swathed too warmly. Now and then he put a little finger into his mouth and sucked on it, laughing, like a baby with a chamomile tea bottle. These manners sharply contrasted with his large beard and tall patriarchal forehead, over which his skin glistened.

In our circle there was hardly anybody who was not indebted to Fernando's generosity. If I ran out of money by the end of the month, I could write him a postdated check. In that respect, generosity, Fernando was not a typical bachelor.

Jean-Jacques, thirty-three, was a post-doc in chemistry from Paris. Exterior: brown hair, neither wavy nor straight, with a life of its own, neither combed nor uncombed, yet both orderly and wild, thrown slightly sideways, but not parted. Eyes: brown, eyelashes and eyebrows strong enough to define his face and to frame his eyes, so that any light that was reflected from them seemed to come out of darkness. Nose: not a remarkable feature. Sharp laugh/contempt lines on the sides of his mouth. His jaded sophisticated air in conversation dialectically turned into its opposite: sudden light in his eyes displayed childlike curiosity and playful love of combination and recombination – perhaps a trait of a true organic chemist, experimentalist, combinationalist, a bachelor at his best – as if learning restored in him some primeval condition of happiness and innocence.

Stature: neither short nor tall nor medium – slightly above medium. Neither fat nor thin, but leaning toward slim. In *Dead Souls* thin men flock around ladies and fat men around gambling tables. Chichikov, neither fat nor thin, oscillates between the two groups, but since he leans a little to the fat side, he spends more time among the money-making people. Jean-Jacques hung around ladies. His air of "I don't care" was intriguing to pretty women who were used to the "I long to touch your nipple" attitude.

Interior: a ladies' man does not need any. A Frenchman especially has no need of any interior since he pays so much attention to the exterior. And to be sure, Jean-Jacques often complained, especially in the morning, perhaps after a night of debauchery, that he felt empty. But as this world is paradoxical, I imagine that he had a good deal of interior life, which kept him relentlessly disenchanted. For a year he worked hard, and then he worked little, and spent very much time in cafes, "permitting" (his expression) women to chat him up.

Robert, forty-four, came to our town from Venice. Italians have cut down 99 percent of their trees, and Roberto wanted to buy a plot of land in Italy and one in the States-typical of a bachelor, to make two parallel plans that will undermine each other – to reforest the lands. He wore green as if he were a forester. Of course, as I looked at him, he yawned, and equally, of course, we tried to carry on a semblance of a conversation. As soon as I mentioned Italy, he exclaimed, "Italians, all crooks!" He flung his chubby hands up – though flung may not be the word, since he did it lethargically as if the very mention of Italy had exhausted him. His large eyes remained dull, eyelids half-drawn. His gray hairs didn't flicker like silver but ate light and stayed dim like ashes. Purple young moons hung beneath his eyes, and from them creases spread around like fossils of rays, rays solidified into a stony setting, if such a thing could happen.

"Cheer up," I said. "Italians are famous for their joie de vivre; at least they know how to joke."

"They used to. Twenty years ago, humor died in Italy. I remember it as a bambino, everybody used to laugh, but no more. Nobuddy!"

I laughed. "Haven't you just cracked a joke?"

"You don't believe me? BBC has done a study on that, so it's true. If Italians did, it would be a lie. Everybody a crook in Italy." He lifted his hands in front of his chest, palms toward me, fingers spread wide, as if waiting to catch a basketball. "Italians don't know notting. They don't know how to walk no more. You tink I'm kidding? We used to promenade. Now the sidewalks are empty, the roads full. Everybody's in a car."

It astonished me that such a great country as Italy should induce so little patriotism. You may have a lot against your country, but during a prolonged stay abroad, you become nostalgic and see the good sides. For heaven's sake, I had something good to say even about my shitty country, Yugoslavia! But then again, I was a beginner at bachelorhood, and Roberto was an inveterate one, never married.

"How come you aren't married?" I asked.

"You don't know Italian women. They talk talk talk, no buddy can stop their tongues, you get a headache listening to dem. You tink Italians marry Italian women? No longer. Mostly German, Swedish, Hungarian, Polish, Yugoslav."

"So, why haven't you married an Eastern European?"

"Solomon in Bible says, Among one tausend men I found one, among ten tausend women, none. Eh?" He shrugged. "You can't find a good woman, I saw it with my az. They all cheat. I know. I screwed many married women on vacation."

"But not all."

"Enough to know. Not even *New York Times* needs to call all the households to find out how many people like Bush and how many Dukakis."

"Don't you have friends in Italy?"

"I used to have a very good firend." His voice was slow as if he were telling me an instructive tale. "We sailed every weekend with women from Holland, Denmark, France. We had so many we did not know what to do wid dem all. He was a Don Giovanni. Two monts after he bot the boat, he got married. A Swedish chick, no different dan di oder Swedish chicks, he took her out for espresso, and dey fell in love. I am not joking, in love! they mved in together, I could see him ony for half an oar here, half an oar dere. He alwasy rushed, they got a baby, then anoder one. Una tragedia. He's finished. No frridom!" Roberto shook his forefinger in front of my eyes.

"But that's normal. Friends get married."

"But not wid a tourist."

"You said not with an Italian."

"Yourright, yourright! That would be the worst."

Robert really did not have good friends, not even among us, and now he stared and daydreamed, not following the conversations, and actually, I, too, let my mind sink into reveries, about bachelorhood and friendship. Friendships shrink as the years vanish. Most men friends get married by their early thirties. The bachelor is left out of the circles of intimacy spun around marriages. Friendships with younger men set him back: the bachelor merely relives the things that may have been exciting but are now a mimicry of the good old days.

I asked John, forty, a computer consultant, "How come you aren't married?"

He interrupted counting his change, mostly pennies, for a tip to the waitress – he always gave precisely 10 percent – pushed his glasses up his nose, and said, "When I had good opportunities, I was too young and unready to settle down, and now I don't have good opportunities."

"But I've seen you with interesting women."

"They are interesting at first, but I am picky."

"So, you are looking?"

"I wouldn't say that. I guess it's too late for me to marry."

Roberto intervened: "Don't ever say that. For a man it's never too late to marry. If you wanted to marry, you could do it tomorrow, I am sure. Just rite yor name, phone nomer, here on the board, with chalk. You'll get twenty offers. I am not kiddin." Roberto shook his head and then propped it up on his palm and looked woefully bored.

The rest of us laughed.

"I have a good girlfriend these days," John said. "I just don't like to bring her here, among you horny rascals. Besides, taking a woman out is too expensive."

Although John was a millionaire from semi-old money, he lived extremely frugally, wore canvas sneakers and irregular T-shirts, watched a Goodwill black-and-white TV, drove beat-up cars, and lived like an impoverished student in a studio. Fear of letting go of money is typical for many bachelors of a particularly cautious type.

As we all raised our eyebrows at his mention that he could not afford to go out with a woman, let alone marry her, John came up with another reason. "She's younger than me, and I'm not sure I could marry her even if I wanted to."

"Don't ever say dat," Roberto said. "Evry woman wants to get married. It may not look like it, but she doz. I know." He yawned. "She plays games, dat's all: una strategia."

Then the other bachelor, Tom, who'd been massaging his receding hairline and staying out of the debate, joined in. "A good book on bachelors just came out." That was typical of him, he had researched everything. He had dropped out of a Ph.D. program in political science when the sixties ended, got an M.F.A. in painting, and now was trying to get into law school, but even law schools seemed to have caught on to Peter Pans. He slurped coffee. "The point the author makes pretty convincingly is that bachelors are the most vulnerably minority in the country – the shortest life span, most suicide, insanity, alcoholism, and the lowest income. Lower even than Black women."

"So, you'd like to get a wife now?"

"I'd like to." He said, quite frankly, a bit unusual for a bachelor, but he was always very honest. He smiled a lot, and sometimes looked very abstracted in his smiles, as if he were holding an inner conversation.

Since bachelors are a restless bunch, soon our being together would be done with. I was about to move to Massachusetts to waste time on a fellowship, Fernando to California where women were supposedly more exciting, John back to Chicago despite horrendous rents, and Roberto back to Venice, or as it turned out later when he wrote down his address, Messina in Sicily (I suppose, another Venice of the South). Tom was the only one staying. Even two other bachelors, who'd joined in the meanwhile, were going to different cities. When we talked about our dispersing, we already felt nostalgic – I guess bachelors are quite a melancholy lot – and we decided to throw a "going-away" party, or as I put it, with a slip of the tongue, "go away!" party.

Before the party we discussed whether there should be Jacuzzis and a swimming pool around, and who to invite.

Fernando said: "I am sick of lousy parties, four guys a woman. Let's invite a few guys and many pretty women."

Roberto said: "Let's invite many gay men so dere won't be much competition for di women, and to women it won't be obvious."

Jean-Jacques and Fernando scrutinized many places – a mansion, a pub, an apartment complex party house. In the end, no place was large enough, except a warehouse which covered a whole city block. There lived Mark, a thin prize-winning pianist, and Martha, his girlfriend, a legal secretary. In conversations she screwed up her eyes sideways like an alcoholic.

The warehouse had three floors and a flat roof, from which you could see the skyline of our town, some geometric pastiche – office buildings. Our town was supposed to become a new business mecca but now had the highest office vacancy rate in the country: as a city it had been most overestimated and now – at the height of the oil bust – underestimated.

Mark and Martha got around their apartment, the second floor, on roller skates. In one corner two ominous black pianos, one large and one small, like the sarcophagi of an emperor and his son, brooded. A soft, pillowy bedroom made a nest in another corner. The kitchen encircled the stairs; the bathroom adorned another corner. Wood planks and large crates of wood, filled with records and books, formed most of the furniture. Thick gray raw-cement pillars stood all around the warehouse, strong enough to support a thirty-story building.

As the date for the party approached, the excitement among the bachelors grew. Instead of spending thirty or so dollars on five hundred invitations, Fernando "rented" for two hundred an artist who'd made posters for Janis Joplin's first concert. Hastily drawn in four or five strokes, a man without feet ran diagonally upwards from the bottom on the recycled paper.

Roberto organized a bash before the grand party, at his home. Jeanette, a woman I'd met in a Brazilian dance club on April Fool's, and I went to Roberto's on her motorcycle. Although we'd arrived an hour late, there were only five or six people there, sitting around somberly listening to Vivaldi. Roberto offered us herb teas, grapefruit juice, pineapples, and spring water. "No tobacco, alcohol, coffee, drugs, dat's my rule. Isn't it great? I feel fantastic!" Two or three people left right away, several others showed up and soon left. For weeks afterwards, Roberto kept describing his fantastic party. He had no need of another one. Instead, he placed ads in the newspapers, offering nature-loving women an exciting Venetian.

The day for the grand party arrived. Two bands showed up. Kornelia, a Swiss guitar player, wanted the stage to be perfectly compact because of her high heels. She wore a miniskirt, flirted, and talked about what a great businesswoman she was. She told that she wrote a novel. I asked her how long it was, and she said fifteen pages. She mistook English novel to correspond to the German *Novelle,* a short story, rather than to the *Roman.* Fernando's debtors carried boards for the stage from the basement, shuffled and reshuffled and nailed them. (Fernando employed his debtors, forgiving them at the rate of five bucks an hour for doing the chores.) Jean-Jacques took off his starched shirt, and with a cigarette dangling on his lip, in the style of Jean-Paul Belmondo, scurried around with a hammer and nails, sweat trickling from his back. "Where's Fernando?" he repeatedly asked.

Four of us carried a large margarita-making machine up the stairs. There were about a dozen gallons of tequila and several pounds of lime powder, but we forgot to buy whatever soda went with it.

In the evening a powerful storm fell; large beads of rain

rebounded from the asphalt like hail. A wind pushed its way through the hissing waterfall, making waves.

At the entrance stood a hired guard, a thin bachelor, admitting only those with the artistic invitations. I thought there should be a big bouncer, but the Greek said that he could always kick in the balls; he'd played soccer for the national junior team of Greece.

Beyond the entrance stood two plastic orange outhouses, like those construction workers use, for us, though we were destruction workers. Mark and Martha had locked their bathroom. After climbing the stairs, you faced the thin podium, and, turning to the right, a bar made of wood planks and crates, and behind it, two debtors, Dick and David, in their late twenties, too young and too energetic to qualify as true bachelors. Dick, with long curly hair, a Grecian profile – that is, forehead and nose in one line – was of the Dionysian rather than the Apollonian predisposition, which served as a theme for the birth of a minor tragedy. David, with thinly shorn black hair, unshaven, wore a ratty T-shirt, which said Freedom Serbs. As a Croatian, I appreciated the World War I slogan since this was before the War in Croatia when I believed that we were all Slavic brothers. The minor tragedy was that the two galley slaves were, after numerous libations to the inexhaustible Greek pantheon, thoroughly pissed, sauced, and sloshed when the first guest arrived. Dick was opening Chinese Dragon beer bottles with his teeth, and later, I don't know why he changed his mind (perhaps he cracked a tooth), he muscled the caps off the bottles with a red Swiss Army knife, showing off his large muscles as if he were slaying dragons. You had to tell Dick several times the number of beers you wanted. While holding the bottles, he'd scrutinize the labels. Who knows how long he would stare, his eyes flickering as if on fire, if you did not say, "Look, could I have three beers?" That startled him as if one of the snakes leaping at him from the label had spoken. The line in front of the bar kept growing as thirsty guests filed in out of the rainstorm. And that was the minor tragedy: the guests, remaining sober for too long, grew whimsical.

Half an hour later when I looked back toward the bar, Fernando's two debtors (one for a meager one hundred, the other for two hundred dollars) were not there. Toni, a star basketball player and high-school teacher of history – not a debtor – replaced them. Debtor number 3 was supposed to help him at the bar. Since number 3 was an AA member, he was supposed to be perfect. With a thick beard, looking like a pirate despite possessing two healthy eyes, he stood on the sidelines and stared at the rum bottles, his eyes twice their usual size, his eyebrows arched high. His girlfriend, a graduate student of English, intervened to save him from temptation. Her sleeves rolled up, her calm eyes intrepidly confronted the oncoming waves of drunks. She served the guests like some sturdy peasant girl bartending a country tavern, and looking at her you'd have no idea that she was an elitist graduate student of deconstructionist literary criticism, with all sorts of meta- and subtextual skills.

Many personages strolled by, bowing to each other, asking each other to dance, winking, letting their T-shirts slide exposing round breasts. Some people smirked, some toasted, some chatted, some leaned against the round pillars trapping objects of desire.

Melissa, a guest of mine, stood close to the entrance and looked on, reluctant to enter the party. She worked as a journalist and book reviewer for our local newspaper. At thirty-two she was the female version of a bachelor. I could not call her a spinster. Why is it that bachelor sounds all right, free, independent, playful, etc. – despite my trying to present the other side of the coin – and spinster does not? Clearly, our society is cruel to unmarried women; now after feminist activism society should be reformed. So isn't there a better term for a single woman after thirty? Bachelorette is too derivative. Independent woman, too political, like a new state. Well, why should not the term bachelor apply to women as well? Anyway, Melissa was a bachelor. She said one could tell that foreign men had organized the party. "I've never seen so many beautiful women. Many women who are disappointed in American men don't know yet about the foreign ones. Boy, are they in for a ride! They come alone or with other women, and the men come alone or with other men; it's as if two nations were meeting on a battlefield!"

I introduced her to Jean-Jacques, but she looked at him skeptically.

A sensible unattached woman meeting an inveterate stylish male bachelor talks to him with caution, if at all, because he either can't love enough to commit – to anything but adultery- or he may have an extensive love history, too many past – and perhaps current – relationships. If he forms a relationship with the new woman, the relationship becomes relative to many relationships; the relativity factor diminishes the chance that the new couple will become relatives and contributes to the bachelor's being unfaithful: entering the new relationship is a breach of faith to the old ones. A bachelor, as a rule, becomes a faithless man. Anyhow, that's what I thought, as I walked away from my hesitant friends.

Fernando wasn't around much. For half an hour he rushed around in his Jamaican outfit, a green-yellow T-shirt with loud palm trees, a straw hat, and a purple backpack, like a student coming home after a hard day of studying at the library. He and his girlfriend, an opera singer, would soon disappear again. It seemed strange to spend so much money (In the end, it turned out to be five thousand dollars; half of it from Fernando, the other from Jean-Jacques) and to stay private at the party.

After Fernando trailed Detlev, a bony German bachelor, thirty-four, a clean-cut type that is common in German department stores, smiling at customers for commission, selling PCs. A follower of Rajneesh, Tantric yoga, he congregated with women to meditate, namely, to insert his penis in them and wait for enlightenment. One is supposed to surpass carnal attachment in the focal point of carnal attachments. But he didn't seem to have gotten very far in his meditation; lustfully gazing at Fernando's girlfriend, he kept asking Fernando for her phone number. And when Fernando refused to give it to him, he shrugged his shoulders as if saying, "It's not my fault that you are so primitive and possessive. I thought you were liberated from the petit-bourgeois standards."

Detlev often sat in cafés alone, his cigarette above his vertical arm, sticking out between his fingers on the side of his head in a posed manner. He stared into space nostalgically, the strong yet sensitive silent type. He rarely initiated conversations with anybody, but if some friends of his were with a woman, he immediately joined them and stared at the woman with a faint smile, a bit of a sideways glance, with his hair falling over his eyes, giving him a girlish look.

Now he said to me, "I vaz danzig all alon, it felt zo good! All bye myzelf!" in a faked, typically German enthusiasm. Almost every culture has its fake ways: Americans – mechanical and meaningless smiles, a habit from too much selling; Germans – enthusiastic breathing while speaking as if divinely inspired – too many philosophers, priests, and dictators had ravished their culture. I may be wrong to make these generalizations, but . . . Anyway, enhanced with some dozen beers, I felt a sudden aversion toward him. "Why are you smiling? You have no right to smile. Your grandfather probably butchered old Slavic women and children in the Ukraine and Byelorussia, threw Jews into the gas chambers of Auschwitz, and you are smiling! Have you heard that the sins fall on the heads of the third generation? That's the Jewish law, and your ancestors killed Jews and should be judged accordingly by Jewish law. Your soul is stained with blood, and it's not only till the third generation that the blood falls, but I tell you, till the fifth. Your grandchildren, poor souls, will also have bloodstained souls."

The guy looked at me, at a loss as to how to respond. His temporary girlfriend in pink, a Tantric nun, came rushing to our side and she asked us eagerly what we were talking about. "Germany," I replied. All the anti-German things I had picked up from my elementary school anti-German teacher popped up in my head and I reeled them off, while I gazed into his eyes, feeling I could strangle him any moment. He said, "You stay away from me, you stay away from me!" True, I was a lunatic. In Europe, we were all born out of the wars, one way or another. If there is shit at the source of the brook, there's shit farther along as well. Walking away, I thought of my violent impulse. What was that for? A rebellion? Isn't it out of place?

Bachelorhood seemed to me to be a prolonged adolescence – at best the Peter Pan syndrome – without conventional rights to be silly, frivolous, flirtatious, and rebellious. Rebellion in a bachelor decays into spite and spite into resentment. If a bachelor should have enough freshness of an impulse – which was rare – to freak out, the question would be: Why haven't you figured out a way to take your complaint to the court and op-ed columns or to take some other civilized option? Haven't you acquired enough writing, debating, and other civic skills? If not, what were you doing all those years with your leisure? And what was I doing all those years at school, if I was to stay a fool?

Near the bar stood a large man, Jim, a Les Amis cook, car mechanic, published poet, and the guru of book collectors. Next to him was Jamie, minus his beard, the book collector junior. They gazed at women and kept talking about first editions of translations.

Jeanette – the motorcycle woman, a seductress by impulse and a passionate dancer – was my date. She praised me on being well behaved. Whenever she went off to dance – I had no interest in dance – she left me her red handbag. Linda, an architecture student dressed almost like a bride, came up to me and asked me whether she looked ridiculous in the dress. I assured her she didn't. Upon which, deductively and seductively she motioned me toward the dancing area (away from the bar), but when she saw the woman's bag strapped on my side, she rushed away from me. She was flushed, but later on came back and leaned out the window to watch the rain with me, and she whispered a poem in Spanish. I looked around because, if by any chance I lost control, it was still too early to blame it on alcohol, and I was not sure how

Jeanette would receive the bridal dress. So, I walked away, and there was Jeanette. She embraced me, while Bruno, a six-foot-six emaciated photographer with a great wingspan, took a photograph of us. Only twenty-five, he planned to dedicate his life to taking pictures of nude women. Wherever he walked, he accosted women, his eyes glazed, and he proposed an art session; most women shunned him.

A hat was passed around. A mild-mannered Arab from Nazareth collected money very nonaggressively. Some people grabbed the lettucelike bills out of the hat while pretending to be giving money. Only about one hundred dollars were collected.

Fernando, who showed up at one-thirty, complained because people had not contributed financially to the party. Jean-Jacques took the loss of money in stride; strolling among many people engaged in petting, he said: "It's almost over, and I feel like it's been only half an hour. A half hour!"

The more the night wore on, the closer to the bar I stood and the more I chanted, "A little more beer, please!" and the less I was able to see, so that I shouldn't report anything further. In the end, I was in the car with Jeanette, who kept praising me how well I had behaved. Who would have expected that of me?

The next morning I woke up with a tremendous headache, and no matter how much coffee I drank and how many showers I took, it stayed. Everybody I ran into after the party said, eyes blinking, "It was a great one, the best one I've been to!"

Now that I've described the party, I look back, and say, What happened? Nothing. Even during the party I'd felt as though at a concert that I'd looked forward to – I regretted that it would soon end without an echo. All those sounds came and went, and what's left? Nothing. That's a typical bachelor feeling after an event. Disappointment, the mode of life of loud desperation. But maybe the party was not in vain. The obvious vanity of the bachelor life alarmed me. The party and the circle of bachelors, together with my broodings, I am sure, contributed to my getting married several months afterward. Jeanette, my date at the party, became my wife. I was not comfortable with marriage at first; some of my friends, especially the Italian, questioned why I had the need.

What is going on now with the bachelors, five years later? None of the ones I described got married, except for Toni the basketball player; most of the tomcats are more worn out, more disenchanted, more bored than before. Some statistics show that a woman in her thirties has little chance of getting married. I think that bachelor men in their thirties don't have a better chance. And unmarried men deteriorate more quickly than women do. A study, I forgot where, shows that – unlike women – the older men grow, the harder it is for them to bear solitude.

On Becoming Naturalized

I used to be proud of taking night walks in dangerous neighborhoods. Ten years ago I lived in New Haven on Mansfield Street, near the Olin factory, where Winchester guns used to be made and some were still being used. In front of my house, somebody was shot dead. One evening, around ten o'clock, when I walked to visit a friend of mine to play chess, four men ran straight at me, from a perpendicular street. I ran, jumped onto the first porch, and rang the bell; the men ran back to their street. I continued to walk the streets, even late at night, and not to cross to the other side if I saw a man or two walk on my side – on the contrary, I would strike up conversations with them. And when a colleague of mine showed up at Yale Divinity School with a smashed-in nose and two black eyes, I thought that he was simply a suave sucker.

In New York, where I lived from '84 to '86, I used to walk across Central Park at night if that happened to be the shortest way home, 106th and Columbus. Nothing bad happened, and I attributed it to my looking like a bum on the prowl myself.

I also lived on 105th Street, close to Columbus. When my roommate, Frank (a Puerto Rican computer operator and photographer), showed me a crack on his baseball bat at the door and told me that he had damaged the bat on the skull of a burglar, I did not believe him. When Frank put thick iron bars over all our windows, as though constructing a cage, I considered him to be excessively cautious, until an apartment above us and one next to us were broken into.

One evening Frank took pictures of a Latin man to put together a model portfolio. When the would-be model came three nights later to pick up the photos, he was shot dead right in front of the entrance to our building. Some dealers had mistaken him for his twin brother, who messed up on a deal. At that point, I certainly became circumspect in the streets.

But I lost that circumspection in Nebraska, Minnesota, and South Dakota, where I had to watch out only when driving – for drunken drivers and stray cows.

So now on July 4, during my visit to New York, at one in the morning, as my train skipped Hamilton Parkway and stopped at Church Street – from where, according to a buzzing and crackling announcement, one could take a train back to Hamilton – I thought that I would prefer walking to waiting in the urinated subway. I would easily find my way to Prospect Park, where my friends lived. Cursorily I looked at the map to see which way to go, without bothering to read the names of the streets because my sense of direction had always been very good.

Cabs drove past me, but I did not wave them down; why spend five bucks? When I reached Coney Island Boulevard, I wondered whether that was the boulevard that turned into Prospect Park Southwest, but it seemed to me that I should walk farther northeast to reach the boulevard that did that. I walked for several blocks along a major well-lit street without running across the boulevard. I stood at a corner, looked around, hesitated. The succession of streets that met at sharp and obtuse angles, I realized, could have switched me around, perhaps only ninety degrees, but enough to confuse me. Anyway, I should have found a broad street that should have ended in a darkness, the park, but there was no terminal darkness as far as I could see down the street with rows of diminishing orange lights. A perpendicular street offered darkness too near to tell whether the park was beyond.

From the other side of the broad street a guy shouted whether I could spare a quarter. I said no and continued to walk, hoping to cross a major street. Another Black man walked toward me, with something tucked above his belt, beneath his T-shirt, some kind of stick or gun, I could not tell. I wore a shirt, had nothing in my hands, and clearly had no weapons on me. In the winter, when people wear jackets, it's not so easy to tell whether you are unarmed, but in the summer, it's easy. I refused to feel tense, although there were reasons to be circumspect. The man passed me silently, sprightly.

Several blocks later, I still had not crossed any major boulevard. I had to admit to myself that my sense of direction had failed me but I didn't admit to being lost. Since I'd had three or four pints of ale that evening, I chose to walk down a dark street to water a hedge – I went north, or northwest.

On my left were low hedges, on my right, along the street pavement, tall conical evergreens, neatly tailored. I rushed to the darkest spot in the street, a stretch of twenty feet or so of solid shadows. What luck to run into it! my bladder thought. My oxhide soles resounded on the cement and echoed. I felt like a soldier, six-two, two hundred pounds, stepping firmly. But something was wrong with the echo, there were other steps in it, not as loud as mine, but faster. The rhythm of other steps jarred and syncopated mine. Somebody was walking about thirty yards behind me. Twenty yards. On the other side of the street another man walked even more quickly. He overtook me and now began to curve around to my side. I passed through the darkest spot in the street, giving up on taking a leak. When I reached a street corner, I barely noticed it was a corner, because the crossing was quite dark. From behind the corner moved a silhouette silently. I still did not run. Perhaps staying cool would settle things. If they want money, I'll give it to them. The man who'd crossed the street I recognized as the one who had passed me by, with an object tucked beneath his T-shirt. He seemed ready to ask me something and did begin: "Could you . . . ?" Before I could think of whether he'd finish it with " . . . spare a buck?" the guy from behind me pushed me, and the questioner struck me at the same time with some kind of heavy object, a lead weight, I guess, although I could not see clearly. He hit me above my ear, I went down on the asphalt, my feet in the air as my head hit the grass just off the edge of asphalt. The blow felt tremendously hot, as though my hair and skin had been set on fire. Two guys jumped on me, kneeling on my chest, each with one knee, and punched me over the head, and the third guy went through my pockets, where I had only ten dollars. I was impressed by their technique – so swift and precise. There was nothing left for me to do anyway, but simply observe their professional technique. Ten dollars, that's not much for this coordination. (That morning I had fleetingly thought, Why carry five hundred dollars in cash? Almost laughing at my impulsive caution, I had left my wallet in my friend's apartment. Not that I would have worried now about a silly wallet with plastic ID's when I could worry about my calcium and carbon skull.)

A thought crossed my mind along with the heat from the blows: These guys might kill me. This could be the end, just like that. A knife could slide into my neck, a bullet could crash into my skull, they could keep pounding till they spill my brains in the grass.

How absurd! Too absurd for it to take place, I thought. Another heavy blow struck my head, the lead coated in rubber, again. Why do they hit me only on the head? I was astonished that I hadn't passed out from all the smashes. They can kill me. I am not going to beg them, but why not, what's there to be proud of? I could talk, could I? "Come on, guys!" I said in a loud voice that did not seem to be mine. It did not sound panicked – it was flat, coming from my throat, deeper than my normal voice. The only feeling that I could sense in it was sadness.

I don't know whether it startled them that I could still talk, They stood up and quickly crossed the street. I wanted to stand up, but instead sat up and watched them go, then stood up.

A car with a Black man and a woman in it stopped. The man rolled down the window, and asked me: "Is everything all right?"

"I was just attacked by three guys, they knocked me over the head . . . "

"You seem to be all right," he said.

"I don't know. Could you give me a ride?" His concern made me feel that I could trust him though by now it was clear that I could not trust my feelings.

"Not really. I need to take my girlfriend home. Good luck!"

I walked. My head burned inside; outside, a strange sensation – I wondered why you never heard that after heavy blows you feel that much heat. I had not been tense during the attack, I hadn't had time to get tense; I had been too busy to get scared, too busy being passive. Now I did not know whether I should feel tense. Wasn't I immunized against mugging, at least for now, having just been mugged?

Dizzy, unsteady on my feet, I waved down a gypsy cab, and said, "Vanderbilt and Prospect Park."

"Prospect Park what?" the cabby asked.

"It runs along the park, on the south side."

"Yeah, but southwest or southeast?"

"South."

"You don't get it. Southwest or southeast!"

"I am not sure. Take me to the Hamilton subway stop, and from there, I could show you."

"How much you got?"

"What do you mean, how much I got? I was just mugged, I have nothing."

"Sorry." He began to roll down the window and press the pedal, but I had just discovered four or five subway tokens in the change pocket – or is it a watch pocket? – of my jeans. The muggers were not that thorough after all.

"I have four tokens."

"That's not enough. Seven."

"But it cannot be far."

"It's far, you aren't even sure where we should go!"

"Wait, I have five tokens," I said. "And fifty cents."

"All right."

He drove, and I felt my head – blood around the roots of my hair. Very soon we were near my friend's place.

As the cabbie watched me stagger, he shouted: "Get yourself some coffee and sleep it off!" He thought I was drunk. It did not matter what he thought.

I unlocked the gate, then the door (I understood security now), and quietly walked into the apartment. Finally I could get rid of the beer; I did need coffee, I needed all kinds of things. When I looked at the bathroom mirror, I expected to see a budding black eye, blood trickling down a forehead, a torn cheek. Instead, I looked the same as usual, not a scratch. But when I spat, blood trickled, oozed, wouldn't break, like a strand of mozzarella, down to the sink. I pulled at the corner of my mouth to peer in. Two purple-black cuts alongside my right molars bled quite liberally, but on the outside, not a bruise. I lifted my hair, against the grain, and saw raw red skin, risen like yeasty dough, with two or three bumps palpably growing and pulsating. I washed my mouth with hydrogen peroxide and the bleeding stopped. My head hurts, so what? If they had pounded my knee like that, it would hurt even more. Perhaps I have some internal bleeding? But I had not passed out. I had heard that brain damage occurs only if you pass out – a suspect formula, but now I believed it.

I made my bed and could not fall asleep for a long time. In the morning my friends, Sasha (a Serb gambler) and his wife, Marussia (a Russian princess from the Romanov line, and a social worker), did not notice anything unusual about me until I casually mentioned that I'd been mugged. I showed them a hole in my jeans, on my left knee. (I had not fallen straight on my back, but sideways and forward – I had instinctively turned to my back, so that my nape with arbor vitae would not be vulnerable.)

"Will you call the police?" Marussia asked.

"I am too dazed to hang around police stations for hours. What could they do?"

"You should go to the emergency room," she said.

"I am an American – I don't have any health insurance."

"Money doesn't matter, you need an X ray."

"If my brain is damaged, to expose it to radiation? I don't see how that would help."

Sasha was preparing coffee on the stove: this time we did not have our usual arguments about the war in the former Yugoslavia. He had argued a typical Serbian line, I the Croatian-and despite it we got along, although we were not supposed to. Neither his Serb friends nor my Croat friends liked to see us getting along. He answered the phone. A son of a cousin of his had drowned in Florida. End of conversation about my head.

That Sunday afternoon I took the LIRR to Hempstead, where I was to teach the following day at Hofstra. I felt every gap in the rails, with pressure in my head mounting. I took three Tylenols, but that did not eliminate the pain.

A week later I dialed my brother Vlado in Croatia. Despite being recognized as a country, Croatia had not gotten its own country code – it used the old code for Yugoslavia, 38. As a doctor in the war in Slavonia, Vlado had seen dozens of dead and treated multitudes of wounded.

"Hullo," he said. "When are you coming?"

I had told him I would visit Croatia to see the war ravages. "Right now we have a civil war in the States, and that's more than I can handle. I don't need yours." I explained what had happened.

"Have you vomited then or since then?"

"No."

"Have you lost any sensory functions, momentarily at least?"

"No. I am often a little dizzy, and if I walk my headaches

intensify. I feel every bump in the road when I am in a car or bus."

"That's all perfectly normal," he said. "And what's the weather like?"

That he changed the topic as though all was settled in the best order amazed me, but then, a Croatian doctor – of course – wouldn't be impressed by a mild concussion.

Vlado had grown up in a village with my grandfather, a peasant, and the peasant obsession with weather had stayed with him. I went right back to the topic of my headaches.

"Of course, you have headaches," he snapped at me, "I have them too. That's part of life."

"How long should my headaches last?"

"Six weeks, probably no more. If it bothers you, take painkillers, but no aspirin just in case there's some micro hemorrhaging. What are your vacation plans?"

Now, three months later, a stream of electricity shivers from my right ear to the left, making a loop through the top of my head. That comes on several times a week.

Then, there is a pulsation in my head: a small artery massaging – and messaging (after a concussion, I am allowed to make clichéd puns) – a nerve to a great echoing effect, as though I had a frog heart instead of the pituitary in the brain. Now, the brain feels as though a hand were slowly squeezing it. The brain supposedly cannot feel itself – it feels only what's around it, so perhaps the pressure is somewhere in the pia mater among the small nerves and blood vessels or even farther out beneath the dura mater, but it does feel as though the pain is squeezed into the brain. The squeezing hand reminds me of mine. During the final anatomy exam (sixteen years ago I studied medicine for a year in Novi Sad, Vojvodina) after I was served a human brain on a platter, the examiner asked me to lift the brain. As my hands shook a little from anxiety, I gripped the brain so the professor would not notice the tremor.

"Careful," he shouted. "It's highly delicate!"

He pointed out my fingerprints, as clear as though I had squeezed a used piece of bubblegum. "Look what you've done!" His voice was plaintive.

"It's dead anyway." I pointed out.

"It's our god," he said. "You must worship it, touch it gently the way a pianist touches the softest pianissimo!"

I am imagining – for no reason, how can I control reveries anyway? – that that brain has replaced mine; it carries my fingerprints. This may be a form of materialistic solipsism: my fingerprints on my brain – do I mean that it's my fault my head hurts? A Stoic said: "A fool blames another, a beginner himself, and the wise man neither." I am certainly more a fool than a wise man, but I would like to think, like a wise man, that there's no need for blame. I had foolishly strayed at night. And the muggers were most certainly despicable criminals. I could drive in the neighborhood where I had been mugged and machine-gun the criminals, if I could recognize them. The image does not excite me.

If I can't readily assign blame, can I draw conclusions from this one case? Can I generalize? Yes: this one case makes me believe most reports of violence.

Was it racial violence? There were no cameras to record it; if I had been killed, there would have been no trials, no noise.

Since the mugging was done so professionally, without insults, almost respectfully, I think it was a purely economic violence. If the men who had nearly cracked my skull (perhaps they have?) – with such good sense of timing, nerve, and cooperation – had been trained alongside other young men in the inner cities and elsewhere to become pilots or engineers – everybody would be safer and better off, including them. I don't think I am just turning the other cheek. If there's no economy, mugging becomes the economy. Not jails, but interesting, stimulating schools with job prospects . . .

Well, I must remember not to slip into the preaching mode. Who am I to preach? I can't even wisely govern my body and its whereabouts, as I have shown – so how can I talk about cities?

And why whine? The headaches might go away; and if they don't, my brother is right – almost everybody has some pain, so what? Not that the concussion is good for me, but, strangely, after the mugging my life took a turn for the better. As soon as I got back to Minneapolis, I had an interview, did well, and got a teaching position. Maybe the blows knocked some sense into my head? Or maybe I do have brain damage, and like a drunkard I feel that I am performing better than usual while in fact I might be worse. I have probably become an American.

Byeli: The Definitive Biography of a Nebraskan Tomcat

❧❧

Making the decision not to castrate Byeli did not go smoothly. At the Fine Arts Work Center in Provincetown, Massachusetts, where I had a fellowship for writing, some idle poets declared that my wife and I belonged to the Mormon sect because we wouldn't castrate our cat. The poets deplored our decision as monstrous because the tomcat would suffer cuts, torn ears, bruises, and he would make many female cats suffer and give birth to too many cats, who would give birth to more, which would cause an infinite amount of suffering, a direct result of our irresponsibility.

Byeli was an orphan. A boy had found him – furry skin and ribs about five weeks old – in the shrubs of Austin, Texas. Jeanette adopted the kitten and, because it was white, she and her French roommate named it Neige, snow.

Before I had heard of Neige, I dreamed I was trying to kick away a white cat with three sickly limbs, away from my tepee.

While Jeanette banged the door on her pickup, the little thin tom strutted into the apartment. I renamed him Snyeshko, snowman.

At two months he roamed as far as three hundred yards from our home and tailgated a homeless former female. It often flared up at him and scratched him but he'd continue to follow it like the white shadow of a black cat. We were not supposed to have any pets at the center, and Byeli – that was his new name, meaning white in Croatian – was very visible: he went to all the cocktail parties and jumped on the tables for ham and cheese. We had once thrown his litter box outdoors to air, and in the sand scattered in the corner from a burst sandbag, Byeli was making a target spot for his crap just as the director and several business-suited trustees came to examine what a worthwhile investment the art colony was. The philanthropic gentry faced a blinking, straining tomcat.

Byeli often visited Tina, who wore heavy paint-smeared black winter coats that dragged on the ground and got pinched under her hiking shoes; she chain-smoked and boozed, painted large yellow canvasses with wall paint and at exhibitions among her paintings she pinned photographs of herself, nude. Byeli played in her apartment on the second floor, inhaling all the noxious paint vapors, and he once jumped from her window, startling the abstract sculptor below.

He hunted ants. He'd follow an ant, gently press his paw on it, and lick it away from its path; disoriented, the ant would run in circles. Late at night he gazed at his ant in the crack of the floor. He poked his paw in the stream of our unshuttable faucet before he went to sleep atop a circular coatrack.

In the early spring we took him for walks, his head peeping out of Jeanette's red jacket below her chin, and during one walk we were all quiet noticing a black van with a sign, Death Nurse. Near the post office several emaciated men with pink hollow eyes, confounded, leaned on their walking sticks, and when they saw Byeli, a shadow of joy lit their faces, and when we left, they still stood there, smiling, as though the pope had just given them a blessing.

After my fellowship was over, Jeanette and I drove to Nebraska to live in a cabin in the woods. Byeli stretched out on the dashboard and whenever he noticed a dog in a car, he growled and hissed.

Sometimes I'd catch Jeanette doing eighty-five to ninety miles an hour. Our right back tire blew before an exit ramp in Iowa. It took me hours to change the tire, since the wheel was rusted on.

A mile off the road Jeanette had in the meanwhile bought a can of diet cat food with extra fiber for Byeli, who was steaming in the pickup – it was a hot day.

"Are you crazy? He doesn't need to diet," I said.

"Sure he does; he's getting no exercise in here."

"All that fiber means is faster digestion; he'll need to crap right away!"

"But see, he loves it!" Byeli crunched the brown, red, and green mini-pretzels, tossing them in his mouth.

"At least we should have a litter box," I said.

"We can always stop and let him do it on the side of the road. He'll ask."

Just then Byeli began to scratch the rubber mat and perched himself conically, his thick orange-seal tail raised and trembling.

"Stop the car!" Jeanette shouted and pushed Byeli from his spot to delay him.

"Let the poor guy do it!" I said.

"Stop the car! I don't want any cat stink in here; you can never wash it out! Stop it!"

"I am stopping, don't you see!"

"You are taking too long."

"So? It's you who didn't want a litter box in here."

Byeli's tongue hung out as if he were a dog. Ordinarily it was pink but now it was red.

"He's thirsty too. You can't expect him to go without water for a whole day," I said.

I stopped the pickup on the shoulder of an exit ramp on I-80. Byeli jumped out and sniffed the dry soil disdainfully – it didn't compare to the fine beach sand of Cape Cod. He ran into the field and hid in a hole with crumbling soil. We called him but he wouldn't come out – for a while. Jeanette and I kneeled in the field along the shoulder and scratched the soil with our fingers, throwing it up behind us, to set an example. But he only waited for us to get over it.

His tongue was red-scarlet, his breath extremely short, his nose dry, his pupils thin, and his eyes crossed. "He's dying of thirst," we both said and took him to a gas station.

I poured water over Byeli's fur; much of it slid right over it and some shrank into round drops. He refused to lick his fur and panted faster and faster. We tried milk; Byeli drank a cupful, but his tongue still hung out rabidly.

At a rest area we took Byeli to a young fir tree, and scratched the soil for him again. He ran away into the field over the fence.

"He's leaving us!" Jeanette shouted.

"I don't blame him."

"I know – you blame me."

"That's right."

"I am sick and tired of your complaining. Do you want a divorce?" she shouted.

"I am considering it."

I was reminded of a French couple, a doctor and her husband, an architect, who had quarreled on a steep ascent of the Inca trail, decided to divorce, and asked me to witness it. Several days afterward, I had run into them on the descent to Machu Pichu, and they were married again.

"Asshole," Jeanette said.

Byeli jumped the fence, ran to another fir, and dug a hole in the dark red soil. All tensed up, he stood, conical and slanted, and produced in that position steamy sticks that piled atop each other like firewood.

Our marriage was saved.

Byeli brushed the soil over the hole from all the sides, building a mound as if over a dear friend's grave.

In Nebraska, we moved into a cabin in the hills, surrounded by oaks, cottonwoods, and a thin creek. At night our kerosene lamp tired our eyes, and a little rechargeable solar powered lamp was a nuisance to keep on your shoulder to read. We pumped water and for showers used a black water tank perched on a tree. We cooked on a wood-burning stove.

The previous occupant was a bachelor who'd taken a dozen years to get his bachelor's with a 4.0 grade point average. He had watched cattle for several ranchers, repaired fences, ridden horses in cattle drives, watched birds, sent his sighting reports to the Audubon Society, read history, kept deer hunters off the hills – and had just gone to a law school in Texas. Outside the cabin, under a roof extended to make an open shack, a black cat, Jezebel, nursed her three black kittens, all males, on neatly piled firewood. The females hadn't passed their swimming exams; the future lawyer said he had drowned them.

According to the country custom, cats were not supposed to enter the house and get spoiled. One hazy-blue-eyed kitten hissed, one purred, and one, a longhair ball, rubbed its back against your palm. We named them, respectively, Hitler, Stalin, and Churchill, and Byeli got one more name, Tito.

When Mike, an Australian blue-heeler, a crafty dog who stole neighbors' shoes, came close to the woodpile, Jezebel clawed him. She also flared up at a horse who brought down his head too close – she flew at its mouth and the horse swung back, startled.

At the beginning of June we brought Tito to the cabin. Jezebel at once made his white fur fly and cut into his right eyelid. By cat law, he was supposed to leave and he did start off for the woods. We locked him in the cabin. They growled at each other through the mosquito screen. At night Tito changed his song; a sorrowful tomcat voice came out, wailing and lamenting, cajoling; his throat vibrated in strange frequencies, possessed by various demons, the souls of his future offspring – as if they all clamored to be released from the prison of being, his scrotum. He clawed at the doors and windows. Jezebel, although her kittens were less than two months old, responded with her high frequency, gentle, questioning cries, but if he approached, she growled and leapt at the mosquito door. He came to us upstairs, emitting his possessed cries, jumped on Jeanette and gripped her shin with his canines. She screamed and kicked him.

To make a studio with electricity, we cleared out an old farmhouse, belonging to Jeanette's uncle Al, who had recently gotten married for the first time at the tender age of sixty-two. Al had no use for the house filled with spiders dead in their own cobwebs, mice traps, mice skeletons. A cracking floor upstairs was caving in under the weight of decades of *Scientific American, National Geographic,* and *Angus* magazines, alongside browning books. Al, although the only one out of five brothers without a college education, enjoyed the reputation for being the smartest, partly because he hadn't gone to college and mostly because he hadn't married, and the fact that he married at sixty-two, nearly on his deathbed with cirrhosis of the liver, could not be taken for a dumb move either.

When I met him – weathered skin, white hairs under a rolled leather hat, pipe in his teeth, resembling a retired Marlboro man – I couldn't understand his slurred Nebraskan speech, nor could he understand my mélange, but that didn't prevent us from having a conversation about the Second World War.

Molding clothes covered his floors: army suits, jeans, gentlemanly white summer suits, all moth-eaten. There were heaps containing Jim Beam bottles, matches, bullets, heaters, burners with melted wires, green TV sets with missing legs, aluminum antennae with dozens of arms thrown every which-way – like dancing Shiva gone mad. In the yard there were sinks, cabinless pickups, guns with rotted handles, dilapidated barns through whose cracks winds imitated owls' mating cries, an old bailer, a rusted tractor with front wheels only a foot apart, and an overturned green car without wheels.

Jeanette and I had burnt most of the junk in the yard, peeled off multiple layers of wallpaper, painted the walls, and gotten the water going in the bathroom; but there was no septic tank and so we used an outhouse, not the most cheerful chapter: resident wasps stung me, always twice in a row.

I took Byeli – Tito didn't stick – to the new place and he bit me. I couldn't kick him because I was afraid he'd run away. He tore out of my hold. I wanted to catch him, and instead of dodging me, he surprised me with a quick leap, tearing deep into my right palm. I bled profusely; my hand swelled up at once as though a snake had bitten me.

Byeli disappeared from the farm during our continued repairs. Although we roamed the hills in a mile radius, we heard nothing of him. We went to our nearest neighbor, Holzer, a rancher, who, as rumor had it, trapped coyotes, and considered it his duty to kill any cats and dogs crossing his path. His pickup had three rifles hung in the back.

We drove to the backyard past several loaves of hay. Large dogs barked and a boy of about twelve greeted us.

"Have you seen a white tomcat?" Jeanette asked.

"Yea, sure thing," answered the boy. "He was here yesterday, in the barn."

His father came out, and we repeated the question.

"Oh yes, I've seen him. He's in the ditch half a mile up the road, dead."

"Are you sure? A white tomcat with creamy peach points and fluffy tail?" gasped Jeanette.

"That's him! If you go up to where alfalfa ends, you'll see him," the neighbor said, glad to be of assistance.

We drove out and Jeanette cried.

Along the dirt road in the green ditch we saw nothing, but over the wire fence of rotting oak posts, we saw a patch of white, bright in the sun, amidst disked soil. We stepped over the fence and neared the cat. It was pure white – no darkening, slightly Siamese, points on the nose, ears, paws and tail.

"Thank God, it's not Byeli!" shouted Jeanette. I was happy too, but the sight of a dead tomcat was not a cheering one nevertheless: the white stranger lay on the soil, his four paws up as if in defense against the sky, his mouth opened a little with black blood in the corners and more black blood in the slits of his eyes. Swarms of black flies with purplish green, radiant wings, buzzed around the cat.

The evening after we had found the dead tomcat, Byeli leaped through the backdoor mosquito screen, a high jump since the rotting porch had collapsed as we had dragged the cast-iron tub over it. Covered with thistles, he jumped on the bed and sucked the blanket – his response to any trauma. As an early orphan, he was a passionate blanket sucker.

We left him at the farm and slept at the cabin. Whenever our pickup pulled out of the yard, he ran after us, down the lane, crying, for half a mile. And when he heard us coming, he ran toward us, and once the pickup slowed down, leaped through the window inside to rub his forehead against us, crying. He rubbed against our legs as we got out, and rolled in the dirt, getting all dusty and gray.

Nearly a mile away from our house, a gray cat lived in an old small building, a former school. Holzer, the neighbor accused of shooting dogs and cats, told me that he had gone to that school with a dozen other children, all grades in one room at the same time. Many people used to live in that country, but after the Depression years most moved out. Rural Nebraska had been steadily depopulating peoplewise and populating animalwise. Holzer's hatted and booted son often interrupted him, "Boy, we got that coyote good! I want to shoot wild turkey tomorrow morning!" Holzer told the fragile-looking boy to bring him a mug of beer – we were at a barn party – which the son did, having gulped one down himself without his father noticing. When the boy wiped his foamy lips, the father, upset yet proud, said, "I told you, don't!"

The gray cat lived in the former schoolhouse with shattered windows in the summer. Byeli must have tactlessly attacked this teacher, and the teacher was gone. Byeli, who had always hankered after cat society, looked snubbed – he swallowed saliva, his blue eyes crisscrossing in intense psychological distress.

We brought Byeli the two kittens, Stalin and Churchill, for company. Fissing Hitler had disappeared. With Churchill Byeli got along grandly, licking his fur for hours while Churchill purred. Of course, Byeli now and then bit Churchill, and whenever Churchill felt the biting was coming, he tiptoed away. Since three tomcats in one place were too many, we gave Churchill to a couple of friends of ours in Omaha, a marriage counselor and his girlfriend, a theology major. Churchill was fed on ratios, according to some formula, once a day, at 8:30 in the morning precisely. What lay in store for Churchill was declawing, castration, and vegetating – he probably wouldn't even be allowed to grow fat in compensation. One Friday, while Paula was bringing in health-food groceries and Jim writing down the exact mileage it took to drive to the co-op and back, Churchill ran out through the open door and never came back. If you are ever tempted to give a kitten to a marriage counselor, my advice is: Don't.

Byeli often went to the armchair where Churchill used to sleep, sniffed Churchill's hairs and cried desolately.

The sleek, thin, and shiny Stalin, like an Egyptian junior god, sneaked around the farmhouse. He passed his boyhood catching grasshoppers. Every five minutes he'd leap through the screen door and crunch his green grasshopper; the antennae and astronomical eyes on the creatures didn't impress him toward mercy at all.

Every morning when I came into the studio, I saw fur, blood, and animal shit on the floor. Byeli slaughtered gophers, mice, rats, birds, and young rabbits who shat from fright. Byeli even ate some years-old mice with rat poison in them, and got sick, his tongue purple; he vomited, ate grass, and recovered.

Byeli and Stalin began to bring in a mouse a day, each. Byeli once played with a mouse for an hour without killing it and when Stalin wanted to join in, Byeli attacked him. We locked up

Byeli so Stalin would get to play some, but Stalin wouldn't touch the mouse. Neither would Byeli when we let him out. With an offended, dignified aura, he sat atop the *Compact Oxford English Dictionary* on the bookshelf and wouldn't even look at the mouse.

Late at night – we had now moved in completely – Byeli brought in a rat, tossed him around, bit him, stuck his claws into him; we closed the bedroom door so he wouldn't bring the rat in our bed. Stalin caught a squealing mouse who had a talent for climbing the wall – sometimes two feet high before falling.

In the morning, as we drank our Colombian Supremo, from beneath the armchair crawled a brown blood-crusted mouse. Then out crawled the rat, swollen like a frog, and moved more with his trunk than limbs, snailing a trail of thin pus and blood. We swept him and the mice outside. The cats paid rent, bringing us animals in prime for eating.

They kept bringing in all kinds of gophers and shrews until they finally understood that we didn't want to eat; and they kept their trophies to themselves, hidden in the barn.

Time and again Byeli chased quick-footed Stalin, treed him, or followed him into holes and burrows. Once Byeli chased Stalin and knocked down the opened door that leaned against the wall, and the door slammed on his foot, trapping him. His crushed left foot was flat and wide like a spatula by the time Jeanette and I came back from Sioux City, where we had seen *Sex, Lies and Videotape* – he must have been trying to get out of the pinch for several hours. To console him, we fed him steak. He gulped a whole pound and wanted more. The following morning we took him to the vet, who amputated two of his toes. The other two recovered. The handicap didn't prevent him from taking his manly trips. We were surrounded by hilly grassland, with our nearest human neighbor one mile away. The stretches between cottonwoods along a creek and the oaks and cedars on the hills were long; coyotes, minks, and bobcats roamed the terrain imperceptibly and a horned owl supervised them. Whether Byeli would survive his trips was always a question, but we let him be a natural cat – better to be Alexander the Great and die young than to be a nobody and die old.

Byeli began to spray. He angled his rear upward, his tail fluffed up peacockily, shook his ass in a quick vibration, and sprinkled the door from the outside, throwing up the piss nearly two yards high. I thought all tomcats did it that way, but later, observing Stalin's much more direct way – puddle formation – I realized that Byeli was a stylist. Perhaps the French name, Neige, would have suited him best after all. Byeli assailed mostly my typewriter and bills. When I filed taxes, my yellowed W-2's stank of cat urine. What the hell, I thought, we should have an organic government.

He destroyed dozens of envelopes and piles of photocopies of my articles and stories – a nasty enemy of literary ambition. I know that the cat is the symbol of libraries and night reading. Many sophisticated bookstores have black-and-white cats silently seated somewhere among the shelves, adding an aura of mystery to book reading. But let me tell you, these are no tomcats; most of them are castrati, the promoters of culture. A library cat has nothing but disdain for country tomcats. I can attest to it. Byeli and Stalin once held a discussion at the threshold to our bedroom, over my black shoes. Lyrically shaking his tail, Byeli scented the shoes with a powerful message that Stalin was under no circumstances ever to enter the room again. Stalin sniffed at the shoe, moaned, and humbly emitted a shot of his ink, printing a petition, which said, Please, your Highness, allow me to pass through to the bathroom to drink water. I will be obedient. Byeli came back to my shoe, meowed, his eyes crossed with indignation, and sprinkled a crisscrossing stream, which said, Application denied. Fuck off.

Two months afterward I strolled in these shoes through a used bookstore, an overpriced one next to a cappuccino shop, with backgammon and chess in the back, and with a quiet black-and-white cat, amazingly clean, wide-eyed, right at the entrance. The former female or male followed me, and as I looked at Heinrich

Böll's *Group Portrait with a Lady,* it sniffed my shoes. I moved to another shelf and the cat followed me; it even growled, low, something you'd never expect of a bookstore cat. It must have finally deciphered the conversation that had taken place between Stalin and Byeli; the cat suddenly ran away from me and hid beneath the cash register.

Byeli took longer and longer trips as he groped through the blond catless countryside of the fall in search of sex. The drought made the overgrazed grass look like a yellow crew cut; the round hills resembled the head-tops of battalions buried above their earlines; the hills also resembled sand dunes of the Sahara, and apparently, sand dunes they had been as recently as ten thousand years ago; the several feet of topsoil lay on sand and rock, and in places the wind had blown the soil off to its sand base. As strong winds blasted, the horizons softened, unlined in a brown haze, while red-tail hawks frolicked, surfing on the rising heat, far more graceful and elegant than the bald eagles several miles north, above the Missouri, near the bluffs of South Dakota. The flight of an eagle compared to the flight of a redtail is like the clanking of the New York subway compared with the buttressed glide of the Parisian metro. In that deserting landscape, we didn't know whether Byeli had scraped any sex for himself.

Hoping to make sex easier for Byeli, we brought the mother cat Jezebel to the farm. Byeli hounded her and beat her so she hid in holes under the house, but the tide turned when she began to attack him furiously in self-defense. He sat around her on the porch, striking poses, semiprofiles, obviously trying to look charming, blinking, but to no avail. She scratched him up so badly that he nearly lost his eye and he got an abscess larger than a ping-pong ball on his right foot. He licked it and licked it until it popped.

We put Jezebel three miles away from us in a barn next to the house of a retired businessman, an Exxon man, who chain-sawed nearly one thousand trees, mostly elms, during the summer. He lorded over the landscape until the fall, when he was felled down by a stroke. His blood vessels, shaped like tree roots, burst in his brain, sympathetically avenging the trees.

Mike, an Australian blue-heeler, lived at the barn, and with a female beagle ganged up to chase Jezebel. She had whipped them both piecemeal when she'd had her kittens, but now, her courage had diminished. She disappeared. A severe December with temperatures minus seventy degrees windchill was blown from the North across the Missouri. We couldn't find her anywhere.

Karma in animal lives tends to be cruel just as in ours. The female beagle, Mike's companion, was shot by her owners on account of being a female (and not a cat-chaser, her true downfall). Mike, her blue boyfriend, sat listlessly and didn't even seek out cats to chase. Jeanette got him company through her voluntary work at the Winnetoon Village Mini Mall Co-op, which offered health foods, massage, gourmet coffee – a customer gave her two Doberman/blue-heeler pups. Having clubbed to death six pups, the owner had grown nauseated and couldn't club any more, and thus the two were selected to live.

We let them stay on our front porch with Mike although they chased our cats, except Byeli, who stuck his claws in Mike's nostrils so deeply that he couldn't get them out – Mike ran and shook him all around the yard, and Byeli hung onto Mike's bleeding nose before he fell off with bits of gray hair on his red claws. The male pup ranged far and was eaten by coyotes.

Mike played with the female pup, and although she was only four months, he tried to have sex with her – Mike, as an American, was sensitive to youth. Lest we have a case of stepfather raping his stepdaughter, we gave her away, to a talented student of mine on the reservation, where I taught at a community college. So that Jerry could take care of the dog, I gave him fifty dollars for dog food. That evening, celebrating, Jerry got into a drunken brawl that landed him in jail, where he got into another fight and plucked a man's eye out of the socket with his fingernails. Afterwards, he became a star student because he had enough time to study and write. Some of my classes I held in jail, on the way home. Jerry read the whole *Decline and Fall of the Roman Empire* and wrote a brilliant story about deer hunting, "To Kill and Kill Again."

Every night the coyotes surrounded our yard and sang Country. Most of them howled but some barked – they must have interbred with dogs. Mike marked his territory and barked so variously that the coyotes must have taken him for a whole pack and stayed farther away. He even broke into the outhouse and smeared some human colors and smells over his fur, and so equipped with war paint, with human authority, he dared cross his narrowly circumscribed boundary into coyote land, like a West Berliner with a diplomatic passport crossing through the Brandenburg gate into East Germany.

One night Jeanette and I heard a shrill catlike, mating sound, but louder, shriller, with a tremolo.

"Come out, the coyotes are killing Stalin!" Jeanette shouted.

We ran out with a flashlight and screamed to chase them away. We regretted we had no gun – we opposed coyote-killing. Our cats showed up. Stalin crawled into a hole beneath the house, and Byeli, electromagnetized, sat on a board of the collapsed back porch.

The coyotes were killing a fawn – that's how the farmers assessed our report of the shrill cries. But in the morning we couldn't find a trace of the skeleton; the coyotes must have finished everything right on the spot or dragged the remains away.

During the severest cold spell that winter, Byeli was gone. We began to count him for dead too, but early one morning he jumped through the first back door – the second one was closed – and clawed and cried. He was cold, shiny, thin. He rubbed his arched back against us, poked his large head under our chins, purred his deep purr into our ears, licked our noses raspily so that they turned red, and sucked the blanket and the sweater on me, plucking the threads. For several days he slept, purred, went with me to the basement where we kept a large furnace going. Every morning instead of praying, I started a fire in the furnace with paper and small wood, throwing in redwood logs afterward – and as flames grew, red and yellow and evasive, I felt more and more alert and warm; it was better than coffee, though of course coffee followed, ground in a little Krups mill and boiled in a fifty-cent Goodwill aluminum percolator, with Byeli still at my side, rubbing against my ankles and howling for canned tuna.

He often sat in front of the electric heater in the bathroom – the furnace duct to the bathroom was rusted and collapsed – basking in the red heat, tilting his body against the base of his grounded thick tail, his eyes closing and opening slowly, his head sinking; he lifted it up when he realized that he was falling asleep. Now and then he slept on the large furnace, where possums used to sleep before we let Mike live with us. Mike killed the possums, leaving their bodies to rot in the yard for weeks before he took several bites out of them. The corpses with erect penises rotted for several months into the spring.

In March near the deserted tree-hater's house, we ran into a thin black cat, Jezebel. She cried as she tried to climb us, with her large claws digging into our jeans. We took her to our pickup. We doubted that it was the same Jezebel, but as she farted her extraordinarily stinky farts and took a crap right at the doorway of Neighbor Holzer, the reputed cat killer, our doubts crumbled – she had crapped precisely there in the fall.

Byeli, a twenty-pound thug, attacked her at once. He was in heat and so was she and so was a little scraggly country cat we named The Forum for Thought after we had adopted her from a farmer with many kittens and a giant Doberman. The dog had closed his jaws over the little calico tabby to swallow her. The farmer kicked the dog, the jaws opened, and we sacked the cat. It was a female. She had two personalities, one indoor, one outdoor; they switched precisely on the threshold of our house. Outdoors she hid in holes, climbed trees, fissed and spat, and responded to no calls. Indoors, she purred several purrs at once, choking with joy, on your neck right into your ears, trying to enter your mind. It took her a long time to gain a continuous picture of the abroad and home. Her stunted growth didn't prevent her from joining in the general heat.

In one day Byeli repeatedly jumped the little Forum for Thought. Stalin, who had for months gently licked her, preparing her for himself, was forbidden to jump her. He watched on as Byeli did. Byeli also raped Stalin's mother in front of Stalin. She had refused Stalin, her son. But Stalin's troubles weren't over: Byeli jumped him too, and grabbed him by the neck. Stalin screamed, his eyeballs popping. The howling, growling, and spitting was too much for us, so we threw the whole sect of Mormons out. After laying everything in sight, Byeli slept solidly for a day in an empty paint bucket and then took a trip.

We heard all kinds of reports. He visited Alfred's farm – a pig farmer a mile east of us – two loud dogs notwithstanding; whipped a resident tomcat; and caught several rats, piling them at the entrance of an empty barn that used to house cows. Nowadays cows stay outdoors even in hailstorms and minus seventy degree windchill, and the farmers believe it's good for the cows – they grow stronger and fatter that way; and if a cow dies of pneumonia, well, that's less bother than building and maintaining barns, now abandoned to rats amidst molding corn. Driving past Alfred's pig pens filled with young piggies – you could tell the season by how large the piggies were – we often asked about Byeli. "Yessir, he was here a couple of days ago."

I saw Byeli behind the town bar, seven miles away, in Center. He was the only white cat in the neighborhood, so there was no doubt that it was him. Byeli leaped into a shed and wouldn't respond to my calls.

"He's left us," said Jeanette. "That's a tomcat for you, a terrible pet."

Two nights later he jumped through the first door and

although the second was closed, shoved it open with a bang. He ran to us and pushed his head under our chins and purred. Jeanette brushed his hair and he bared his long teeth, relaxing his jaws. We feasted him with chicken livers.

In the litter box he stood upright, with his front legs leaning straight on the tall edge, and he was so full of imperial dignity that he didn't bother to bury his crap. The little Forum for Thought, who monitored the action, buried it for him. She followed him around like a suspicious cop.

We bathed him to rid him of his new fleas, but when his fur dried, there seemed to be more. He ran out, rolled in the weeds – he knew the right kind – and the fleas were gone. He slept in the sunshine near the window, his paws crossed one over another; or, as a true stylist, he slumbered with one of his paws in the pool-table pocket, his head on the cue ball for pillow, or with all four legs spread wide, his head hanging down from the table, his balls showing shamelessly, his long and muscular body stretched. He looked like a bodybuilder.

Time and again he yawned, expressing pure boredom, some kind of existential ennui. But ever since he had learned about sex, he couldn't be bored for long. Although Jezebel was pregnant, several days before she was due, he howled his lewd propositions at her. She spat back at him and meowed in alarm. He grabbed her neck with his long teeth, and she accepted the game, lifted her behind, pushing her awkwardly stretched paws against the floor, alternately, now one, now another, claws sliding and screeching. She growled and Byeli did his thing, crouching over her. She cried more and more shrilly and during orgasms she tore away, her claws sparking at him. Instead of withdrawing, he'd run after her, slap her, and jump her again. To have some quiet, we threw them outdoors, but it went the same way. We separated Byeli from her, whacking him with a broomstick, and he throated strange, desperate, muted howls. He pissed over the ending of my novel about the decline of Communism. To save my manuscript, I let him approach her again. He must have jumped her several hundred times in four days and nights. She couldn't take it anymore and we separated them in earnest. For a break, he attacked Stalin leaving in his skin a couple of claw-layers; Byeli had no need of trees for sharpening claws. Stalin sat bleeding under the bed. No doubt Byeli would have killed Stalin if we hadn't separated them. After all that, Byeli just collapsed from exhaustion.

Even before attacking Jezebel, Byeli had been in poor shape. We had found him on the road, near our mail box, three-quarters of a mile away from our house. He just sat there on the road, sunken, dirty, will-less. If we had continued driving, I believe he would have let us drive over him. His fur was gluey. He limped. "Something terrible has happened to him," Jeanette had said. I thought that he was limping because his two-toed front paw couldn't take so much running; it was swollen. But later I discovered a black hole in his back thigh, a deep bite – perhaps from a horned owl's talons.

During his gradual recovery he got those sexual seizures.

So when he collapsed after the orgy, he really collapsed. I was away to a powwow and a conference on Indian education in Bismarck. On my way up, the towns were shrouded in brown clouds of soil dust. The powwow took place in a no-smoking ball room of the Radisson Hotel. When I came back, Byeli's balls were swollen and blue, his whole back was swollen with abscesses; he couldn't urinate; water dripped out of his penis, drop by drop, when he tried to walk; he couldn't jump, he didn't purr, but his eyes were alert. When I came home, Jeanette said, he livened up. He began to recover quickly, but to be safe, we took him to the vet, who examined him under anesthesia. His blood and temperature were normal.

At home, Byeli strolled, his fur began to look better, he slept, but grew bored and constantly begged to be let out. We forcibly kept him inside for two more days, giving him the pink liquid antibiotic through an eyedropper. Some pink stayed on the fur by the sides of his mouth.

It was springtime and on a sunny day we let him step outside to sit on a plank of wood. We planned to keep an eye on him so he wouldn't go away. Jeanette filled a large bottle with milk from powder and walked to the corral to feed two orphan calves. They were orphans because their mothers hadn't licked them at birth and they didn't smell like any mother's saliva. The orphans' ears, wet from sucking, stuck straight out of their heads parallel with the ground. After the calves had finished sucking the milk from the large bottle-nipple with their round and long gray tongues, they nudged each other under the stomachs, as they would their mothers had they had them, and proceeded to suck on each other's dicks. Jeanette called me out, and while we laughed at the calves, Byeli left.

"Well, let him," Jeanette said. "This warm weather is good for him."

I agreed.

Three days afterward, in the premature dark of heavy clouds right before a storm, he suddenly showed up, with sheet lightning trembling behind him; the windowpanes shuddered with the thunder. He was silent. He looked well. I brushed him for a long time that evening. He purred looking me in the eye, relaxing his eye lenses; he didn't suck the blanket. He nudged his wet nose under my chin and rubbed his forehead with short hairs like those on a toothbrush against my ears. In the morning he took a look at his children; there were ten kittens nursing between two mothers. The kittens switched mothers and the mothers didn't care: a Communist upbringing. He jumped in, trying to grip Jezebel by her nape, to have sex amidst the family. She wouldn't go for it. His children didn't even greet him. He was not needed.

He sprinkled an armchair before the door, with his tail trembling, and he cried with a certain degree of charm. He wanted out. "Why do we put up with this?" Jeanette asked.

In the sky-clear morning we let him outdoors. On the fourth day of his renewed absence, Jeanette said he probably wouldn't make it this time. I went into my room; Stalin began to growl.

Stalin now lived mostly in a large empty barn but whenever it was windy the hooting of the wind through the cracks terrified him and he came home. Byeli jumped through the high door. Jeanette shouted, "Byeli!" I ran out to see, happy because Byeli was home. But lo, there was a terrible stench with him; his back legs and tail were brown and black with blood, pus, dirt, shit. We washed him with a towel and soap; he cried and bit Jeanette. I held him by the scruff of the neck, surprised that he was so light, that he offered no resistance, that there was no strength in him. I laid him on the floor gently. He wanted to drink the soapy water. I ran to get him clean water, but he had no strength to drink any more. There was a terrible fear in his eyes. There was a big black-and-blue hole in one of his legs. His hair on that leg was almost gone, and when you pulled the skin it stayed up.

"My God, he's dying! He came home to see us before he dies!" Jeanette shouted.

She had often said that, whenever he was hurt, but now I was afraid she was telling the truth.

"Gangrene," I said.

The fear in Byeli's eyes made me feel how empty my stomach and my arteries and lungs were; his fearful eyes hollowed me. There had never been much fear there before, and now, I saw a vast fear. His large pupils begged for something, for help; he wanted to be brushed and comforted, perhaps he knew he was dying and wanted to die with love. But it was close to five o'clock and the vet would leave after five, so we rushed Byeli to him.

As we put Byeli on the white metal examination table, he shrieked. His eyes were large and he wailed with such despair that I turned sick from that voice. The last thing he wanted now was the table where his toes had been cut, thermometers stuck up his ass, syringes in his muscles, scrapers in his ears. We were leaving with that cry and his eyes on us, as if we were abandoning him forever.

And we were, although the vet told us there was a chance he would live.

A day later when Jeanette came home from work, she wept. "Byeli died at the hospital last night, around midnight."

I said the conventional words, "He lived a full, good life – it's natural."

I picked him up at the vet's. He came in a carton, the whole package amazingly light. Jeanette and I dug a hole in the ground struggling to cut through cedar roots. I took him out of the box. His eyes were half open and there was a blue film over them, blue-gray, and you couldn't distinguish between the pupil and the iris. I touched the short hair on his head. Jeanette didn't want to touch him because she wanted to remember him warm. He was frozen and stiff in death, neither peaceful nor dignified, neither tormented nor joyful, but dead. A thing eighteen months old. There was much of Byeli still in his long whiskers and his teeth, which stuck out on the side below his sunk cheeks. We put him in the ground, his four paws up against the sky.

No cats showed up for his funeral.

We buried him in the soil – mud to mud – and put the log of a collapsed tree over his grave, but we said no prayers, because he had been a pagan.

Many large white birds descended on the brown ploughed soil, where Al had sowed oats behind the grave, and they ate before flapping off for the North.

It took me a long time to get used to Byeli's not existing because his ghost kept leaping everywhere for me, and I would almost reach to scratch his forehead, so he would close his crossing eyes and enjoy.

But there he is below the log, his eyes half open and blue.

In the Rand McNally Gap

A friend of mine bought a cheap hill in Slavonia, stood atop it, and shouted, "This is *mine!*" The hill bulged out of a tedious section of God's country, good for nothing except oaks. He built a cottage on the hill with the tranquility of Jonah, expecting disaster to strike elsewhere. But just as Jonah lost his gourd, my friend lost his hill. The Serb irregulars set up cannons there to bomb a village three miles away, then Croat guards took it over, and now the UN troops lounge there, and though my friend can again visit his hisdom, he no longer jumps and shouts, This is mine!

His example taught me nothing, however. My wife, Jeanette, and I had accumulated books, papers, documents. I used to think you could dump papery things safely with your friends. I had left a box of college papers and rough drafts for stories with my friend Dan. I often wished I could retrieve those drafts, but Dan's mother had thrown my papers away, taking them for her deceased husband's law-court sketches. "All the better," I said to Dan, "I have a clean start." Maybe it was all the better then, but now I could not take another clean start – I wanted a shelter.

There was an even better argument for buying a house: if

Jeanette and I lost our jobs – which we now did – we could stay somewhere rent-free.

In search of a new domicile, Jeanette and I crossed the Missouri River, from Nebraska into South Dakota, and drove into the Rand McNally gap, so called because one year the authoritative mapmakers had skipped central South and North Dakota since the major towns of both states could be included in the maps of neighboring states. Marketeers had concluded that that part of the country would not sell but would perhaps irritatingly clutter the road atlas. Mostly Sioux Indian and poor farmers lived in the Rand McNally gap. The Sioux had the lowest per capita income of any group in the States, and the farmers, not much higher. Although they fed the country, many farmers lived on food stamps, until banks would force them out, after quickly selling the land, tractors, bailers, furniture, in a frenzied auctioneer glossolalia. The farmers witnessed their being sold out as though it were an estate sale, of somebody dead and buried.

Newspapers ran debates about whether the land should be turned over to the bison. The houses would be torn down, the roads would crack and sink into the soil, dust would cover them, and the prairie would open up for the bison to roam from Canada to Kansas, stimulated by Indians' bullets or spears, arrows, and other prickly things.

Despite the threat that a stampeding herd of fat bison might trample down our new domicile, Jeanette and I looked for a house on the banks of the Missouri. We started from Yankton, an old outpost for western expansion of *wasicus* (the pale people). Because the reservoir, Case Francis, had submerged old roads and houses, we could only sporadically approach the "river," fenced off in state parks and controlled by the Army Corps of Engineers. We finally managed to dip our feet in the river in Springfield, a town that used to host the University of South Dakota before the campus was turned into a state penitentiary. Since the town economy boomed because of the prison, the cheapest house there went for fifteen thousand. But, five grand was all I could afford.

We drove on to Running Water, where the effect of the dam thirty-five miles down the river was slight. Rapids twisted and sucked a couple of bald trees under, sticking them into the muddy bottom. The cricketing marshes with cattails, flopping beaver tails, and fluttering red-winged blackbirds made us yearn for a house there. But the houses we saw were fashioned after the architectural ideal of a mobile home. We knew there must be large houses above us in the treed hills. The river had sunk below the high plains, carving steep banks, inverse mountains, almost a thousand feet high. In the bluffs of limestone, cliff swallows whistled. Dozens of bald eagles from Canada perched there in the winter – the bluffs protected them from the northern winds and opened them to the sun. The Nebraska side, even higher, hid Devil's Nest, a failed resort project. The rusty cables of a ski lift spanned the bank. Hypermodern houses lay scattered among trees and hills, and the cheapest of them, though its roof was caving in, went for thirty thousand dollars. Jesse James used to hide in these hills, and now they served as a setting for ghost stories on the adjacent Santee Sioux Reservation.

Highway 50 on the Dakota side passed through – or over? – the famed 98th meridian. I read in the *Economist* and elsewhere that the 98th meridian best marked the beginning of the High Plains. West of the meridian the rainfall was so low that it was only good enough for rough grasses. Indeed, the landscape did suddenly change. The hills rolled in wider swings, the grass was yellower, and the buzzards blacker. God's country. *Wakan Tanka* country. The wind swooped down at us like a continuous word, uninterrupted by lips, unsmeared by spittle, neither lisping nor limping, sweeping. After God's presence passed, Moses could not dare to look, because he would die. And here, a dry palm of God had swung, and you could look for but could not see the wind. It took courage to draw a deep breath, because the sacred was in the air.

The earth and the sky caressed each other. Trees and sumac

poked the sky, and the sky blew down the earth's hair, bending it, and abandoning it startled and tilted, bare and cold. The sky's eyes floated, feathered, and marveled at the beauty of the earth's fuzz. The earth's ears, furred, pricked, and shivered at the sky's cold touch. The sky and the earth sniffed at each other. When the earth was too cold, the sky threw a white coat over it; when the winds were too tired, the earth bade them lie down and repose in the grasses, where they would pick up the dry smell of prairie flowers and the damp odor of mole burrows.

Where we had been hitherto, the sky was far away and above, and the earth was below, under you, but now that had changed. The sky was right upon us; it hung low and rolled in the soil, fat and satisfied. We walked in the sky. And the soil stretched far away; even though the earth was flat, you knew and felt it to be high, a steady mountain that did not need to prove itself.

Our road again neared the river, narrow by the Missouri standards – half a mile to the Nebraska bank – with sand islands. In the previous three years Jeanette and I had often canoed down the river, and the sandbars were different each year, each month. When the water rose, the sand slid off and floated down and climbed into a new islet. One islet disappeared, another arose. The islets moved around like animals. But here, trees had sunk their roots, nailing the sandbars to the earth.

We hit Greenwood, a desolate town with a dozen cement houses on a slope, pale green and blue and pink – traditional reservation colors. It used to be a settlement for the Yankton Sioux, who burned the village because they did not want to live in a government project. The American Indian Movement had ghosted the town. Close to the river stood a turn-of-the-century whitewashed Episcopal church amidst a recently mowed lawn. We opened the unlocked door that scraped against the tilting door frame and floor; the door wing stayed straight, rectangular, but the rest shifted and tilted into irregular quadrangles. The floors bulged as though made of yeast and set atop an oven. Strewn around were old papers, church records, magazines, molded and moth-eaten red and blue sweaters and brown pants. "Should we buy the place and renovate it?" I asked. Jeanette laughed at that. "In several years this will be an historical site – if the state had more money, this would already be an historical site – and we'd have to leave."

After Greenwood the road grew rougher, rocks sticking out, washed out – only the base, the under-the-road, had remained, deteriorating into a steep path, almost too much for our first gear, which shot us up past an abandoned farm, a big olive-colored house with gaping doors and glassless windows. Four shaggy electrical wires ran to the house like profiles of long waves, swinging and singing in the wind. The chimney, blackened outside, had weathered many a thunderbolt. "Should we buy this house?" Our Chichikovian question arose once again. No, we did not want to be exposed to God's anger atop a hill.

"But we could keep donkeys here," Jeanette said.

True, that was a powerful argument: I saw an army of ears moving like windmills. And beyond, in a huge lake pressing against a tall dam, among brown hills, broken white clouds swam below wholesome ones.

On the road to Case Francis, Fort Randall casino winked at us from the sovereign Indian land – the federal restriction on gambling did not apply. White gambling mafia through Indian proxies opened up the hall, ripping off – and up – the Indian nation. Alcoholism had already decimated the reservations, even before the casino opened. So just as it had appeared that the Indian nation would rise, proud and sober once again, the casino leaped up with its shiny devils dancing to the tune of coins, accompanied by their muse, alcohol.

We drove through Fort Randall (est. 1976, the youngest incorporated town in South Dakota), past a sadly tailored tourist park, like an interstate rest stop, and on, over the dam. A thin slide of dark water shimmered into the depths.

Nowhere on the south bank could we see any houses. So we turned back to Nebraska on Highway 12, and to beat the tedium, we drove seventy-five miles an hour – nothing arrogant from the human perspective, at first sight. Two young rabbits ran across the road, and in trying to avoid them, as they changed direction, I killed them both, one with one tire, another, with another, soft thumps. I cringed and slowed down, and then, at sunset, I was back at seventy-five, narrowly missing a deer, and then trying to miss an orange tomcat standing in the middle of the road, on the orange stripe, his tail lifted, his balls proudly swollen, as he stalked a gopher. I braked, honked, swerved – and crushed him. I did not speed up again. The country road was not fenced off from the fields and groves, so that driving on it meant murder. Road-kill here was so common that in a Yankton bookstore a book of road-kill recipes was a best-seller.

We crashed near Winnetoon, Nebraska, at Jeanette's uncle's crumbling ranch house, with wiring burning in the walls and sending pleasant waves of stray voltage through the floor so that when you touched a blanket at night, sparks, not only of static, gave you a start. Whenever we neared our cats (one exactly like the one I had killed on the road), they ran.

A week later we drove toward Fort Randall on the Nebraska side, through Niobrara, a town that had been flooded and then transplanted up from the bank of the river into the hills. We crossed from Knox to Boyd County, beneath electrical wires on the Boyd side. Here Air Force jets flew low in stealth maneuvers, testing radars, penetrating the sound barrier, hurting your eardrums. Two thousand people and hundreds of thousands of God's other creatures who lived in Boyd County – the size of Kuwait – did not officially constitute a populated area, and so five states agreed to build a nuclear dump site here. Signs along the road: New Orleans, Keep Your Garbage to Yourself; Honesty Will Prevail; Dump the Dump; Health is Better than Wealth; Dope Pusher, Dump Pusher, Same Thing; etc. We drove through Minowi, pop. 6, and wondered how many families lived there. One and a half? One-third? A trailer-bar stood atop bricks in front of an outhouse among stripped pickups.

In Lynch, pop. 385, we admired an old movie theater, resembling half a bread loaf, and ordered eggs with hashbrowns in a restaurant. Half an hour later, seeing that we were fidgeting, the waitress explained that because she had run out of eggs, the cook had gone home to check whether her hens had laid any. They had. Sunset-colored succulent yolk soaked my dry toast and hashbrowns, the best eggs I've eaten since my childhood in Slavonia.

We drove into South Dakota, bought local newspapers and read Burke and Gregory police reports: Told the party to close the garbage lid. Issued a speeding ticket to a party from Wisconsin. Told the party to bring out the garbage after the weekend. Told the party to turn down the volume. Told the party to chain their dog. Told the party . . . "My God, do you want to live in Gregory?" Jeanette asked. "If you peed in the yard, you might get a citation."

Along the road we saw drive-in theaters. You think these are dead? Come to the Rand McNally gap! Every twenty miles, along Highway 18, there's a drive-in, showing movies just released and barely yet reviewed in the *Los Angeles Times.* Most of these towns were well kept, too prosperous for us. But we found a town, Fairfax, that promised a lot, literally. All the streets were unpaved, and only Main Street was graveled. We talked to a café owner – in general, café owners knew even more than bartenders and ministers. Not everybody went to the church, not everybody went to the bar, but everybody visited the café. Alfred told us right away that nothing was to be had in the country. "But here in town, yes, there might be something. Hell, I'll sell you my house," he said when we had finished chewing his frozen food, quickly burned for us.

Alfred's house was solid, at first sight, and at second, there was not too much wrong with it, except that it was filled with other houses. Whenever a farm was auctioned away, Alfred would, for a hundred bucks, tear down the farmhouse. He alone had torn down twenty houses in Gregory County. Large farms ate small ones. Young people left, nobody new moved in, and so, old houses served nobody. The interior of Alfred's house suffered five cast-iron bathtubs, two furnaces, hundreds of electrical sockets, a hundred pounds of rusty nails, several roofs (shingles), a dozen water basins, ten stools, hundreds of pipes, carpets, door frames, wood floors, and an ice-cream making machine out of order.

The barn was stuffed with floorboards, and so was the yard. As the house came with three lots, we could build two or three used houses from the materials.

"How much do you want?" I asked.

"What I paid for it. Twelve hundred."

Maybe I could have bargained, but twelve hundred for a house struck me as a pretty decent thing.

"I'll help you take the garbage out!" He thereby solidified his offer.

Next week as Jeanette and I crossed from Boyd County to South Dakota, I said, "It's great. We didn't kill anything today." I turned to Highway 18 and accelerated. Behind a curve a young blond man in a black jacket waved frantically at us. I stopped. He shrieked. "My brother is dead. Dead! They killed him!"

"Who? What?" We looked to the side of the road, where a blue car dug its nose in the ditch; beyond it lay a twisted motorcycle and a red body in black leather. "He's dead. Dead!" The blond man was tearing at his hair, screaming. Against the car leaned five Indian girls, ranging in age from ten to fifteen. One bled from the mouth.

"They killed my brother! My little brother!" He screamed, pointing at them, and trembled in frustration because they were too young for him to hit. "How could you do that! Damn you!"

I seated three of the girls in our car – the two hurt ones and the youngest one – to take them to the hospital and to call an ambulance. Jeanette stayed behind to help the motorcyclist flag down other cars. I drove straight to Fairfax, to the café, but Alfred would not take over. I called the Gregory ambulance from his phone and drove on to Bonesteel, because that's where the children's parents lived. The parents were in the bar, from which they stumbled, blinded by the sun. I told them their kids might be hurt, two of them, and that they should go to the hospital with me. The father threw out the one who said her arm might be hurt, although I protested, to make space for a buddy of his. As I looked at the scared girls, I wondered what chance in life they had. Their parents had probably had the same kind of terrible start. The vicious cycle of alcohol use had started long ago, with the fur trade. What could deliver the poorest people in the country?

It turned out that the kids had been on their way to see the Fort Randall casino. The fourteen-year-old who was driving fell asleep at the wheel, and she woke up as her car smashed the motorcycle. Her car had swerved into the oncoming lane, hit the cyclist, dragged his body into the ditch, and had driven over it. The girl with the bleeding mouth was all right – only a cut lip – but still in shock. The man and his buddy fell asleep in the waiting room, and when they woke up, they walked to another bar in town.

I drove back to the accident scene, and there was Alfred, who did not want to help at first, but curiosity had gotten the better of him, or the worse of him. He'd examined everything there, the corpse, the rubber stripes, the marks on the car.

Farmers gathered around the corpse and the two girls. If they had not been underage and the farmers had not had a sense of shame, a lynching might have ensued. Dragged into the ambulance to be tranquilized, the motorcyclist screamed at the girls, "You be damned till you die!"

Jeanette said, "Let's go back to Nebraska. I don't want to live here. It's horrible, horrible. I'll never forget his mangled face! It's a horrible start."

Several hours later after drinking iced soda in Fairfax, I gave Alfred twelve pieces of green paper and in turn got a house and the confirmation of ownership: a jagged notebook paper, signed in Alfred's shaky handwriting. Everything he did was a bit shaky; perhaps he had overtrained his muscles tearing down houses. He was hard to understand because he talked softly and slurred his words.

Once we signed the deeds and paid the thirty dollars to the lawyer, I asked, "By the way, what's my new address?"

Alfred scratched the red skin between his light-brown crew cut and his ear, along the white line formed by a pencil that usually resided there. "We don't go by addresses. We go by people's names, not house numbers."

"How about the mail?"

"We use P.O. boxes."

"I'd still sort of like to know my address."

He laughed and shook his head, found the pencil in his pocket, put it on his ear, shook his head further, as though that was a very odd thing to say, but since I was an outsider, a city slicker, he'd accommodate me on that trivial point. We went into his restaurant and from a drawer beneath his kitchen knives he drew out a bundle of papers, wrapped in plastic. The old deeds stated nowhere what the address was – but finally he found the address on the town map: Johnson's Addition, Lots 4, 5, 6.

"Lots? How about the house?" I asked.

"Lot Four? Six? I'm not sure."

"Fine, I'll call it Five because I like odd numbers. How come it's Johnson's Addition? Was there a Johnson?"

"To tell you the truth, I don't know. I am a newcomer myself. I moved here thirty years ago."

But at the courthouse, nobody asked me for the address. I said, "I need to register the transfer of deeds."

The clerk said, "Whose house?"

"Alfred's."

"I think the plumbing's bad." Everybody in the county knew everything about the house. We registered the transfer of deeds in two minutes.

Next, we wanted to turn on the electricity. Jeanette and I drove to Bonesteel to the nearest Rural Electric office. On the way, we waited as a semi dragged on a broad platform a big green-painted house – two stories, a four-pronged attic, windows on each side. The house hovered and tilted over the highway, creaking, as the semi turned down a dirt road. Half the county was without electricity for the afternoon because this house was being moved.

So the Rural Electric agent was not in his office in Bonesteel that afternoon, but the next day, since he'd heard from the post office master, with whom I'd had a casual chat, that people had moved into Alfred's house, he turned on the electricity – without signatures, without anything. The bill came in the mail a couple of weeks later, with a slip of paper asking us for five dollars to join the Rural Electric, a contribution for a mountain-oyster annual feast – where people eat young bulls' balls fried in flour.

Next, the phone. We talked with several US West agents on the pay phone on Main Street. Address? We gave them Johnson's Addition, Lots 4, 5, and 6. No, nothing on the records. Who lived there? We gave them the names. No, it would not work. No Alfred, no Trautman, no Johnson. They asked for the nearest neighbor's name and phone number. There was nobody on our block. On the next block? No next block – just a field. Across the road? After all that failed, the agents advised us to get the legal address with the district number, from the court in Gregory.

The court confirmed that Johnson's Addition was the legal address and gave us the district numbers, but despite two phone jacks in our house, the US West agents did not believe that the house existed. They sent their repairman, a local man from Bonesteel, and the phone began to work a week later.

The water, too, worked, but we had to refrain from using it at first. Since the pipes, looping outside the house, would burst when temperatures dropped below minus thirty, Alfred had decided to move them into the foundation. He had bored holes in the cement, cut off old pipes, and stopped there. "Half the job's done," he said. We bought books on plumbing. No big deal, really, if you were willing to crawl.

Cleaning the place was a much bigger task. We threw out the sinks, bathroom mirrors, bathtubs, sockets, wires, lamps, aluminum, and even the ice-cream machine, a heavy devil that nearly brought down the front porch as I rolled it, and dumped it, crushing the aluminum and wood underneath.

We made a hill of junk, but that was no embarrassment. A house next to ours was collapsing, window frames torn out, bricks sliding out, and a heap of old tires rising in the yard. East from us, past our three cedars stretched the yellow prairie. Across the road, there were two old houses – one boarded up, another aging peopleless – and one new trailer with an aluminum chimney, smelling of cedar, where a retired laundryman lived. He came over one day, a big goiter-like tumor on his neck, and spoke like a computer – a voice dispersed in his vocal cords. White goose bumps stood out on his crimson face and neck. He suffered from multiple sclerosis. He had run thirty laundromats all over Knox and Boyd counties in Nebraska, and he retired, a rich man, though you couldn't tell it by his trailer house. He began to visit almost every day, chatting with me while I cut and fitted boards for tables and bookshelves and pipes for chimneys. He asked me whether we would be willing to sell our lumber to his nephew, a construction worker from Kansas City. "We'll see," I said. We thought we might use the wood to panel the ceilings, walls, floors: everything would be wood, to create a cozy cabin feel. Later we settled for sheetrocking, so I don't know why I had not sold the lumber. The lumber rotted in the yard, alongside an aluminum weathervane – a wind-direction bull with a bullet hole in its chest.

Jeanette and I moved in our books, boxes of papers, documents, and other papery things. We did not have a real lock – a padlock would do since we had nothing valuable. Certainly, it would cross nobody's mind to steal this essay.

We moved in a bed, chairs, etc., and distributed them into two bedrooms and a large living room. There had been four rooms, but Alfred had torn down the wall between two of them. Where the wall used to be, we placed a long cabinet that could work as a bar. We had a bathroom with a deep cast-iron tub, which emptied in the yard through a plastic pipe as did a sink near it. Soon we would hook up the sewage and have a twentieth-century house. The laundryman showed me where the sewage hookup was. He knew because even he used to own the house, some ten years before.

After being here for three weeks we don't know many people – we don't even know yet whether they are xenophobic, which may mean that we are. Every night we have made different plans. We planned to set up a chess colony, so chess addicts from Washington Square Park could spend several healthy months here. Then, a writer's colony. Then, if we gathered enough money and bought eight cheap houses, we could house eight homeless families. With welfare money, gardening, and farmhand jobs, the homeless could make it here better than under the bridges of Chicago and New York. The population of the dying town dropped from 240 twenty years ago to 120 now; just yesterday at the road corner at Highway 18 we saw a fresh grave being dug. Somebody departed. Now it's 119. Or with us, 121!

Why should there be dying towns, with good houses, when fifty million people are exiled and half a billion homeless?

Jeanette and I marvel at how the world works, as we watch brown clouds of dust roll over the deserted streets. We imagine that we might be part of a new wave of people turning away from big cities to set up abodes in prairie towns, from where, via computer modems and fax machines, you could keep in touch with the world – daily admiring the flights of the bald eagle and the red-tail hawk – better than if you lived in Manhattan and had no time to read and write and breathe.

But when I look out at the dusty street, without footprints and fresh tire marks, I wonder who is crazy, the urban USA or us. I am tempted to exclaim, "Come all you poor exiled and homeless people to the Rand McNally gap and set up your garden!" But, listening to the howling and yelping of a pack of coyotes at twilight, a hundred feet from our house, past the three cedars, I think that whatever is to be said – and it might be much different from what I have said – they have said, much better. *He who has ears to hear, let him hear.*

The Fence Posts

Visiting my hometown of Daruvar, Croatia, in 1986, I was taken aback when a friend told me, "Go back to the States! We'll have a war here. Serbs have lists of all the Croatian households. At night they will slit our throats." I thought he was crazy. Now I think I was crazy not to see the warning signs.

Four years later, I returned to Croatia with my American wife, Jeanette, and my Croatian friend Daniel to celebrate Croatia's declaration of statehood. As we approached Yarun, on the outskirts of Zagreb, we saw lights and rising smoke, then we smelled piglets, oxen, and lambs roasting, and beer and plum brandy. Here, among half a million Croats, there were very few Serbs, because they feared the outburst of Croat nationalism. The Croatian red-and-white checkerboard flags swayed in the rising smoke amid crowds cheering and shrieking songs that had been prohibited for forty-five years. Now and then the singers glanced about mistrustfully, as if Tito's cops from the old days might swoop down on horses and club them.

I hid my bearded face after Daniel said beards were a sign of Serbian nationalism. From the shadows where I stood all evening, I saw only four beards.

A few drunks in the crowd frothed at the mouth, but nothing violent happened the whole evening, an accomplishment celebrated by the press the next morning. But on my way home, from a crammed bus, I saw the corpse of a motorcyclist carried into an ambulance. Perhaps the man died recklessly, drunk on alcohol and nationalism. I worried that he had foreshadowed Croatian liberty: a Hell's Angel smashing into a Serbian truck on a dark night.

Until the age of twelve, I didn't even know there were nations. My parents taught me that I was a Baptist, everybody treated me like a Baptist, and that was that. Then I heard about Croats and Serbs on a radio show. I asked my mother whether I was a Croat or a Serb, and she said she thought I was a Croat, but not much of one, because of mixed marriages. Still, excited that I could have a new identity – be a new person, be born again, something highly thrilling for a Baptist! – I ran over to a friend's house. I found him plucking grass from the cracks in the pavement so that it would look clean for May Day.

"Danko, I'm a Croat. Are you a Serb?" I asked.

Danko dropped his lower jaw. His mother frowned, her lips vanishing into a blade-thin line. His father's heavily browed gaze nailed me to the ground. I realized I had said something absolutely wrong – that nationality must be a greater and dirtier secret than sex!

I quickly forgot the whole business, but was reminded of it a couple of years later, in 1971, when friends from Zagreb explained to me how Croatia had enough oil and foreign currency from tourism to do beautifully on her own, and how Serbia stole the money. It was the Croatian Spring, the spring that Yugoslav federal police attacked students demonstrating in Zagreb, cracking skulls and clavicles. In the attack, a man from my town disappeared; his father, who never heard from him again, walked around town obsessively, his hair completely white.

After 1971, friendships often split along ethnic lines. Some Croatian friends of mine distanced themselves from me because I was a Baptist and my last name was common in Serbia. I believed you could rise above such divisions and have some kind of pan-national, global identity. So I went to study in Novi Sad, Vojvodina, a Serbian province with a large Hungarian population. My roommates were a Croat, a Muslim, and a Bosnian Serb. The Serb constantly quarreled with the Croat and the Muslim. He told me I should change my speech so I would not sound like a Croat; otherwise, I would fail my anatomy exam, which a Montenegran Serb would run. But what happened instead was that the examiner threw my Serbian roommate out of the examination room and invited me to be his assistant because he was so happy with my answers. He was not a nationalist.

I became good friends with my Muslim roommate, and got along fine with the rest. Most people, it seemed to me, were not nationalists. So what is happening now is all the more incomprehensible.

Recently, my hometown of Daruvar was bombed. I wonder if the house I was born in is still standing. But will I grab a machine gun to fight the Serbian *conquistadores* and defend my fatherland? I don't feel that Slavonia (eastern Croatia) is my fatherland; I could get along with neither the Croatian Catholics nor the Serbian Orthodox, who both despised Baptists. Growing up, many children were forbidden to play with me, and in some homes, parents told me not to step over the threshold because they wanted nothing to do with the *new believers.* In fact, I didn't get along with the Baptists, either.

How could I be a patriotic soldier? I have always detested the military. Despotism comes to mind when I think of the Yugoslav military and the Yugoslav police, both Serb-dominated. In Daruvar, where Serbs constituted only one-third of the population, the entire police station was Serbian. If you criticized the Serbian hegemony, you could be jailed as a nationalist.

In order to get ahead, some people pretended to be Serbs. I knew a Croatian banker who subscribed to all the Belgrade political journals in Cyrillic, gave his sons Serbian names, and advanced in his post. My uncle was promoted in his Belgrade firm after claiming that our family might be Serbian.

I faked high blood pressure to evade military service and won a temporary reprieve. I immigrated to the United States when I was twenty, after quitting my medical studies, but the Federal Army continued sending draft notices to my address in Yugoslavia. For years I did not visit because I was in effect a deserter.

I considered myself a pacifist. When I was interviewed for U.S. citizenship, I said I would not bear arms for this country. The interviewers, who clearly wanted me to pass the test, told me that if I did not say yes, they would annul my application. They reasoned with me that bearing arms did not mean that I would *have* to shoot; I could shoot into the air. So I said yes.

Meanwhile, I feel I have betrayed my native country. Perhaps I should go to Slavonia and protect my people, my relatives, my friends. Beyond that I don't know whom to defend. Perhaps Hungarians (I'm nearly a quarter Hungarian), Czechs (also a quarter), Croats (a little more than a quarter), and Slovenes.

My story of malingering is common. For decades, many Croats took pride in tricking military recruiters. Serbs, on the other hand, would hang themselves if rejected for service. I had wondered why it was so easy to trick the recruiters. Now I know. The Serbian administration must have been happy to see the Croats demilitarized, untrained for the type of showdown we are having now.

There were few Croatian officers in the Yugoslav Federal Army – partly a Croatian failing, and partly a Serbian success in repressing Croats. For example, the military used only the Serbian version of the Serbo-Croat language, rather than both Croatian and Serbian. I've heard stories from many Croats who did serve in the army, but were abused for speaking Croatian.

Croats got only blame for any kind of military involvement, so naturally they felt that a military career was not a good option. My Serbian high-school history teacher gave numerous lectures about Croatian atrocities in World War II, but never mentioned any Serbian misdoings. Jasenovac, a concentration camp thirty-five miles south of Daruvar, stood as a blight on the Croatian nation and was amply talked about at school, in the papers, in the streets.

Last summer, I went with my wife and a Serbian friend to Jasenovac. A gigantic sculpture of a flame rose over a meadow where the multitudes were slain. Dozens of storks flew over the fields. A nearby village – where old people in rags, and chickens and pigs roamed the dirty streets – exuded somberness. The camp museum contained surprisingly few objects from the victims. The guard invited us to see a documentary about the camp, explaining that the footage was not from Jasenovac. Images from German concentration camps flashed at us – bulldozers piling up emaciated corpses – accompanied by a soundtrack of howling winds and human cries. Several Serbian families were also watching the documentary, their children at their knees. Their faces hardened; lips vanished. No doubt they believed the scenes were from Jasenovac. The educational film, designed to inspire Croat-hatred, was a complete success.

Visiting Auschwitz in Poland, Jeanette and I saw mounds of victims' hair, glasses, luggage, and furnaces and tools of torture – an overwhelming amount of evidence, unlike in Jasenovac. On a map of all the concentration camps in Europe, Jasenovac was listed only as a train depot, along with dozens of others.

I certainly believe that thousands of Serbs were killed there. Many contemporary Serb historians estimate the figure of Serbs killed on the territory of World War II Croatia to be 700,000. When I was a schoolboy I remember the figure stated by Serb teachers as 120,000. Tudjman and several other Croat historians recently estimated the figure of Serbs killed by Ustashas as 40,000 to 70,000.

The best respected Serb historians – Aleksa Djilas and Kocovic – claim that Croat soldiers took part in killing 390,000 Serbs, the total number of Serbs who perished in Croatia and

Bosnia and Herzegovina at the hands of Ustashas, Muslims, Germans, Partisans (who killed a fair number of extremist Serb royalists and their civilian supporters), and typhoid fever. If the Croatian Ustashas killed more than half of the Serb victims, the figure realistically should still be estimated below 250,000 – otherwise, what could one make of the Serbs' claim that they had sacrificed rivers of blood in fighting thirty German divisions in Croatia, Bosnia, and Herzegovina?

On the other hand, teachers were not allowed to tell us that in Bleiburg, Austria, Partisans killed at least 20,000 Ustashas and Croat Home Guards who had surrendered in accordance with the Geneva POW convention. The Partisans ploughed the corpses into the fields or transported them to caves. At least 30,000 more Croats were executed at the very end of the war: perhaps 20,000 perished in a 250-mile forced march, known as the Trail of Crosses. Chetniks and Partisans had killed tens of thousands of Croats and Muslims, civilians and soldiers alike, during the war. The total number of Croat and Muslim victims at the hands of Serbs and Partisans could be around 200,000, and according to many Muslims and Croats, twice as many.

Most statistics seem to be in one way or another manipulated by political tendencies: a war of numbers, propaganda on both sides, is taking place. No matter what, the history of former Yugoslavia is much more complex than we were taught.

Teachers neglected to point out to us that in Yugoslavia's war against the Nazis, the leaders were Croats – Tito, Ribar, and others – and that the Croatian government in World War II was not democratically elected, but a puppet. Croatia was split between the Communists and the Nazis – and most people avoided both. Families split. My maternal grandmother divorced her husband because he wouldn't join the Partisans with her; he not only stayed out of the armies, but also preached against all of them, for which he did time after the war.

After censorship slackened three years ago, the Zagreb media brought out the other side of the story of World War II: caves filled with human skeletons, remains of Croatian victims killed by Partisans and Serbs. Children stared at pictures of smashed skulls next to the pornographic pictures of oral and anal sex that flooded shop windows all over Serbia, Croatia, and Hungary. The brutality of the Croatian and Serbian media, which irresponsibly blurred World War II with the present, contributed to bringing about the war; many people have suggested that these journalists be tried as war criminals.

The current crisis, as I see it, comes from the bad teaching of history, rather than from bad history. The winner writes history and the loser rewrites it. After World War II, Serbia took the role of the winner and the writer of history, though it was no more responsible for Germany's defeat than Croatia was. And now Croatia, the loser, has been attempting a rewrite. It could almost be seen as a high-school writing competition, if the consequences were not so grave.

If the first victim in war is the truth, it seems that both world wars never ended in Yugoslavia, but have continued quietly, behind the scenes.

On the phone, my brother in Daruvar tells me that our older sister, Nada, was hit by a Yugoslav mortar. A piece of iron penetrated deep into her liver. She underwent surgery without antibiotics, nearly bleeding to death. When she was in critical condition, the Serbs bombed the hospital; she was transferred to the basement, which has terrible hygienic conditions. She could have been killed; it is still not certain how well she is doing.

Her husband, Kornel, a metal factory worker, suffered a heart attack three years ago. I don't know how he's handling the constant bombardment. My second brother, a theology student in Switzerland, says that he could hardly hear Kornel on the phone because the explosions were so loud.

Last summer Jeanette and I visited Nada and Kornel. Nada had given birth to five sons – one died of heart failure – and one daughter, and now was a gray old woman at the age of fifty-five (twenty years older than I). Now and then, her neck and eyes twitched. She raised her children in relentless poverty and feared for her husband's heart.

Their five children dream of going to America. But the four boys will have to join the Croatian or the Federal Army. One of the boys, I remember, used to take his father's lesson – *turn the other cheek* – so literally that every day he came home with bruises, a bleeding nose, black eyes. Children beat him and ridiculed him for his religious beliefs. Kornel protested in vain to the school principal and the police. Finally, he tried to reeducate his son. *Fight back,* he said. But Daniel remained averse to violence. Will he change now? I wonder. Shouldn't he?

And shouldn't I go over there and join?

There may be a better way to help. Boris, a Croatian friend of mine, who was teaching at an American university, called me a week ago and said he could secure dialysis machines for the town of Pakrac, where bombs had destroyed the kidney ward. I admired my friend's scheme. But a day later he called to say he was quitting his teaching post and going to Croatia to fight the Serbs. Better bullets than dialysis, apparently.

I called up Ivo Banac, a prominent historian from Yale, and he advised me, "Yes, all kinds of terrible things are happening. Everything is true. Just write it down."

On the phone, a Croatian acquaintance told me that Serbian guerrillas had mutilated old men and forced them to eat their own testicles, plucked out their eyeballs and forced them to eat their own eyes.

A Serbian friend of mine tells me of a friend who fled Belgrade because the Serbian police slaughtered his best buddy, a leader of a peace protest, in his bed.

I try to see the bright side: at least there is a peace movement. Could Croatia have a sensible peace movement, or would it simply be a push for surrender and slavery?

Guerrillas have killed many journalists, so, when a Texan friend of mine, a journalist, told me I should go to Yugoslavia to gather stories from the front, I laughed at him. As though a press card meant anything there! And how would I live in Croatia? I'm broke. Moreover, who would give me a press card? The newspapers I called either already had journalists there or did not want to send any.

So, the phone is as close as I get to being there. Almost all the Croats I know in this country have overstepped their phone allowances. One man is so much in debt to the phone company that he's hiding from the FBI. In Yugoslavia, he probably feared that the UDBA, the secret police, would jail him. Here, it's the FBI. I guess you re-create your psychological reality no matter where you go.

I bought a shortwave radio. Last night the BBC reported from Pakrac, where my older brother works as an eye surgeon. From a nearby mountain, Serbian guerrillas had shelled the town and demolished the hospital. The interviewers reported from the lunatic asylum's basement, where inmates wail, crap, and live in a horrible stench to the melody of mortar fire.

Sixteen years ago, my brother took me for a visit to the asylum because I wanted to become a psychiatrist. I met there, as I was supposed to, Jesus Christ. If I had finished my medical studies, that is probably where I would have worked.

I called my brother, who told me the road to Pakrac was walled, so now he treats the wounded in Daruvar, where he lives, twenty miles to the north. A doctor friend of his had been killed when his ambulance team was hit by a projectile. My brother was so depressed that he'd stop talking in the middle of a sentence. Thinking we had lost the connection, I'd ask, "Are you there?" Several seconds later, as though the answer required thought, he'd say, "Sure."

To understand all of it, maybe I need philosophy. "War is the king of all," said Heraclitus in fifth-century B.C. Did he mean that from war come all the good things: freedom, law, order, happiness? (And bad things, too, no doubt.) But I am no philosopher. And I am not ashamed of not being a philosopher.

What can philosophy do, anyway? It's a wizened old man or woman on a deathbed. Croatia needs five thousand ground-to-air missiles and fifty American or French fighter planes to survive. But if I have to give up philosophy, what will become of my essay? Sure, I could give up writing. I could have given up writing even before I began. In college I wrote something I called a novel, got a fellowship, and a prominent editor asked to see my work. After she read it, she told me to quit writing. It was a mess. I'm sure it was. But I liked the synthetic way of thinking that writing gave me – words, memories, images, ideas – a melting pot. Now I can't help putting the pot into the fire, the civil war, six thousand miles away.

When my wife goes out I make phone calls. Like a child, I have to call up stealthily; otherwise, my wife will bring out a pen and show me that one call a day means twenty dollars, and a month of that, six hundred, and since I am now unemployed . . . But that's unimportant compared to what I've heard on the phone. Although the Croat government claims that about two thousand people have been killed so far, my older brother thinks there must be at least ten thousand dead among the Croats alone. That's the consensus among the doctors he knows.

For a while, instead of calling, I wrote letters but didn't get any replies. I sent $130 to my friend Daniel in Zagreb. A letter did come back from him: he gave the money to a psychiatric asylum, though I know he's poor. Maybe, as R. D. Laing said, those in the asylum are the sanest. (Or perhaps the least guilty.) Daniel has sent me my membership card; I am now a member of the Vrapce Psychiatric Ward. I suppose it's better than being a member of a political party.

Another call. While our sister Nada was still in the hospital, two bombs exploded near her home. One smashed the gate, shattered the front windows, and blasted holes in the wall. The other smashed the door and Kornel's pickup. Fortunately, Kornel and his kids were in the back room. Kornel had been building the house with his own hands for thirty years. He had worked for ten years to afford the pickup. For Kornel, the worst thing in all this is that he cannot drive to the fields anymore to visit his bees and winterize their hives. Once a corpulent man, he now sits at home, thin, eating nothing; there probably isn't much to eat anyway. He says it's all the same to him whether he lives or dies.

A week later his son, my nephew, tells me over the phone that Kornel's brother, a carpenter, made Kornel and Nada a present of two coffins. "This way, if you get killed, you won't end up in a mass grave."

I recently got a letter from my friend Boris, the one who gave up his teaching post in the States to join the Croatian Guard. Instead of joining the Guard, he helped in an old people's home in Zagreb. His letter was filled with anecdotes. When supplies arrived, Daruvar got only stretchers for the wounded and a neighboring town got only hand grenades; so the towns exchanged their goods – a stretcher for a grenade.

A hearse broke down on the way to the cemetery; the procession of five hundred mourners took a detour to a car-repair shop and waited for five hours before going on to the graveyard. Touched by the anecdote, the German government shipped to the town a new hearse, a Mercedes, but the townspeople were enraged, not thankful, because the money spent on such an expensive car could have been better used in a town where the average salary is fifty dollars a month.

Anticipating the arrival of UN troops, the town parents, particularly the mothers, urged that a brothel be opened on the outskirts of town near the army barracks so the soldiers would leave the native daughters alone. But once the brothel was opened, the town fathers began frequenting it; the mothers are now urging that it be closed.

In a letter two weeks later, I learned that Boris now works as the liaison between Daruvar's town council and the UN troops. Daruvar has become one of the four major centers for the UN troops in Croatia.

But despite the newly dispatched UN troops, I recently heard a report from a village near my hometown: a Croatian peasant, returning home from the woods with a bundle of branches for winter, found the severed heads of his wife, two daughters, and a son stuck on the fence posts of his home, drenched in blood.

Rings and Crucifixes

A Visit to Eastern Croatia in November 1992

In thick night fog, when I stepped off the bus in my hometown Daruvar, an oily rancid odor of burned-out houses hit the inside roof of my nose, between my eyes, but the house silhouettes stood no more crooked than several years before.

I walked to the house of my childhood – the yard gate and the house door were unlocked, odd for a country at war. Soon my mother, brother, and sister-in-law, all grayer than before, regaled me with stories of bombs bursting in their vicinity. "We often hid in the basement, but we knew that if a half-ton bomb hit, it would go straight through the basement. When the school was struck, the power of the explosion, the air blast and the sound, knocked us out of our beds." I admired them for not running away from Daruvar – as most townspeople had done in the worst times – but they said that if they had left, they would have lost their jobs (my brother as a doctor, his wife as a school principal) and their house would have been looted. Still, to stay, with the possibility that Serbs would invade the town and go door-to-door slaughtering, struck me as imprudent. "It's a matter of pride," Lubitza said, "you would not feel right if you let your fears push you out of your home."

I always thought that Lubitza was a Serb orphan – her mother was tortured and slain in front of her when she was four years old, in World War II, and I had simply assumed that Croat Ustashas had murdered her mother – because it had not been politically correct to talk about Serb atrocities while history teachers, invariably Serbs, had recounted Croat atrocities relentlessly. Now I learned that it was Serb chetniks who had murdered Lubitza's mother because she would not tell them where her Croat husband was. The new light on Lubitza's past made me understand why she would be brave now, although she used to be so timid that she could not address our Baptist congregation without a tremor in her voice from stage fright. Now she sometimes addresses assemblies of townspeople with confidence.

At dawn I was eager to see the destruction. On my block only one house was burned out. In the park two blocks away the rheumatism ward at the hospital was demolished, windows sagging, floor lines crooked, all the glass gone; steam came out of a crater ten feet wide along the foundation. I thought that the bomb had dug a well, but I was told that the half-ton bomb of the Yugoslav Air Force had cut the waterline. As a boy I used to take baths here in big oval marble tubs, much more pleasant than the oak tub at home. (The town used to be a hot-springs spa during the Turkish Invasion and even in Roman times, and most Daruvar townspeople took pride in our public baths.)

After my walk, I told Vlado that the damage was less than I had expected. "All right," he said, "let me give you a ride."

Outside Daruvar we saw a dozen burned-out houses where the Serbs who had joined the paramilitary (chetnik) forces used to live. Above the windows frozen tongues of black soot clung to the stucco walls; the roofs had caved in, but few walls had collapsed. Croats and Serbs had built homes like fallout shelters, from brick, stone, and concrete. Some peasant houses of raw bricks had collapsed into heaps of rubble as a consequence of the so-called *ruchni rad,* "handiwork": the destroyer placed a candle in the attic, turned on the gas, and several minutes later, after the gas had arisen, an implosion made the walls cave in. Many Croats rejected the notion that they should have to live with neighbors who had left town to shell and kill them; consequently, although the Croatian government pleaded with the people to leave all the houses intact, several angry townspeople went around doing the *ruchni rad*.

My best childhood friend, Danko, a Serb, was now a chetnik. Almost every day we had climbed pear and cherry trees, cracked green walnuts, made bows and arrows, talked about pubic hairs and God – his Communist parents had taught him faith in God was a sin. During my last visit two years before we had drunk late and talked; he said somebody – on no account would he say who – had come by to persuade him to join a nationalist Serb party, but he would not. He had boasted a firm house and wondered why I still had not built one. And now he was in a fascist army, probably slaughtering Croat peasants – I did not see his house, but I would not be surprised if it was gone.

Vlado and I drove up the Doljani hill through a forest of beech and oak trees. Vlado said, "Here, in that yard on the left – that's where Hnoychek took the picture of a dead Croatian soldier among bullet-riddled cars. He took it while the battle was going on!" The picture showed up in *New York Times* – without Hnoychek's name – on 4 September 1991, one of the first Croatian war pictures. "Hnoychek sold his pictures to foreign journalists, in the Hotel Intercontinental in Zagreb, for one hundred dollars apiece so the journalists could pretend that they had visited the front. They just hung around, drank whisky, told jokes, and stole stories from other guests, the newspapers, and the radio." That did not strike me as a bad way to report, considering that in Croatia alone, in six months, twenty-two journalists had been killed by chetniks and the Yugoslav army.

Ten miles south of Daruvar, as we passed a forest of thick oaks – used in making French wine barrels – and began our descent into Pakrac, Vlado exclaimed that the town looked much better than several months earlier. "Tires, glass, bricks, and burned-out cars lay on the pavement and in the ditches." Even now, every fifth house or so was completely destroyed, most in battle, he said, or by Serbs from the mountain. Like Berlin before 1989, Pakrac was now a split city. Serbs controlled the eastern hills beyond the river Pakrac, Croats the western hills and the downtown.

As we walked around my brother's demolished hospital – he used to run the ophthalmology clinic – stepping on shards of glass, staring at grenade holes, Vlado talked about how Serbs, some of whom used to serve on the hospital board of directors, had targeted the hospital with mortar from the hills to terrorize Croats and force them to leave the region – ethnic cleansing.

Among crumbled buildings near the hospital stood a tall crane. "Are they rebuilding already?" I asked. "No," Vlado answered. "Now, see that spot three yards above the cabin? That's where one quiet Serb bureaucrat – a sweet man during peacetime – crouched as a sniper and shot several bed-ridden patients on dialysis through the hospital windows before a policeman shot him. The sniper fell, but his foot got caught in the crossbars of the crane. He remained hanging by his foot, crows ate his flesh, and when his foot rotted and slid out of the boot, he crashed below." Now the orange crane looked unbalanced, as though it would collapse, like a skeleton bending over, spitting out its tongue.

We drove on, to Lipik, two miles south of Pakrac. Retreating Serb tanks had blasted Croatian houses; the town was utterly destroyed. Several glum people walked in the streets. Jokingly, I said: "The funny thing is, the people look cheerful." Vlado said nothing, but a couple of minutes later, when we saw another glum group, he said: "You are right, they do look cheerful." He was not joking. Clearly there was a gap in our sensibilities – mine spoiled by peace, his by war.

We walked into the hot-springs park among Austrian baroque buildings, where two years before I had sipped cappuccino and practiced my backhand slice on clay courts. The spa building was pockmarked, windows shattered and burned out, soot smearing the light pink; the metal roof, collapsed and pierced by shrapnel and bullets, lay rusted and twisted outside and inside the building.

"On the lawn here,"Vlado said,"twenty soldiers lay dead after a battle. Starving pigs, abandoned by peasants who had run away, came by and ate the corpses. Later, Croatian soldiers killed the pigs, but although they would not eat them because the pigs had eaten men, they cut open the pigs' stomachs and found wedding rings, watches, and crucifixes. Then they poured gasoline over the pigs and burned them." Beyond the circle of black grass stood trees without branches, mutilated by grenades.

We stepped over a two-inch-thick layer of broken glass and metal sheets into a hotel. Leaves from the outside piled up against a kicked-in door with a boot mark. "Look,"Vlado said, "the radiators are intact. Next time I might bring along a pipe wrench!" I laughed. The idea that people thought everything belonged or should belong to them had subverted Eastern European socialism – workers had practically dismantled and looted their factories. You could declare free-market economy, but how would the people suddenly change? The first thing the Croatian army did upon liberating a town near Sisask was to rob the bank. The occupying Serb soldiers looted villages and town, and the Croatian liberators took whatever was left over. Vlado was surprised, not that bombs had not blown away the radiators, but that soldiers had not stolen them.

On the way back, Vlado and I saw UN soldiers escorting Serbs to the Croat side of Pakrac and Croats to the Serb side – to show them their homes. The people needed to know whether they still had homes where they could return when the fighting was over.

A sign on one home read, "This is a Croat home, Owner Juro Juric"; a pale red-and-white fragment of a chessboard, the Croat emblem, stuck to the crummy mortar. The refugee had correctly estimated that Croats would hold on to that part of town.

We were stopped by the UN soldiers – Nepalis – and later by

Croatian soldiers, a routine checkpoint. I wore an untrimmed beard, now a sign of Serbdom. Both my last name and my middle name were commonly Serbian – when becoming a U.S. citizen, I chose Alexander for my middle name because as a child I used to like it, after Alexander the Great, and I thought the child in me should have more say about such matters than the adult. But despite my appearing to be a Serb, the soldiers let me go on without hesitation. So, a Serb as well as a U.S. citizen could travel easily here.

Along the road I saw bunkers that Serbs had built secretly and under the auspices of the Yugoslav "Federal" Army, to facilitate the conquest of Croatia. A forest hill was shaved because Serbs wanted to survey the access roads to Pakrac. From several people who had served in the Yugoslav Federal Army years before I heard that all over Croatia the army had practiced attacking every Croat village and defending every Serb village, invariably. So when the war occurred, the "Federal" Army was ready. While I internationalized my identity by studying foreign languages and moving abroad, Serbs had, under the guise of Yugoslavism, spread their nets over a quarter of the Balkans. I should have understood Serb dominance a decade ago – although everyone was prohibited from singing nationalist songs, Serbs could still sing Serbian songs freely while anyone singing Croat songs would be jailed.

Why was the war taking place? Although Serbs were a minority in Croatia, they formed the majority in management, politics, police, and the military – a privileged minority, like whites in South Africa. Especially since Tito's death, Serbs had begun to dominate Croatia as a closed and often unscrupulous power-circle. Serbia routinely appropriated the foreign currency from tourism in Croatia and even illegally printed several billion dollars worth of currency for distribution only in Serbia. From 1990 to 1991 all the republics of the former Yugoslavia – except Montenegro, with majority Serb population – wanted some degree of independence so that the Federation would become a Confederation, but Serb President Milosevic rejected the notion of confederation because Serbia wanted a strong centralized government – naturally, in Belgrade. Milosevic aggressively abolished autonomy for Kosovo (90 percent Albanian) and Vojvodina, and with the dictatorially controlled votes of the two regions, boycotted a Croat, Mesic, who was supposed to take over the rotating presidency of Yugoslavia for a year, starting in May 1991. Serbia formed a separate Yugoslav presidency, which meant that de facto Serbia with its controlled territories (rather than the remaining republics) split from Yugoslavia – or schemed for full military dictatorship. When Croatia and Slovenia declared independence in June 1991, they simply stated the obvious, that Yugoslavia had split apart. Serbs then started the war not because they had been oppressed, but because they wanted to keep their control of all the republics. If Croatia wanted to go her way, she could, after Serbia seized huge chunks of Croatian territory. U.S. policy for preserving the integrity of Yugoslavia reiterated by Baker in Belgrade, on the eve of the Slovenian and Croatian Declaration of Independence, signaled to Milosevic that the international community would not react if Serbia occupied Croatia. Milosevic needed only a pretext so that the occupation could pass at first as a move to preserve Yugoslavia and then as a move to protect the Serb minorities in Croatia.

And the tactless new Croatian government under Tudjman gave Milosevic a pretext. The new government of Croatia should have reassured the Serb population – if that was possible – that their rights would not be violated. Instead, Tudjman's government laid off many Serb policemen – not all, enough would remain to correspond to the Serb 12 percent share of the population – and trained Croat recruits. It is true that there had been too many Serb policemen and that Croatia was effectively under Serb occupation, but one can't just fire people. According to inflammatory stories from Belgrade, Croat government would not only dismiss the Serb police, but would organize massacres. Most Serb police, even before they could be laid off, formed Serb militia, withdrew into Serb villages, and collected heavy artillery from the Yugoslav

Federal Army. They began to ambush the new, untrained and lightly armed Croatian police; commandos from Serbia joined to help. Serbs may have lost police jobs, but the people being murdered and ambushed were Croats, and it was Croats who were threatened, not Serbs.

Soon after the aggression by the Serb militia, the Croat government did recognize all Serbs as citizens of Croatia with equal employment rights, constitutionally. But now there was no dialogue between the two sides and Serbs had no intention of pursuing the legal route. Serbs in Croatia read only the Belgrade press, which was notoriously manipulated by Milosevic's cabinet. The Serbian nationalistic indoctrination made the Croat government's conciliatory moves toward Croatia's Serbs impossible. Milosevic exaggerated the degree to which Serbs were threatened in Croatia so that he could occupy parts of Croatia in order to "protect" the Serbs the way Hitler moved to Sudetenland to "protect" the German minorities.

Even a year before my trip, Serbia had occupied one-third of Croatia. Population exchange had taken place between the Serb-held territories and the rest of Croatia because most people went over to the side of their nationality out of fear. However, hardly any Croats remained in Serb-controlled territories, while many Serbs did stay in Croatian-controlled territories.

No matter how the war had come about, it disturbed me that the country of my youth was now a divided one, and that I could not travel freely, and I wondered how the people who'd stayed were able to handle it all.

When Vlado and I returned to Daruvar, I went to a barber, a Muslim from Serbia, who used to cut my hair throughout my youth. As he combed my hair, he talked. "When the sirens wailed and we expected bombers, we turned up the volume on the radio and said to our daughter, Time to dance! We taught her steps and sang with her – we thought we had fooled her. But another day when a bomb went off close to home, she rolled down the curtains, and said 'Time to dance!'" The barber's face in the wavy mirror glistened with pride. "Everybody has a story about how he survived a close call."

My nephew Davor, an M.D., gave me a ride to Vinkovci in Eastern Slavonia, where I wanted to see his mother and my sister Nada, who had been severely wounded a year before. As a child Davor had been so hungry – because his parents could never buy much meat – that the first word he had learned was *meso* (meat). As a six-year-old he ran away from home to fish. He had kept his childhood sense of wonder (two years before I could keep him wide-eyed and smiling with stories about the United States). But now he was absent-minded – and amazingly overweight; under stress he had reverted to his childhood fears of starvation. North of Daruvar we passed through Batinjani, a village from whose cemetery Serb cannons used to bomb Daruvar in the valley; when the Croats fired back, Serbs complained that Croats had no respect for the Serbian dead. Two years before, my wife and I had enjoyed the idyll of old women geese-herding and bread-baking in the brick ovens in the yards. The cherries hung low over the wooden fences into the street and nobody minded us eating them. Now, only a gaunt peasant stood in the middle of the road, between burned-out houses.

Before chetniks had planned to occupy the area, they had lied to the Serb population that Ustashas were coming to slaughter them. Chetniks had tortured several Serbs who had refused to leave; after that nearly all the Serbs left. Then, without fear of killing their faithful own, chetniks comfortably bombed the villages, killing Croats and Czechs. Upon taking the villages, chetniks had chopped off many Croats' annular and little fingers to force them to show the three-finger Serb sign for the rest of their lives.

During the war Davor had stayed on the front lines outside of Osijek. He had to certify the causes of death after several massacres. I asked him what it was like.

"I'd rather not talk about it," he said. That was a change since December 1991, when he had phoned me to visit Croatia at once to report to the world what atrocities Serbian armies had committed on Croatian peasantry. "As soon as I remember the details, I feel nauseated."

Even doctors are liable to suffer from post-traumatic stress syndrome, and clearly my nephew did. When I tried to visualize him digging with a scalpel through bloated purple corpses to find bullets and blades, I could not blame him in the least.

We drove north past Vocin – where Serbs had massacred dozens of men, women, and children, in November 1991 – into the Slavonian Podravina region; poplars and willows lead to small cemeteries with dark cedars and blue porcelain Virgins, red roosters, white goats, muddy cats, and hunched peasants in wooden shoes and brown clothes, lighting candles – their hands and the flames trembled as much as the last leaves on the poplars before falling off in the wet wind. You could see why Podravina had given birth to Croatian naive art.

After taking many back roads to avoid Serb-occupied villages and roadblocks, we arrived in Vinkovci – a hundred miles east of Daruvar and only ten miles north of Vukovar, where the Yugoslav Federal Army slaughtered several thousand Croats, mostly civilians and POWs – and walked into Davor's childhood home.

Kornel – my brother-in-law, Davor's father – opened the door, his hair completely white, and soon Nada, my sister, dismounted a bike in the street and walked in. She pulled out a sleeping bag, a Caritas gift. When Kornel found that the zipper had a break in it, he said, "Instead of throwing this into the garbage, as people in the West normally would, they send it to us." I was astonished. So what if the zipper does not work? When winter comes, it would still keep him warm.

Nada complained that her scar burned and had grown in size. During one of the first bombings, Nada's son, Tom, had run out into the streets to take pictures, but once a bomb burst near him he jumped into a ditch and crawled around the house. Nada ran out, calling him back, until shrapnel hit and scorched her side. Her abdomen filled with blood and she passed out.

"Don't worry," Davor now said, "your tissues are growing back. Perfectly normal."

I was glad to see that she was plump; she had been thin two years before.

Although Kornel did not seem fond of charity, I opened my bag with presents from my mother – ten pounds of walnuts and three pounds of cookies. Mother had collected three bags of walnuts, and wherever I went, she sent them along; she also sent along a vacuum-packed sausage. When Kornel saw the sausage, he commented, "German donation, isn't it?" in a dismissive voice.

I had sent Nada and Kornel several hundred dollars to help them during the war even though I was unemployed, so I wondered how they had used the money. "We bought all the new window panes and some jars for honey," Nada said.

Kornel and Nada took me out of the house to stare at a burned-out and gutted house. "A Croat policeman lived here," Kornel said. "Serbs fired a phosphorus bomb to kill him, his wife, and two children. The flames were twice as tall as the house, but the man and his family jumped out unharmed."

Then Kornel pointed out a grenade hole in the foundation of his own home and his utterly shattered brick-laid garage. "In the garage Croatian soldiers set up a cannon. Once the Serbs located the origin of the firing – the cannon was withdrawn by then – they blasted the garage. They are very precise. Professionals. And they are very close. The new Serb border is just three hundred yards away, in Mirkovci." He pointed east over the shrapnel-cut vines of his garden toward white UN tanks.

"Are the UN soldiers doing good work?" I asked.

"Terrible," said Kornel. "Here Russian UN soldiers who'd made two dollars a month back home smuggle gasoline and all sorts of goods to the Serb side, and Serbs give them money and women. They escort the expelled Serbs back to their homes here and make sure nothing happens to them, but they help no Croats move back to Vukovar and the Serb villages. The whole thing is a disaster – Boutros-Ghali comes from Egypt, General Nambier from India, and since Yugoslavia and those two countries founded the non-aligned movement, the two UN leaders look after the interests of whatever is called Yugoslavia. In Western Slavonia, by agreement Croat troops withdrew from the area they had liberated, and the UN protected returning chetniks – so the snipers are back. People are disgusted with the Blue Helmets here. In a brawl between several Blue Helmets and some drunks, Croat policemen who were passing by took off their uniforms and beat up the soldiers."

Where the garage had been previously, Kornel was now building a church, next to the black rubble. Fresh red bricks stood out of the foundation. Since Kornel could never get along with any churches, he now wanted a church of his own, as though one needed a church to worship. Thinking money would be wasted on bricks, I gave Kornel only fifty dollars. "For the bees!" I said.

During the war Kornel had biked out of town to look after his bees in the fields at least once a week: even a light shaking – like a chicken walking on a beehive – could disturb the bees, make them panic and die, according to Kornel, but his bees survived the constant shaking of the ground amidst explosions. Selling honey, Nada and Kornel made three times as much as his fifty-dollar-a-month pay.

But poverty was not foremost on Kornel's mind. He talked on: "You think you can get used to grenades, but not so. When Nada hears an explosion, she trembles, and can't stick her head out the door."

Nada smiled at that. It struck me as pretty normal that if a bomb nearly kills you, you won't welcome its sound.

"But when machine-gun fire flared around, that was music! We all relaxed. Bullets could not pierce the walls. Soldiers ran back and forth past the house, their boots stamping the ground, shouting, 'There he is! Shoot! Catch him!' "

Then Kornel almost wept because one of Davor's childhood friends, who used to come by to see how Kornel was doing, had run with two Croat soldiers after a couple of Serb soldiers and tripped over a mine wire. Several mines went off, blasting him and his comrades – their body parts flew and their blood splattered the houses flanking the street. Barely enough of them remained to fill a basket, let alone three coffins, and people did not know which fragments to put into which coffin.

"How do you get used to living with howitzers pointing at your house?" I asked. "Are there any explosions these days?"

"Sure, almost every night a couple of times – that we can live with."

Davor and I made sure to be out of Vinkovci before nightfall.

Later on, Davor and I passed a train without a single passenger on it. Snipers had killed passengers before. After a UN checkpoint around ten o'clock, five miles north of Daruvar, we entered a heavy mist and smelled sharp smoke. Davor sped up. "Somebody has probably set another house on fire. And there could be snipers along the road – chetniks the UN is sponsoring to come back." Since there was no road divide and no marked edges, we nearly slid off a couple of times. Davor said that if we ran into a chetnik roadblock, we'd have to crash through it. He became tense, and considering how well he knew the terrain, this made me tense. But soon we emerged out of the misty village to a Croat checkpoint.

Before taking off for Zagreb, I walked to the office of Hnoychek the photographer. I planned to organize an exhibition of war photography in Minneapolis. I found him drunk. "My wife has just given birth to a son," he said and shrieked with joy. "Let's have a drink to celebrate!" He was in no mood to sort out his photos and write out the titles. Tom, my sister's son – whose photography had nearly caused Nada's death – hadn't mailed me his photographs. At first I was sad that I could not organize the exhibition of war photographs and that I would not have good photos to accompany my essays, but then I changed my mind. If the motto "One picture equals a thousand words" was true, writers should simply genuflect in front of photographers and move out of the way before their Canons. It struck me that there was almost a civil war between photographers and writers, with writers underarmed.

In Zagreb I visited an engineer, a Serb, one of my best friends. He complained that he lived in Croatia, a fascist state where elections were fixed, and where Serbs could not be comfortable. Commonly – see Misha Glenny's *The Fall of Yugoslavia* – the story about Serbs in Croatia is that they have all been sacked from their jobs and therefore had no choice but to fight. While that's true of the police, it's not true of most other occupations. A large proportion of Serbs had kept their old jobs – and many of those who lost them would not have if they had not joined the Serb paramilitary forces. Since my friend complained so much and he used to teach in the States, I said, "Why don't you go back to the States?"

"Are you crazy?" he answered. "Here I have this apartment within walking distance of my easygoing teaching job, a good Italian car, and then, there's Europe. In two hours I can be in Austria or Hungary, in three in Italy. No, thank you."

"So how can you claim this is fascism if, as a Serb, you feel so comfortable in Zagreb?" He had gotten an apartment cheaply in Zagreb through a connection, a Serb relative in the Housing Department. By contrast a Croatian friend of mine, a native of Zagreb, who worked as a machinist for the Zagreb Utilities Company, lived in a cramped attic like Raskolnikov; his turn to be awarded an apartment never came up, not even now under the new Croatian government although he had served in the Croatian army.

"What did you do about all the alarms during the war?" I asked the engineer. "Did you go into the basement shelter?"

"Not once. It was a well-known fact since the '86 Referendum that Serbs had planned to form their western border from Virovitica through Daruvar and Pakrac and so on, so Zagreb would be well out of the range."

"And you could go by that?"

"The Croat government could, too – and that it did not share the information with the inhabitants, but excited them with sirens, shows you that the government wanted to develop the war psychosis."

My friend left me with the impression that with such reliable information as he had, in the middle of Zagreb he was better off than a Croat. Later on, when I mentioned the '86 Referendum, several Croats said that Serbs had made all kinds of plans and agreements, none reliable. However, I saw for myself that the oil refinery just outside of the imaginary Serb western border, in Kutina, was left completely intact although MiG jets could have easily smashed it – Serbs had followed the plans from 1986. So Zagreb Croats had spent the war unnecessarily rushing to shelters – and perhaps Tudjman, the Croat president, planned it so as to recruit many angry young men into the Croatian army.

In the evening in the Hotel Esplanade I met with Bozho Kovachevic, a childhood friend, who worked as secretary of the Croatian Social Liberal Party, the second most powerful party in the country, with some leftist tendencies, which had won 30 percent of the vote in the recent elections. (The Croatian Party of Rights, the right-wing party, had won only 6 percent of the vote, the lowest right-wing percentage vote in Europe – right-wingers had won more than 20 percent in France and 30 percent in Serbia.) Bozho showed up in a black suit, red tie, white shirt, a picture at odds with the old hippie I remembered – as youths we used to take night walks talking about Communism and religion. "We can't meet at my place," Bozho said, "because a missile intended for the presidential palace demolished my apartment. In our living room we have a hole larger than the window."

When his Albanian wife, Elisabeta, joined us and talked about selling antiques, we walked to Jelacic Square, to have supper with the top members of the Croatian Social Liberal Party, in honor of the new Croatian ambassador to the EEC. Next to me sat the wartime major of Osijek – Kramaric – who examined a picture of himself yawning in tomorrow's papers. He was mad because, despite working eighty hours a week, he would appear lazy. To the left of me was a professor of philosophy who kept talking about how oppression in moderation can stimulate – its excess debilitates as does its absence. Croatia with its Croatian Democratic Union (CDU) and Tudjman in power had the right amount of things wrong-perhaps a little too much – to stimulate us to work well. Maybe we would all become artists now, he joked. Fanciful talk proliferated, as we sipped shots of whiskey, and Bozho commented to me, "In case you want to know why we are not the leading party, here's the answer! We theorize and gossip rather than make concrete plans the way CDU does."

You would think by the mood that there was no war out there, but Elisabeta handed me a letter from Sarajevo. Here is an excerpt from it in my translation:

November 4, 1992

Dear friends,

Can you imagine a university professor climbing trees in the park, breaking branches, and making a small fire in the streets to bake bread? – amidst constant firing from all sorts of weapons? That's me.

After a bombing on our block people walk out and conclude that five people have died and ten have been wounded, and then go back in. You see a woman without half her head or a man who carries his arm like a loaf of bread or crawls clutching his severed foot, under his armpit – right in front of your window! Literally, one wrong step separates you from death. If the city survives, it will be a city of the mad and the maimed.

I have forgotten what electricity is. Radio and TV seem to be abstract objects whose function nobody knows. While I'm writing, sniper bullets hit the roof and the house-front; the tanks firing half a kilometer away make the building sway. Last Sunday a grenade hit our wall and now we are freezing because we have a hole the size of the window. Kids were at home – L.

in the corridor, F. in the bathroom – and only thanking to Allah Akhbar nobody has suffered a scratch.

But the worst thing of all is hunger. Until it happens to you, you can't comprehend it. I watched hunger on TV, convinced that it could not happen to us. So, I can very well understand satiated Europe's indifference to our plight.

I haven't seen any potatoes, tomatoes, and eggs, not once, since seven months ago. The humanitarian aid with which the world washes its hands gives us only rice and a can here and there, once a month. Everything better is stolen and sold in the black market.

If you receive this letter, try to get me some money, somehow, because all my savings are outside of Sarajevo, which will be under blockade until the last penny gets sucked out of it. (The only currency that works is the deutsche mark.)

There's a chance to mail us something via the Jews, Adventists, or Caritas. We would really enjoy a sack of beans – they're as expensive as gold here – and we'd love oil. You have no idea how long it took me to beg for food. I have lost seventy-two pounds, but that does not worry me as much as our kids' hunger.

Love,
S.M., Sarajevo

"I'll translate the letter," I said, "and publish it in the *Minneapolis Star Tribune* but I won't publish the man's name because the letter might place him on the Serb blacklist, so if the defense of the city collapses, they might slit his throat."

"You are absolutely right," Elisabeta said.

"No, you're absolutely wrong," said a silvery politician, who, unlike many of his colleagues, did not wear a tie. "How much worse can it get? If you publish his name, the chances are that some aid will get to him directly, and he'll pull through. If you don't, he might not pull through anyway. And besides, the city will not collapse." He walked away.

I concluded that the newspapers, if they decided to publish the letter, could keep the author's name and address confidential in their files to relay any money raised to him. And, the half thousand words – uneven letters, some hollow inside, from the vigorous typing – could fit in my essay better than a picture.

The following morning as I walked past shop windows – kid gloves and snakeskin boots – along the newly paved mall in Zagreb, it struck me that Zagreb seemed strangely immune to the war not only in Bosnia, but even in Croatia itself. Only in the farmer's market, where people stood hesitantly with single onions and single apples in their hands, did I realize that Zagreb kept up the appearances while suffering from poverty. The war had impoverished Croatia. Fields were not harvested; tourists did not come to the Coast; because of the arms embargo against Croatia, Croatia armed herself at three times the normal price; 400,000 Bosnian refugees – for a country of 4,500,000 would be comparable to the United States receiving 25,000,000 refugees – sapped food and energy, so the prices went up.

Many shabbily dressed people standing disoriented in the squares were Bosnian refugees. They exchanged stories, shared newspapers, stared absentmindedly, smoked, and waited . . .

Croats who had sacrificed to help refugees resented the world press attitude that Croatia had betrayed Bosnian Muslims when at the same time the United States admitted only three thousand Muslim refugees. It seemed to me that Croats harbored remarkably little resentment toward the huge influx of refugees; most of the resentment was reserved for Greater Serbia, whose territorial ambitions had squeezed their throats and bellies. Of course, in neighboring Bosnia and Herzegovina, Croats resented the influx of Muslim refugees because if the Muslims remained, the towns now with a Croatian majority would become Muslim. Since in Bosnia, Croats made up only 17 percent of the population, they were particularly sensitive to becoming a minority even in the few towns where they were the majority. So Bosnian Croats these days refused to accommodate new Muslim refugees and expelled many old ones, and Muslims expelled many Croats. The two underdogs, instead of fighting together against Serbia, began to fight each other more and more. Serbs, controlling more than 70 percent of the territory, divide and rule.

In a café I watched Belgrade TV, via satellite dish. Milan Panic spoke: "Albanians in Kosovo complain that they aren't allowed to study in Albanian. I think they should be glad they have the opportunity to study in Serbian, a world language. What's a diploma in Albanian worth when one goes to the West? To sweep the streets and clean the toilets. But in Serbian, on the other hand . . . " A waiter laughed and said mockingly, "*Govori Srpski da te ceo svet razume!*" (Speak Serbian so the whole world can understand you). The famous Serb saying revealed Serbian ethnocentric arrogance.

For me, even ten days in my old homeland became oppressive. I understood very well why I had left the "Former Yugoslavia": the tensions, the police, the spying, the propaganda, the nationalist hatreds – they had all been there, repressed, illegal even to speak about. Now everything was spoken about, but nothing made any kind of constructive sense – I could not see where the new Croatian freedom and Greater Serbia would lead. In the region where people were used to looking backward, into the distorted past, hardly anybody seemed able to predict anything, to look forward to anything, and the aura of the country to me was just as glum as it had always been. I wanted to relieve the glumness by visiting the coastal town, Split; however, it would take me two days – rather than the normal, pre-war eight hours – to get there because first I would have to to go Rijeka in the north and then take a boat. Serbs occupied a stretch of the coast, although they were not the majority along the coast anywhere; they had destroyed a key bridge near Zadar, and so Croatia was split in half. Although by the UN agreement from the year before, Serbs were supposed to withdraw from the occupied stretch of the coast, they had not done so. The UN seemed to be intent on making sure that Croatia complied with her side of the agreement, not to press militarily against the Krajina Serbs, who were free to violate their agreement by keeping their gains.

Frustrated with travel in my paralyzed homeland, I stepped onto a Zürich-bound bus and sat next to a quiet Muslim from Sandzak in Serbia who claimed there were no problems in Sandzak and refused to say anything more, probably afraid that I might be some kind of spy. So, to cheer up I read *Tom Jones* by Fielding until I hit this passage:

> *"The result of the whole was a kind smile from Mrs. Western, who said, 'Brother, you are absolutely a perfect Croat; but as those have their use in the army of the Empress Queen, so you likewise have some good in you. I will therefore once more sign a treaty of peace with you, and see that you do not infringe it on your side . . . '" (Book VI, Chapter I)*

I did not mind the insult to Croats but did the similarity to the present. Fielding wrote this in 1749 when Croats served Austria to whom they were bound by various agreements which, on the surface, guaranteed Croatia autonomy similar to the one enjoyed by Hungary, but which gave Croatia effectively the status of an inferior province. Even later, after 1848 when Croatia practically defeated Hungary to protect Austria, Austria drafted an agreement with Croatia, on the surface granting Croatia equality with Hungary but in fact handing Croatia over to Hungarian rule. After the First World War, Croatia joined Serbia and Slovenia to form Yugoslavia as equals, but since Belgrade became the capital and a Serb king the ruler of Yugoslavia, Croatia basically became a province, with Serb military officers in control – the patterns of Serb military control over Croatia remained until 1991. When would Croatia gain the clout not only to sign agreements but to have them carried out without becoming inferior? The United States had recognized Croatia a year before but still failed to appoint an ambassador to Zagreb. The United States along with her allies had done her best to keep Croatia and Bosnia and

Herzegovina from importing heavy arms, thus insuring that Serbia – on the surface unrecognized as a country – would remain a regional superpower. What kind of recognition for Croatia was that? When would Croatia select skillful and eloquent diplomats, ministers, presidents? So far, watching American TV programs, I had hardly ever heard an eloquent Croat make a case for Croatia – moreover, Croats got invited disproportionately fewer times to appear on American radio and TV compared with Serbs and Muslims even while the war raged in Croatia. Croatian President Tudjman rarely got invited anywhere because of his ill-repute for right-wing tendencies although he, as Tito's commissar, had done more than most of his critics to defeat the Nazis in the Second World War. Why did Tudjman fail to display his left-wing credentials? So, with such unskilled representatives, Croatia of course stood no chance of entering decent agreements and following them through.

With thoughts like these, I closed the comic classic, *Tom Jones,* which in Croatia did not sound humorous – nothing did. Although worried for my friends and relatives in Croatia, I was glad to be leaving. At the border, the Croat policemen waved the bus on, without checking a single passport – nobody had checked my passport on the way in either, amazingly liberal (or negligent?) for a state at war – and we went on. Across the border muddy fields stretched flat beneath low clouds which crumbled into falling chunks of fog.

JOSIP NOVAKOVICH moved from Croatia to the United States at the age of twenty. He has won many writing awards, including a National Endowment for the Arts fellowship, an Ingram Merrill award, a Vogelstein fellowship, and the Cohen/Ploughshares award. His prose has appeared in *The New York Times Magazine, Pushcart Prize XV* and *XIX, Paris Review, Threepenny, Cleveland Plain Dealer,* and elsewhere. Story Press has recently published his *Fiction Writer's Workshop.* He teaches writing at the University of Cincinnati.

This book was designed by Ann Artz.
It is set in Bembo type by Stanton Publication Services
and manufactured by Bookcrafters on acid-free paper.